'A Chance Meeting'

And sometimes we ask!
Will we?
Tell me, how you are?
Tell me, where to start?
Tell me, what's in your heart?

A Chance Meeting

A Novel

By

David Lawrence

Visit us online at www.authorsonline.co.uk

An AuthorsOnLine Book

Copyright © Authors OnLine Ltd 2004

Text Copyright © David Lawrence 2004

Cover design James Fitt from a photograph by David Lawrence ©

All rights reserved. No part of this publication may be reproduced, stored in a retrieval system, or transmitted in any form or by any means, electronic, mechanical, photocopy, recording or otherwise, without prior written permission of the copyright owner. Nor can it be circulated in any form of binding or cover other than that in which it is published and without similar condition including this condition being imposed on a subsequent purchaser.

ISBN 0 7552 0131 0

Authors OnLine Ltd
40 Castle Street
Hertford SG14 1HR
England

This book is also available in e-book format, details of which are available at www.authorsonline.co.uk

About The Author

David Lawrence, a Bristolian by birth, with a great love of Cornwall, brought about by long hot summer holidays in the county as a child.

Now fifty something, and, after over thirty years of working in the telecom industry, he held on to a desire to write.

He still had in mind, hand-me down accounts of stolen family fortunes in the distant past by some unscrupulous ancestors, their livelihood having been in the farming industry, as depicted in the cover photograph, these vague tales were passed onto him by his mother and other long since departed relatives.

Having embellished the story somewhat, added a modern day plot or two, sprinkled a large measure of romance over the entire saga, and as a result here is the adventure.

Acknowledgments

Nanette and Ted, for striking the flint that lit the fire to 'A Chance Meeting'

Carole, always by my side, keeping me going, even when I wanted to, and at times when I felt like giving up!

Alan, on the end of that phone, some times its hot, thanks!

Ceri, for not judging!

Barbara, for being the one that read it first, and liking it, and as always being there, together with John, never rejecting me or turning me away, standing by me through your own troubles. 'When I wouldn't choose myself as a friend, you are always there'. Thank you, it's been over thirty years.

Bernice and John, for listening, I owe you one, but John, I'll never pay!

The boys, for believing in this, we'll have a few more pints!

Janet and Colin, you're both in there somewhere.

Mum and Dad, if you're looking down, I know you both believed in me.

Melvin. What I would give for just one smoky night in your bed-sit. Never to be forgotten.

Sid and Betty, here it is!

To those I've missed, I'm sorry, you know who you are, and thank you, I couldn't have done it with out all of you.

And last of all. The Real 'Mrs Louise Shaw'. Out there? One day?

Now for the musical contributions that drove me on, when all else failed, the sound of other people's determination, kept me going.

Kevin Montgomery. Jars of Clay, Wood, Paul Thorne, Chicago, David Gates & Bread, Toto, Foreigner, the thunder lives on!

The Players

Andrew Jackson. Extremely wealthy having recently inherited a vast fortune has been living on his own since returning from America, where he had to prove his right to the inheritance. A very sensitive and somewhat insecure person, due in part to his upbringing and newfound wealth.

Kate. Andrew's former wife divorced after the settlement in the States, and now a permanent resident in America.

Louise Shaw. A stunningly beautiful auburn-haired former work colleague of Andrew's, and one-time friend. Andrew had been fond of her for a number of years before she left the company. That fondness would not go away.

Sarah Shaw. Louise and Gary's daughter aged 6. Striking looks passed on through the female line of the family.

Gary Shaw. Louise's husband, big and powerful, thinks with his fists, takes no messing, but is hiding a sinister secret connected with his job.

James Shaw. Louise and Gary's youngest child, two years of age.

Jill. Louise's close friend in the tiny village of Chillingston where they live.

Phillip. Andrew's close male friend and confidant, always available at the other end of the phone.

William Jackson. Andrew's eldest son, always a kind word coupled with wisdom that many older men would envy.

Natasha. William's partner, considerate and very sensitive.

Peter Jackson. The younger son, a quietly spoken man - more a man of action than words.

Sophie. Peter's bright and pretty companion.

Christine and Bryan. Andrew's older and trusted friends, Christine often referred to as an 'adopted sister' following the death of Andrew's true sister Rachel. Christine's husband Bryan, full of wit and humour but a man crossed at one's peril.

Alex. A mutual friend of both Christine and Andrew, his true past was unknown to either of them but he could be relied upon to have contacts in all of the right places.

Trevor and Diane Morrison. Louise's parents, very middle class, well educated, and very self-motivated, extremely dependable.

Jackie. The elder Morrison daughter, a strong and supportive female.

Inspector Jones. The unexpected arrival of officialdom in the form of this man, not the brightest of policemen and at times seeming to struggle to do his work due to the somewhat unhelpful assistance given to him by his short-term colleague.

Marcus Rimes. The Post Office official assigned to help the Inspector, but Rimes was concealing a dark and frightening part of his own private life, which he was to pay for dearly.

Jan Van-Elderman. A blond-haired Dutchman who has a habit of disappearing, a ruthless thug. Jan has a score to settle with Gary, or anyone who should happen to get in his way.

Sergeant Mitchell. The Cornish police officer tasked to keep an eye open for Louise and Andrew, only Sergeant Mitchell was often to be found in the pub. When two murders take place his eyes were firmly closed.

Mrs Baxter. The housekeeper of Andrew's large Victorian house in Scotland.

Len Shaw, and his nephew Mark. Trouble comes in two's, and these two not-so-bright individuals turn up looking for trouble after Gary's funeral.

The Greek connection.

Stavros. An old and trusted, worldly-wise man from a distant Greek village - a touch of a rogue about this man, but he could always be relied upon to get someone out of a tight fix.

Marie. Stavros's third wife, young, very attractive, and of English origin.

Nana. Stavros's beautiful daughter, a slight Greek complexion to her stunning features, educated at the very best of private girls' school and fluent in many languages.

Andreas. The eldest of Stavros's children, full of questions and an eagerness to travel.

Demetri. The younger son, only a half-brother to Andreas, but a full-blooded sibling to Nana, he was a man of few words, but strong actions.

A Chance Meeting

Never be afraid of the words.
'I'm Fond Of You'

Chapter One

It was the first Friday in December and it was an extremely cold day; a strong northerly wind had been blowing uninterrupted for the past few days. Exposed and unprotected it cut like a knife. The Christmas rush was already well under way, except for myself. For I was of the opinion that there was far too much hype; it always starts too early and, after all, it's over in just one day. I'd fought my way through the crowds of Christmas shoppers and made my way to W H Smiths, dodging as many people with their overflowing bags as I could. I was upstairs looking for my new year diary, without a lot of luck I have to say, when from about three aisles away I heard a woman's voice calling a child. Not much in that, you may think, but I hadn't seen the owner of that voice for almost six years. I still recognised the voice of Louise Shaw after all this time. I felt uneasy about looking round to see if it was the person I thought it was, when all of a sudden some of the old feelings rushed back.

I looked down, and standing by my side was a small girl wearing a red three- quarter-length coat, trimmed with a black fur collar. I would say she was about five years of age. She looked up into my eyes and a smile formed on her lips, an inquisitive smile that should have told me instantly who she belonged to, but my mind was gripped almost with fear of seeing the face to whom the voice belonged. It was a struggle for me to smile back, but you could say I managed a nervous grin. The little girl continued to look up and I felt as if her big blue eyes were burning into me. I looked at her again; not only did she have the most beautiful deep blue eyes but her hair was long and auburn, with a tight curl.

The woman's voice again called, "Sarah", and it was then I knew this would be more than a chance meeting. I looked down again, to find the little girl had gone. Could I have been daydreaming, or was it just wishful thinking? Then I heard a man's voice calling the same little girl's name. But this wasn't in soft, warm tones, it was coarse, and almost to the point of anger.

"Get over here now," he said. "If you don't do as you're told, you're going to be in big trouble!" he continued.

It's best I try and get away, I thought. I looked with more intensity for my diary and was almost at the point of giving up when I found what I was after. Gripping it tightly in my left hand I turned to my right, ready to head for the cash desk. As I turned, there she was, standing right in front of me - the owner of that voice.

"My," I said, as I stumbled for words, "fancy seeing you here, and after all this time." I could feel my voice trembling and it was difficult to string together the simplest of words.

We stood just for a moment and then she spoke to me in her soft, warm, caring voice.

"It's nice to see you, as well," she said, just slightly sarcastically. "It's been a few years, hasn't it? You're looking well," she continued. By now her voice was quiet, not the calling mother's voice, and a smile had formed across her whole face. My mind was racing back to the last time I had seen her. It seemed such a long time ago now. At the time I'd had feelings I shouldn't have had and I'd allowed myself to be misled; and it was me that had suffered, alone, I thought.

"You haven't phoned me for such a long time, I thought you'd left the Country," she said.

"Yes, I used to ring you didn't I?" I said, still with that nervous stammer in my voice. "And you're right, I did leave the country for a while," I continued. "I stopped phoning because I thought I was getting in the way."

From what seemed like nowhere the little girl came running to her side. "And this must be Sarah," I said, relieved I had something else to take my mind off this beautiful woman who had come back into my life, and I was able to put the old feeling temporarily back in the depths of my mind.

"I see you've already met," Louise said. "Well, she could have found a far worse place to hide!"

That comment gave me the reassurance I needed; it made me feel relaxed, as in the old days when we'd first been friends.

Now it was my turn to look at this woman to see what physical changes had taken place over the years. I saw very few. She was dressed in a smart navy-blue suit with a white blouse and a full length black coat that was undone. She always had a good dress sense; she hadn't gained any weight and had held onto her very petite size ten, no, size eight, figure - my ex-wife was size ten and Louise was smaller, even to the point of being tiny. I put it down to being a mother and being on the go all of the time. The years had been kind to her, and I still found her very attractive.

And the years had given her two babies. I had learnt that some time ago. I had longed to see her and had forced myself to stop phoning; I was hurting myself, and didn't want to get in the way, as I had told her.

"You really haven't changed in all this time," I told her, now I was beginning to gain some confidence. "It really is so nice to see you," I continued, "I often think about you and wonder what you have been doing."

"Oh, not a great deal," was her reply. "You don't get much time to yourself when you have two small children, and I live in a tiny village miles from anywhere - not that I'm complaining."

I was just about to ask if she saw any of the other people who we used to work with when I heard a man's voice.

"There you are!" he said, and continued, "I've been wandering round looking for the both of you."

I looked round to see a big man pointing at the little girl.

He was about six feet tall, with very short dark brown hair and a growth of beard that indicated he hadn't shaved that morning. He was dressed in jeans, tee shirt and an open leather jacket; hardly the best clothes for this time of year, I thought. He looked extremely fit and appeared to be carrying no excessive weight: his large frame filled the gangway.

"I told you to come here," he said, anger in his voice. With that, Sarah pulled in tightly to her mother.

"It's alright Gary. She's with me now and not lost," Louise told this enormous man. By now he had come closer to us; he was so big and almost blocked out the light.

His massive hands were gripping the top of a pushchair, which had a very small boy asleep in it.

"Who's this you're talking to?" he asked, in that very intimidating voice.

"Oh, someone I used to work with," Louise replied.

I'd met this man once before at a wedding party many years ago, but then he had very little to say, not just to me but to everyone. He had stayed by the bar all night and as a consequence I just thought he was a quiet big man; our meeting now was beginning to prove he was anything but.

"Well, what's his name?" he asked, in a very demanding way.

"This is Andrew," Louise replied.

"Andrew this is Gary, my husband," Louise said, and went on, "I haven't seen Andrew for … " at that moment she paused and I could tell she was trying to remember the last time we met. " … it must be five years at least," she continued.

"Well, I think it's more like six," I added, and I put out my right hand to shake Gary's, but he declined.

"Yes, I remember you," he said, as he took a step closer to me. "She used to talk about you. Do you still fancy her now she's turned into a lard-ass with two kids?" With that comment he gave Louise a slap on her backside, prompting her to exclaim, "Don't do that, it hurts."

I began to feel extremely uncomfortable. I could sense an atmosphere. I certainly wasn't helping it and may even have been the cause.

He looked down at me, straight into my eyes, no smile on his face and his brown eyes peering into mine. "You used to send her cards and letters didn't you?" he asked. Before I could reply he continued, "You haven't done that for a long time now, have you?"

No, I hadn't sent any correspondence for a considerable time. I had never received any replies, and as a result I had felt a little rejected. But now I was getting the message. It was quite simple. Don't!

I felt intimidated, well and truly put in my place, given a warning not to do anything like it again. I was speechless and a little frightened.

"Come on," Gary said. "I want a drink and these kids want something to eat." He turned the pushchair and started to walk away; he had only taken a few steps when he stopped to look back at me, "See you again sometime, mate!" he said, meaning: I never want to see you again. "Now come on, I want to go," he said in a raised voice.

The little girl ran off after her father and I was left alone with Louise. I looked into her blue eyes and could see the years of unhappiness. Her smile had all but disappeared. I wanted to say something to ease her obvious pain, but was unable to choose the words; anyway, what good would they do, she was going to have to live with this forever, I thought.

I was about to say goodbye and walk away when she came close to me, put her arms around me and kissed me on my right cheek.

"It's been so nice to see you," she told me, "please ring me." She paused, then continued, "Wednesdays are best, in the morning."

It felt so good; her arms wrapped around me, the smell of her perfume. I was unable to resist the temptation and slipped my hands inside her topcoat and put my arms around her. She felt so warm and firm and I remembered the last time I'd held her: it was to say goodbye all those years ago. I'd never wanted to let go, and now I felt the same, only this time we were in Smiths and not a pub. This time her husband was only a short distance away and it was possible he could look back at us at any moment.

"I can't promise anything," I said, "but I will try."

"Please try," she said, with a longing in her voice.

We released our hold on each other and she walked away, almost at a run to catch up with her husband. As she got to him I heard her say, "What about these letters?" His reaction was to tell her to "Shut up and get a move on."

"I never had any letters or cards from Andrew," I could hear her say.

"I know you didn't and you won't." Now he had stopped and was pointing his finger at her. "Just remember who you belong to; me, and not old lover-boy."

I'm not sure if I was meant to hear that comment, but it reinforced his earlier statement.

I stood and watched the little family walk away, all of a sudden feeling very nervous, but the danger had passed and they were on their way. I made my way to the cash desk and paid for my diary, then put the change into my pocket and headed for the exit. Outside, the cold December air greeted me, forcing me to button up my coat. I looked up and down the road expecting to see Louise and her family, but they had gone, disappeared into the throng of Christmas shoppers.

I made my way back to my car, by now feeling excited. I needed to ring my friend Phillip. Over the years I'd wanted to see Louise so much and now I had I couldn't wait to tell someone. Phillip had known how I'd felt about her for all of the years I'd known him. I dialled his number from my mobile phone and he answered with his usual greeting.

"Ah, Andrew, how are you on this bloody cold Friday?" he asked.

"You'll never guess who I've just met!" I blurted out.

As always Phillip had a quick reply: "The Queen," he said.

"No, not the bloody Queen," I said, "but someone much better."

"No, you're right, I won't guess so you had better tell me and put yourself out of your misery," he snapped, almost impatient with me.

"I've just seen Louise," I said, the excitement still in my voice.

"And where was this?" Phillip asked. "Before you tell me, just calm yourself down and take some deep breaths; I don't want you to burst a blood vessel." He went on, "I'm not sure this will do you any good, you know."

I went on to tell him where we had met and gave him all of the details right down to the clothes she was wearing.

"And how did you leave it," he asked, concern in his voice now, for it was he who had said years ago, there was something in her that I wouldn't forget; how right he had been.

"She wants me to ring her," I told him. "Next Wednesday. But I don't know if I should," I went on. "I'm not keen on making a fool of myself again as I did all those years ago."

"But *she* asked *you* to ring her, you say," Phillip replied, and continued, "*You* didn't suggest it did you, so what have you got to lose? It will be on the other end of a phone, and the big man won't be about, will he?"

"I'm not sure. I'll have to think about it over the weekend," I said.

"Andy, there's nothing to think about. You've waited so long for this, you have to ring her." Again he sounded impatient with me. "I know just how much she got under your skin. This time you'll take it very carefully, I'm sure."

"Well, that's it then. It has to be done. I'll talk to you later."

"Ok," he replied.

The weekend was slow to pass and I found it difficult to concentrate on anything I tried to do. I'd been on my own for three or four months since returning from America and I hadn't really settled into a new routine. I spoke to Phillip over the weekend but tried to stay off the subject of Louise: seeing her once again had stirred my thoughts of the past and I found myself waking in the night from dreams of her - not for the first time dreaming we were sleeping together. But we never had, we'd never even had a relationship. I'd wanted to be friends, but as I have said I got the wrong end of the stick after I'd had my shoulder cried upon, and things had gone sour for a long time.

I was married in those days and my marriage was going through a difficult period. It did get resolved and we had managed to be happy for another few years, then just recently my financial situation had changed. I no longer needed to work and after the trip to America my wife had decided to stay and make a new life for herself, with, I might add, a new partner. I returned home very disillusioned. I didn't like the States that much; it was fine for a short break, I could manage that, but after more than a month I had a need to be back in the old Country.

I'd spent some time in America to sort my new-found wealth and my wife

Kate loved it and very soon adapted to this new, fast lifestyle. I came home, and most of my friends couldn't understand why I came back. "With all that money you could go anywhere," they would tell me, but England was my home and whether it was rain or sun this was where I belonged; travelling long distances didn't suit me.

Upon my return to this Country I'd bought some property. Scotland was always a favourite place and I'd managed to find a little place just the other side of Ullapool: I say 'little place' but it was in fact a large Victorian house set in several acres of farmland and surrounded by forestry. These days it wasn't hard to get to and most of the time I had little else to do. But in fact I'd only spent a few weeks there at the most; the long dark nights drove me home, to the comfort of my house in the suburbs of Bristol.

When our children were small we had spent a lot of time in Cornwall and become friendly with a farmer there. He'd had some barns renovated and converted into apartments. At the time of my return from America he was having some difficulty in selling them. I'd always liked this particular spot and it was a pleasure to be able to help him out. I'd invested a considerable sum: not only did I purchase the buildings but also the swathe of land that is bordered on both sides by Royal Duchy land - I knew I'd never get any trouble with my adjoining landowner! I'd been able to leave the farmer in residence and he paid me a peppercorn rent; not that I needed the money!

I kept all of the apartments and put the letting side of things into the hands of a local estate agent, ensuring I had right over others until I could find a cottage as a more permanent base.

I was looking forward to spending some of the summer there. All I required was good weather. Being alone wasn't too much of a problem; I enjoyed my own company, liked to go walking along the coastal path and I thought the boys would come down for weekends to keep my spirits up if I needed them.

Monday and Tuesday dragged. I found it difficult to even sit and watch the television. I played music, read the paper from front to back and then back again, and talked to Phillip on the phone. Tuesday evening Kate rang from America. We had remained very good friends; after all, you can't be married to someone for twenty years and just walk away, can you? She asked what I had been up to since I'd been home; it had been well over four months since I'd seen her. We chatted for twenty minutes or so and she told me it was unlikely she would be back in the home Country for Christmas and she closed saying she would call before or on Christmas day.

I made for bed at about eleven thirty but found it impossible to sleep. I was tossing and turning all night long through fear and excitement, one and the same emotion. Eventually I did drop off to sleep, reassuring myself with the thought that Louise may not even be in if I did phone.

I was up a little later than normal, just after seven. Since I had retired from full-time work I'd tried to keep at least a small part of my old daily routine. After a shower I took a walk to the local newsagents, got my copy of The Times and made my way back home. It was cold and there had been a very hard frost. I looked at the headlines on the front page of the paper: another government minister was involved in a scandal, something to do with backhanders; two people had been killed in a bombing somewhere, and right at the bottom was a line about the Post Office. Just how busy they were at this time of the year; a reminder for us all to post early for Christmas, I thought.

I was taking more interest in the headlines than where I was going and promptly slipped on a very icy patch and landed on my back. I fell to the floor with such force that as I put out my hand to break the fall I hurt my arm and took some skin off the back of my right hand before bumping onto my backside. I gripped a wall and pulled myself to my feet, then bent down to collect my paper, which was about to be blown across the road. I gathered it together and very gingerly made my way home, now looking exactly where I was going.

Once indoors I had a look at the extent of my injuries. I had a big bruise on my right buttock and had removed some of the flesh from my forearm as well as my right hand. I'll live, I told myself. It was now nine thirty and I settled down in my favourite chair in the conservatory to have a read of the paper, a cup of coffee and some toast. I thought if I sat still long enough then at least the pain on the right side would go away. I was wrong; while I sat I felt comfortable but when I got up I could hardly move. It took a considerable time for me to get out of the chair just to go and make another cup of coffee. I'd been sitting for almost an hour, and during that time Louise hadn't crossed my mind at all.

Ten thirty and the sun was now out. I made my way to the lounge, sat down in an easy chair and picked up the phone. She may not even be in, I told myself. Her number was scribbled in the front of an old address book. Carefully I dialled it, but first I dialled 141; I didn't want to antagonise Gary if he should answer. It did cross my mind I could be set up: maybe she had told him she had felt pestered by me all those years ago. "Too many 'ifs' and 'buts'," I told myself out loud as I pressed the last digit of her number. Now it seemed like an age before I even got to hear the ringing tone come back to me, and it would have been easy for me then to hang up, but after four rings the phone was answered.

"Hello." At the soft voice of Louise my nervousness disappeared and, as in the old days, I found no problem in replying.

"Hello," I said, "and how are you today?"

"It's you!" she said, pleasure and excitement now in her voice. "You kept your promise," she continued and I could tell now, just the phone call was making her happy.

"I've just put baby James down for a sleep, you've timed it just right. Now tell me what you've been up to since I saw you all those years ago," she said.

"Well, that's a long story. I'm sure you would get very bored," I said. "I need to know about you and that lovely family you have. It's alright for you to talk, is it?"

"Oh yes, Sarah is at school, Gary's at work, I've got all the time in the world to talk too you, if you've got time for me."

"What can I say, I'm very flattered." I went on to tell her about my fall when I was coming back from the newsagents. I exaggerated the story somewhat and I could hear her laughing, so much so that when she stopped she was crying. "Are you alright?" I asked. "I didn't mean to upset you."

"I'm fine," she said through her tears. "I don't get much to laugh about these days. You always had the ability to make me smile. If I were there I'd be able to soothe your injuries." She paused before continuing, "I've missed you so much."

"Not half as much as I've missed you and our telephone conversations," I told her.

"What about your wife? Kate, wasn't it? How is she these days?" Louise enquired.

"Now that's a question," I replied, as it had caught me a bit by surprise. I explained the situation briefly; I didn't want to go into great detail at this early stage of our renewed friendship. By the time we finished we had talked our way through three-quarters of an hour.

"You will ring me again, won't you?" came that asking voice I just couldn't resist.

"Of course I will," I replied. "Same time next week? But I don't want to cause any trouble between you and Gary. After all, he's a big bloke!" I finished.

"Yes, and don't I know it," was her immediate reply. "I'll have to go now, I can hear James, and I look forward to next week. Bye."

"Goodbye," I said, and she was gone.

I hung up the phone. I'd had enough excitement to last me a week. I felt like I was in heaven. My next call was to Phillip.

"I've been expecting a call from you," he said. "How did it go? Was she there? And what about the big guy?" not stopping for me to get a word in edgeways.

"So many questions," I said. "She's fine, and no, Gary wasn't there. In fact she didn't say much about him at all."

"And are you going to ring again?" Phillip enquired.

"Same time next week," was my prompt reply. "What I will do between now and then is anybody's guess," I said.

"You need a job to take your mind off her," he went on. "Too much time and money on your hands. Oh, by the way, did you explain why you don't work anymore?"

"Well, I didn't quite get round to that," I said, and continued, "but I'm sure I'll be able to cross that bridge when I come to it."

"Well, the best of luck to you. It's well overdue, and she's a fine looking woman if my memory serves me right. I'll have to go now, but speak to you soon." And he was gone.

A week can soon fly by, and the next one did. I was able to concentrate more as a result of getting that first call out of the way, a week later and with far more ease I rang again. The first things she asked me about were my cuts and bruises. This call was longer and I'm sure we were both far more relaxed.

On the next occasion I rang, Louise reminded me, the following week would be Christmas week and it may be best if I didn't phone, as there was a possibility that Gary could be about and it may be best if I didn't call until the New Year.

I told her it would be very hard for me to keep going for three weeks without hearing her voice.

"Don't worry," she said, "you'll be in my thoughts over Christmas and the New Year."

"But I can't even send you a Christmas card." It felt like a one-way affair and as I said the words my mind went back to our meeting in Smiths at the beginning of the month.

"Did you send me cards and letters?" Louise asked.

"Yes!" was my somewhat stern reply. "I don't understand why you never got them."

" Well, never mind for now, just have a nice Christmas and a happy New Year," she continued. "Are you going away?"

"Yes, I'm gong down to Cornwall for a few days and my sons William and Peter are coming as well. I think their girlfriends will be with them, so we will fill the apartment." I had briefly explained that I'd come into some money and had made some investments in the property market. I never went into too much detail or said just how much money I'd inherited.

"I'm sure it will be good fun," I said, "and Phillip said he will be down to see the New Year in with me. It would be nice if you could be with me."

"Oh!" The comment took her by surprise. "I don't think I'll ever get to see your place in Cornwall, as much as I would like to," she said.

"Maybe one day you will," I said, with a longing for her in my voice.

"Maybe one day!" And for the first time she closed the conversation with, "Take care my dear. Goodbye." And I was alone again.

Chapter Two

Christmas Eve

Christmas Eve was on the Wednesday. The week had rushed by with surprising speed, as it does at this time of year. I'd had plenty to do: last minute shopping and collecting the necessary groceries to take away. At one point I found myself sitting by the phone. It was an awful job not to pick up the phone and ring her. Some of the last words she had spoken still lingered in my ears, 'Maybe one day.' I quickly put thoughts of Louise to the back of my mind and got on with packing the car to make the week to ten days I was going to spend in Cornwall as comfortable as possible. It couldn't be, I told myself. We are destined to be just friends, with the possibility of the occasional meeting. I had loaded the car by twelve fifteen and after locking up and saying goodbye to my neighbours, I was on my way.

The twilight of the winter evening was creeping up the lane like a cat stalking a bird as I approached the track that leads towards the apartments, the blackness of the night rolling over the hillside like a blanket. I arrived at the apartment about four o'clock. The darkness had already engulfed the courtyard, the surrounding buildings looked black and overpowering in the dim afternoon light and a frost was beginning to form.

Now one of the little but expensive luxuries I'd indulged myself in was my liking for sports cars. The 'One day I'm going to have one of those' had arrived and it was a treat to drive my Porsche 911. But though it's fine having a Porsche, when the traffic is heavy and slow you can't go any faster than the man in front of you.

Next to arrive was my eldest son William, along with his girlfriend Natasha. I already had a meal well on the go, as it must have been getting on for six o'clock. The three of us sat and had a drink whilst waiting for my youngest son Peter and his companion Sophie to arrive, which they did at about seven with tales of traffic chaos and reasons why the car wasn't running correctly. In unison we all told him to shut up; we were all here for a rest and to get away from our everyday problems.

Christmas Day

Christmas day dawned fine. We were all up by eight o'clock, had a light breakfast and exchanged presents; then the girls gave me a hand to prepare dinner, which we had agreed would be an evening meal. We even managed to go to the pub for a drink. The place was packed and we made comments about not being so many people about in the summer. Kate rang from the States during the afternoon and went on for over an hour telling us just how cold it was, but all the same she didn't miss the English winter. Everyone spoke to her and agreed, somewhat reluctantly, to go over in the summer. But there was nothing stopping her from coming home really.

I was out on the patio after dinner on that cold Christmas Day taking some air, my thoughts on Louise and her family, wondering what sort of Christmas she was having. Maybe playing with the children, most likely at one or the other parents. Of course it was made all the more difficult for me because I hadn't been able to ring her that week. I was trying to console myself with the thought, two weeks would soon pass, when I felt two small hands cover my eyes and offer a penny for my thoughts. It caught me by complete surprise and for an instant I imagined it was Louise. I turned in my surprised state to find William's girlfriend Natasha standing on the patio.

"I'm sorry," she said, "I didn't mean to startle you. You must have been miles away. Are you coming in? You've been out here for ages and its very cold," she said as she wrapped her arms around herself.

"Yes," I replied, and continued, "You're right, I was miles away. Just a few more minutes and I'll be in with you."

With that, the patio doors opened and William stepped out.

"I wondered where you two had got to," he said, with a smile.

"I think your Dad was thinking of home," Natasha replied, "I'm going in; it's too cold for me out here. Don't be too long!" And she was gone, leaving William and I alone.

"You ok Dad?" he asked, "You've been a bit quiet." He put his right arm around me.

"I'm ok son," was my reply.

"Are you sure? Do you miss Mum?" he went on. "Or is there something else on your mind?" He wasn't going to give up, he could see through me.

"Yes, I do miss your Mother, and the old times, I suppose," I said, with a need to tell him about Louise. "Its not just that." I paused, "I've seen an old friend and started making contact with her." I went on to tell him about the phone calls I'd made.

"I had noticed, Dad," he said. "Well, only time will tell what will come of it Dad, you could do with some female company."

"Yes, you're right, but I bet her husband wouldn't agree with you," I replied light-heartedly.

"Oh shit Dad, she's married. Has she any kids?" he asked.

"Yes," I said, "but I'm not even sure of where it's going. At the moment it's just a phone call once a week and it may not progress any further."

"But you would like it to, wouldn't you?" he said. Now he was digging, trying to get at my feelings.

"Well, son," I started, "as you get older you learn to be patient. I'll take it slow. The last thing I want to do is break up a marriage. Even with all this money I've got, I realise I can't buy happiness. Maybe I'm destined to spend the rest of my life alone. I wouldn't be the first millionaire to spend my time without any company. We'll have to wait and see what comes of this potential friendship, and your mother may need me; nothing is certain in this life."

"But would you have her back Dad?" concern in his voice.

"I still love your Mother, you know, son," I said, I think to his surprise. I went on, "She may need me, as in the past. All of this money has brought its problems, and now none of us can just walk away from it. It's ours after all these years; it's what so many people work and die for and I used to work for. I don't want it to change me, you or Peter; just because you can have anything you want doesn't mean you have to have everything."

The evening was spent watching some of the customary offerings of rubbish on the television, until someone suggested a game of Monopoly. That was fine and the game continued well into the night, with a considerable amount of alcohol being consumed by everyone.

Towards the end of the evening, and I'm still not sure if it was the drink talking, William suggested I needed a new career to take my mind off the money. Various options were discussed, from buying a chain of hotels to investing in some pubs, then Peter came up with the idea of an investment in a garage come workshop. By now my mind was too confused to concentrate, or even argue against such an idea, and at almost 1am we went our separate ways to our beds.

Boxing Day

I awoke at eight on Boxing day morning, and looking out of the windows I could see we'd had another hard frost: everywhere was white, the trees bare of any leaves but laden with particles of ice. Off in the distance I could see smoke rising from a farmhouse chimney. I made some tea and waited for William to come down, for he was never far behind me. I think I usually make so much noise I wake everyone in the apartment.

I sat on the small seat by the patio doors and my mind went back to what we had been discussing last night. Slowly I regained my thoughts. It wouldn't be such a bad idea after all. Peter had finished his education at university, and William and he had always had an interest in cars. I could well afford to set them up in business; certain rules would have to be followed, but William was right, I did need something to take my mind off the money. It would also occupy my mind in-between the Wednesday phone calls to Louise, and if they were to fizzle out then I would have something to fall back on.

Sure enough at 8.45 William was down, and after taking a mug of tea up to Natasha he came and sat on the small sofa with his own tea.

"That was good fun last night Dad," he said, as he stretched his arms and the night's sleep out of his body.

"Yes, I enjoyed the game as well," I replied and continued, "I've been thinking about what you said last night, you know, about getting a job."

"Yes, but Dad you don't need to, do you?" was his reply.

"Well, I think you were right first of all. I do need something to take my mind off this money, and we could use a business as an investment, something like the way we inherited ours." I paused, for now he was interested. He wasn't happy where he worked, and spent long hours in his own workshop; a hobby on cars can soon turn into a small business.

"Well, what sort of money would you be thinking of putting up as capital?" he asked.

"How about we start at say one million," I said. "That's for the right premises and all the equipment required to get the business going. I'd be looking for some sort of reasonable turn-round within, say, twelve months. I must add it will be your business, I would be purely a sleeping partner. You'd have to get an accountant and everything would go through the books. What do you think?" I finished.

"I have to say I like the idea of being my own boss and I know for a fact that Peter is keen on working in the motor trade. We'll all have to have a chat, but if you're up for it Dad, then I am." With those words he was up and took my hand. "Yes let's go for it, what have we got to lose other than a million pounds!"

The five of us talked it over during breakfast and the girls got as excited as their respective partners.

"But first you've got to have that skiing holiday the four of you booked. What time is your flight?" I asked, trying to change the conversation from cars to something I felt equally uncomfortable about.

"We fly out at ten o'clock in the morning, on the twenty eighth," Peter said, and continued with, "Why don't you come with us Dad?"

"Now you should know better than ask me that," I said. "Anyway, Phillip is coming down and staying for a few days, so I wouldn't be able to come out with you."

After breakfast we took the short drive to the beach, and had a very bracing walk along the soft sandy shoreline, and for a time I thought of other things, and not Louise. I made up my mind I would ring the solicitors tomorrow and get the ball rolling on this new and exciting project. I would have almost two weeks to sort something out while the children were away.

Back at the apartment we had our traditional Boxing Day lunch: cold meat and chips. They had to be oven chips as I don't have a chip pan in the apartment, and by mid-afternoon my sons and their companions had packed and loaded their cars and, with a few more goodbyes, were ready for the journey home. Natasha, a far more sensitive girl than Sophie, shed a few tears; I suppose at the thought of leaving me on my own. Then they were on the move.

Soon I had just the night and a chill wind for company, and my thoughts again went back to Louise. I poured myself a large tumbler of malt whisky, and sat by the patio doors, looking at the flickering lights far off in the distance and the blackness of the night. It crossed my mind I could go home, make apologies to Phillip, and invite him to my other home, but I also felt I needed to stick this out. Alone I might be, but a day would soon pass.

As the evening moved along the children rang to say they'd arrived home safely, and their words of 'Happy New Year' were still in my ear as I hung up, and the previous thoughts of Louise came back to me. I'm afraid then, temptation got the better of me. I found the receiver in my hand. I just had to hear that soft voice. I'd made a note of her number and carried with me in my wallet. That, too, was by the phone and as I pressed the last digit my heart began to race.

If Gary answered I would hang up. I didn't need to exercise the same caution as I did when at home, as this line was ex-directory. The ringing seemed to go on and on, and I was almost at the point of hanging up when it was answered.

"Hello," she said, and then she was silent.

"Have you had a nice Christmas?" were all the words I could string together.

"It's you!" Louise said very softly in an excited tone, "Yes thank you very much, have you?"

"Yes," I paused before continuing, "but I've missed you."

She went quiet for a short while and then replied with, "I know, and I've missed you. I can't talk for long, I'm just getting the children ready for bed, and Gary is due back from the club any minute."

In my semi-drunken state I told her I needed to hear her voice, and I was looking forward to ringing her when I returned home.

"And I look forward to speaking to you in the New Year. I'll have to go now, please take care and have a happy New Year."

"And you, I'll be thinking of you," I told her, but I also had a hundred and one other things I wanted to say to her.

"Goodbye," she came back with.

"Goodbye," I returned, and she was gone.

I finished my drink and watched some television, but had no interest in it at all, so as the clock ticked away I made my way to bed, knowing I would have to give the place a bit of a clean-up in the morning.

December 27th

And that's exactly what I did. The morning passed very quickly as I busied myself with the housework. I also had to give the other apartment a clean, as that one would be shut up for next few months, at least until the spring. At times my mind did wonder to my phone call last night. I'd got the response I wanted, so she hadn't forgotten about me during this spell away from the phone. I would need to work on building the friendship in the coming months, for I wanted it to progress, and it would have to be Louise who called it to a halt.

December 28th

As planned, Phillip came down for a few days and we spent a great deal of the time discussing the 'ifs' and 'buts' of my new and exciting relationship. We must have talked through every conceivable scenario and situation, before we decided this new friendship would have to run its own course. We did seem to spend a lot of our time leading up to the New Year in the pub, and I think that maybe a chain of pubs might not have been such a bad idea after all, as Peter had suggested.

The locals as always made us very welcome and we saw the New Year in with a great number of them. Neither of us can remember just how we got back to the apartment on that cold frosty first day of January.

January 1st

It was very late when I awoke and I had the most awful headache. We both decided it would be best if we returned that day to our respective homes. Phillip had to go to work and I needed to get the ball rolling if the boys were going to start the business, so after a fried breakfast we packed away our belongings and set of on our separate ways. Firstly I had to call on the agent who managed the apartments for me; I knew his wife would give them a good clean and keep them aired in readiness for my next visit, whenever that might be.

The children called me on the mobile phone installed in the car as I was driving homeward along the motorway, again wishing me a happy New Year, and I explained I would be seeing the solicitor later in the week with regard to the garage. All were happy with the arrangements I planned to make and we agreed to meet when things had progressed to a more constructive stage; for their part they would start looking for suitable premises when they returned from holiday, and would keep me informed of any progress.

So that was how I occupied my time between arriving home and the first

Wednesday in the New Year, and it very much helped having something to do because it helped to take my mind off her. Still, she was always there, and on the Wednesday morning of the second week in January, when I phoned her from my lounge, I felt better than I had in a long time.

It was ten thirty and I had a coffee on one of the small tables. The phone couldn't have rung more that three times when it was answered and this time a little girl's voice said, "Hello."

In an instant I thought I had a wrong number, but I was very quickly proved wrong, for in the background I heard her voice and the words, "Give the phone to mummy darling!"

"Hello, is that who I think it is?" she asked, and just the sound of her sweet voice gave me the greatest of pleasure. We picked up from where we had left off on Boxing Day evening. She told me in great detail about their family Christmas: she'd spent a lot of time alone, Gary was out with his mates from the football club or just in the pub with his other mates. It prompted me to pass a comment about him not being a great family man. In the past her reaction would have been very defensive, but not now, all she would say was the club and his mates seem to mean more to him.

I told her very briefly about the business that was beginning to take shape and I felt encouraged by her reaction, wishing us luck in our venture.

After forty-five minutes we closed our first call of the year, and I said I looked forward to next week.

"Me too," was her reply.

Soon enough the next Wednesday was with us and I happily called and received the same greeting, our calls were getting longer and more intimate, and she told me she felt she could tell me anything. As the calls progressed she did, for on one occasion she seemed a little edgy and I enquired if I'd been rude, or if she felt I was going on about the garage too much, maybe boring her. Her reply took me a little by surprise but wasn't totally unexpected.

"Oh its not you!" Her tone was firm. "You know, it's one of those weeks," she said, and continued, "I always get a bit edgy. It's not helped by being on my own for so long, and the children have been playing up a bit. Gary doesn't help much." She paused. "I'm sorry, I didn't mean to unload my problems onto you."

"That's ok," was my reply. "I think we can tell each other anything and we shouldn't be offended or too upset. It'll take more than a bad week to put me off ringing you."

"Thank you," was her reply, in what now seemed a more relaxed way.

Chapter Three

And so we talked our way through every Wednesday morning in January and also February, getting to know each other at the end of the phone. On the first Wednesday of the next month I could wait no longer, I had to ask her the question that had been in my heart for what seemed an eternity.

"Can I see you again?" I asked.

The silence was painfully deafening as I awaited her reply. And I thought: I've blown it this time, I don't know this woman at all; and all sorts of other thoughts crossed my mind as I hung on waiting for her words. I felt I had to know and added, "A simple yes or no will do."

"I've been waiting for you to ask," she replied softly, and paused. "Yes, I would very much like to see you again, and not in Smiths." Her words reverberated around my head. I hadn't wasted my time phoning her, it had been worth it.

"There's a chance," she began, "that Gary will be going away for a week this month. Do you think you can wait until then?" She must have heard my sigh of relief to the positive answer I'd received. She continued with, "Just a drink?"

"Well, perhaps we could go for dinner." I stammered, still in a state of shock.

"Yes, that would be really nice, somewhere quiet and out of the way," she replied, pushing my ego to new heights.

"Well, when shall we say?" I asked.

"I'll tell you next week," she said, and went on, "I'll know then when Gary's going to be away. Can you wait until then? You sound so excited."

"Yes to both of your comments. Next week will be fine." By now I was even shaking with the excitement.

We finished our conversation, agreeing the following week would be one of the longest.

My next call was to Phillip and I told him time and time again we had made plans to go out for dinner. He, as always, wished me luck.

The next week flew by, partly because the boys had found a suitable property to start their business from. We had to act quickly to secure it, and then there was the task of buying all of the necessary equipment to furnish the workshop, not that I spent a great deal of time at the new premises. I was given a list of jobs to do and got on and did them, in no time at all it was Wednesday and I was by my phone.

"Next Tuesday!" were her first words when she answered the phone.

"And what if it wasn't me?" was my reply to this somewhat cheeky woman.

"I knew it would be you, you always ring at the same time," she said as she laughed down the phone to me. "I'm so looking forward to going out, do you know where we can go?"

"Yes, I've just the place in mind, very quiet and secluded." I told her, and continued, "Am I that predictable then?"

"No, not predictable. I would say," she paused to gather her thoughts, "reliable, that's one of the qualities I like in you."

And so my most wishful secret was given life. I would meet her at the railway station at 7.30 in the evening, and we would go for dinner at a restaurant of my choice. It was to be a treat, from me to her. She made a comment about it changing our lives, but little did either of us know just how much truth there was in that comment, and what was to unfold during the coming weeks.

Chapter Four

Tuesday

My heart was pounding. My throat, dry with nervous anticipation as I pulled up outside the Railway Station at 7.30. There was no sign of her on this Tuesday evening in March, a mild evening for this time of the year. I almost felt relieved she wasn't waiting, for it gave me the opportunity to regain my composure. Perhaps the train was late, I thought to myself. I could give it a few minutes on the double yellow lines and then I would drive round the block.

At that moment my car phone rang. It was my eldest son William and he was to take my mind off of the waiting: Had I heard from Mum, and what was I up to. I hadn't seen him for a few days and he was concerned about my absence from the garage. Our conversation went on for almost ten minutes. I explained what I was doing, but not the secretiveness of it. Before I cleared down he wished me luck and said he had to go and would call later in the week if I didn't see him.

I looked across at the station entrance and standing just to the side of the main doors was Louise. I couldn't believe my eyes. Even from this distance of fifty yards she looked stunning. She was wearing a knee-length green and red tartan skirt and black lines separated the colourful squares. Her dark green jacket was unbuttoned, and underneath she was wearing a roll neck jumper of a deep red that matched the red in the skirt, and was pulled outside of her skirt accentuating the flatness of her tummy. Over her shoulder she had a small black bag which matched her black high-heeled shoes. I got out of the car and took the short walk across the taxi stand to greet her, a small bunch of flowers in my right hand.

As I got closer I could see she was wearing make-up, not a lot as she didn't require much, just sufficient to highlight her deep blue eyes, a dusting of blusher and some pink lip gloss; enough to keep me transfixed on her beautiful features. Her long, wavy auburn hair was held back in place by two small clips just above her hairline, and to complete the picture her nails were done in the same pink as her lips.

"Oh, I thought I'd been stood up," she said, with an air of surprise about her.

"I'm sorry, I was on the phone to one of my sons," was my answer. "I do hope I haven't kept you waiting. You look beautiful, and these are for you," I said as I passed her the flowers, and her face gained some more colour.

"No, you haven't kept me waiting, I've only just got here and thank you these are lovely," was her slightly embarrassed reply as she held the posy in both hands. "You look very smart yourself."

I'd put on a navy suit and a shirt and tie I thought matched well. I don't have the need to get dressed up much these days but I wanted to look my best. I put out my right hand so as to lead her to my car, and she came forward and kissed me on the right cheek and slipped her hand into mine. I felt I was in heaven; her lips were warm and she was very gentle and her small hand gripped mine for security.

"Thank you," I said, surprised at her fondness, and turned and kissed her in return. Her skin was soft and warm and the smell of her perfume filled my nostrils.

"You still use the same perfume," I said. "It's the same one as all those years ago."

"Do you like it?" she asked, "I don't have many and don't have much need for it as I don't get out and about much these days."

"Yes, I do like it and you're out now. I'm going to take you for dinner at my favourite restaurant," I said, as we walked towards my car.

"Is this yours? A Porsche!" she exclaimed, a real look of surprise on her face. "I've never been in one of these before."

"Yes, it's mine alright," I replied, for now it gave me an intense feeling of pleasure to open the door for this exceptionally pretty woman. She made me feel good and I wanted to savour every second of being with her.

We arrived at the restaurant at eight and pulled up in the car park, and as I got out of the car and walked round to open the door for Louise a man looked across at me from the other side of the car park. He was just getting into his own car, and winked at me. I'm not sure if it was because of the car, or because he had set eyes on my attractive companion, but I made my mind up it must be because of Louise, for I have to say I had a job to take my own eyes off her.

We made our way up the slight incline of the car park to the restaurant entrance, I opened the door and we went in.

Just inside the door, to the right, was a small table similar to a lectern, behind which stood the head waiter, who welcomed us and asked whether we had a table reserved. When I told him my name he replied with, "Of course, sir" and took us to a table tucked away in a quite corner. It was placed under a small window and we were able to look out over the fields and down to the river. The evening light was beginning to fade and the glow of the sun going down over the distant hills highlighted the redness and warmth on Louise's cheeks.

The table was small, about two-foot square, just sufficient for the two of us. We talked about her children and she explained to me that her mother was baby sitting for the evening. She'd told her mother she was going out for a meal with a girlfriend and said her mum had passed a comment about being a bit over dressed for a pub meal. Her mother had also said she had been more cheery these past few months, and her smile had broadened as she said, "I can't think what that can be down to, can you?"

I told her in more detail about my grown-up sons, and how well the new business was doing. We ate and talked all night and the service was impeccable as always. I'd been in the past but on the previous occasions I'd been alone or with my sons, now I was in the company of this immaculately turned-out woman and I wanted it to last forever.

The night passed and I can't even remember what we had for our meal, I was so bewitched by her smile and presence. At no time did we run out of conversation.

I thought the details about my income would keep for another occasion. Anyway, I feared it could lead to the end of us as friends. Over coffee I asked the time of her train back. Ten fifteen was her answer. It was now nine thirty, and a good twenty-five minute drive back to the station.

"I could run you home," I offered.

"No, you mustn't," was her instant reply, "It's Gary you see. You know he is away for a few days, but the problem is too many people see what's going on in the village - you know how neighbours like to gossip - and your car would stand out like a sore thumb. Honest, I'll be alright on the train, I can get a taxi back from the far end to home."

"Ok, if you say so." I felt there was no point in pursuing the issue, as so far I'd had the most wonderful evening.

I settled the bill and we made our way out into the car park. It was March and by now the chill of the evening had come down, and as we headed for the car she took my arm and pulled her little body close to mine. All of a sudden I felt like a schoolboy on his first date. I opened the car door for her to get in and as she slid herself into the leather seat, she looked up at me.

"I've had the most wonderful evening you know," she told me. Her face was beaming, and that was the way it remained all the way back to the station; every time I looked across at her she had a contented smile across her entire face.

I pulled up in the station yard, where I had stopped to pick her up.

"Can I walk you to the platform?" I asked.

"Yes," was her reply, "but once I'm on that train you must go."

We walked hand in hand across the car park, into the station building, and onto the platform.

"Only five minutes and the train will be here," she said, looking up at the station clock, still holding my right hand with her left, the bunch of flowers in her right.

"Can I ring you tomorrow?" I asked, but really I didn't need to ask.

"You'd better," was her reply, just as the train pulled in. "I'm not sure if I'll sleep very much tonight," she told me. "This has been a bit like a dream."

"And for me," I replied. I opened the door of the carriage for her and she stepped aboard, then hesitated, turned round and stepped back off the train. I wasn't sure what was going to happen next, and what did, took me by complete surprise. She put her arms around me and kissed me long and hard on the lips, her arms wrapped around me pulling me close and tight to her.

"That's something special. Just for you," she said as she let go and got back on board the train.

"Now go and I'll talk to you tomorrow. Take care, bye, go!" she said in a forceful way I couldn't argue with.

I turned and walked back across the foyer to the exit, telling myself not to look back. I didn't want her to see the huge smile I now had across my face. I felt as if my five foot four stature had grown, and now I felt ten feet tall. I'm afraid I couldn't resist it, I had to look back. She'd found a seat and was sitting by the window, her own smile telling me everything I needed to know. She waved her right hand and then gestured me to go on and so I did, but very reluctantly.

Now I was alone again and I stood and looked across at my car. Two lads were looking at it and by time I'd got to it they were quite close.

"Nice motor," one said. "I bet you can pull the tarts with this, can't you?" the other added.

"Thanks," I said, "it's nice of you to say so, but I do prefer ladies." I continued thinking of the lady I had just spent the evening with. I pressed the key fob, opened the door, and Louise's perfume came out to greet me as if she was still sitting in the car. I was close enough to get straight in, without any problems.

"Well, fuck you. You tosser," was their aggressive comment as they made off into the night, giving me a two-fingered salute as they went on their way into the darkness of the poorly-lit streets. But my mind was on other things, or I should say another person, as I sat and thought of her standing on the platform holding on to me. I was able to reflect back to those six years ago, when we said goodbye. She'd felt the same then and I'd wanted to tell her then that I loved her but I'd left it too late, or the time wasn't right. Now I felt exactly the same, if anything my feelings were stronger. I drew comfort from Phillip's words: "You'll take it more carefully this time!"

And so if I had a plan, then it was going to plan, if not, then it was down to luck. I heard the engine of the train roar into life and looked at my watch; ten-fifteen and she was on her way home, and that's where I headed, with my head full of what we would say in the morning.

Chapter Five

Wednesday

I slept like a baby. I didn't even have a night-cap when I got home, just put the car away and made for my bed, the impression of her face as she had sat opposite me etched in my mind.

It was seven o'clock when I awoke, came downstairs and made some tea, looked at the post and went back upstairs to take a shower. A brisk walk to the newsagents and I was back indoors just as the rain was starting to fall. I settled to read the paper but was unable to concentrate; I had to ring her, and in my eagerness to call I made my first mistake in all the months I'd been phoning her. I needed to make sure she got home all right and also to confirm I hadn't been dreaming.

"Yes, I was home by eleven and no you weren't dreaming," she told me. "If you were, then we both had the same dream." The words came from her lips as if I was still opposite her in the restaurant. "Did you sleep ok?" she asked.

"I did," was my reply. I wanted to ask her about the way she felt for me, but even on the phone it was difficult to summon up the courage.

"Do you think we could do it again?" I asked. "I know lots more restaurants like that, they only cater for very intimate couples," I told her. A sigh came back down the phone, then silence. "Are you ok?" I asked.

"Oh yes I'm fine. I just never had such an intimate dinner before," she said with an air of wanting in her voice. "And yes, I'd love to go out again, that place was just fine."

There was a pause and I could hear something or someone in the background, then that voice. "I'm back." It was Gary. I felt frightened and I was miles away.

"I'll have to go," she said very softly. "Next week, call next week, ok?"

"Take care," was my reply, "goodbye," and she was gone.

As a result of arranging this very secretive meeting and the way I was feeling about Louise I'd let a lot of my day-to-day things slip into disorder. The upside of these secret phone calls over the past few months was a boost to my own self-esteem. I'd started my running again, not far, just a few miles, but the effect was beginning to show on my physique: my stomach was flatter and felt firmer than it had for years. Once again I had a purpose in my life. On the other hand I had mountains of paperwork to sort out and some bills to be paid. I made up my mind this was the best way to occupy myself until I could ring Louise again.

I spent the rest of the day doing just that and as a result I came across a bill which needed to be paid. How I'd left it unattended I'll never know. I looked at the clock in the study; it was gone five o'clock, too late to go to the bank now, I would have to go tomorrow, I told myself.

I fixed myself some supper, but found it difficult to eat; no company can very easily take away your appetite. I left most of it and was just taking the plate out into the kitchen when the doorbell rang. I made a detour to answer it, and upon opening it found it was my youngest son Peter.

"Anything to eat?" he asked. "Well, if you're not going to finish this, then I will," he said, taking the plate from me and heading in the direction of the lounge. In no time the plate was cleared.

"You ok, Dad?" he asked.

"Yes, I'm alright," I said, feeling quite pleased with myself, the thoughts of last night still in my head. I wanted to share them with someone, but before we could get into conversation he stopped me.

"That's good then," he went on, almost in a hurry. "Can I borrow the keys to one of the apartments, I've seemed to have mislaid mine," he finished.

We were making our way in the direction of the hall and I was just about to call him a donkey when the phone rang. I reached into the kitchen and lifted the receiver. Now, my situation has taught me not to answer the phone with the number and often it's best to let the other party speak first.

I answered with "Hello" and wasn't expecting the reply I got.

"I fucking knew it!" And I knew the voice; it was Gary. In the background I could hear Louise crying, "No! Gary, No!" then the receiver was slammed down and my right ear was ringing from the shock. There was a deadly silence and a realisation there was nothing I could do.

"You ok Dad?" my son asked as I replaced the receiver. "You look a bit, no, not a bit, but a lot, shocked."

"Oh, just a wrong number," I said, numbed from the aggressive manner in Gary's voice.

"Those keys then, Dad." He was persistent. Something in me wanted to jump into the car and drive up to Louise's house. Maybe I would be able to explain what had gone on.

Thoughts of Louise would fill my mind for the rest of the evening, long after my son had gone. As he was leaving he said, "I'll get a new set cut, see you in a week or so."

"Don't lose those," I shouted as he manoeuvred out of the drive, and in reply I got a thumbs up and he was gone.

It was to be a very poor night's rest for me, wondering what would have gone on when that phone went down with such force. He wouldn't hit her, I kept telling myself. I was up in the night at about two o'clock, made coffee, back to bed, tried to read a book, but I was in no frame of mind to do any reading.

Thursday

Six o'clock I was up. I would have a break from my normal routine. I had to go to the bank and afterwards I would risk a ride up to the village where Louise lived; I had a rough idea of where her house was. Showered and dressed, and after some toast, I was about to leave when I thought I would try to ring Louise first. This time I withheld my number, but all I received was the busy tone. My mind was full of all sorts of thoughts as I set off on my way.

What I had forgotten was that Thursday is one of the worst days to try to park anywhere, let alone outside the bank. I asked myself if the entire world was out to do its shopping. Easter was in two weeks, not tomorrow, what the hell was going on?

I found a place in the car park at the back of the bank and made my way via the narrow lane to the side of the bank. People were everywhere. If parking wasn't bad enough the bank was full; the woman in front of me had a child in a pushchair and he was screaming his head off. I felt like offering to give him something to complain about! The little old lady in front of her couldn't find her bank book and all in all the day couldn't get any worse, and I wanted very much to just get out of there.

My turn came and I went up to the cashier, a very pretty girl behind the screen, smartly dressed in the bank uniform. She would have been about twenty or maybe twenty-one. I looked at her left hand as I passed my bill over to her. She wasn't wearing a wedding ring. "Good Morning, Mr Jackson," she said as she glanced at the bill I was paying. I replied with the same, but I'm sure she could tell it was anything but good, and judging by the lengthening queue it was not going to be a good morning for her either.

"The bank is very busy today, is the world coming to an end?" I quipped.

"No. It's always like this on a Thursday," she replied. "Anyway, we don't see you in here often these days Mr Jackson."

"No," I said, "I've got most of my affairs sorted out, just this one bill I forgot." With that I felt someone pass behind me and almost give me a nudge. I looked round and could see a man standing at the counter about three people away, his back to me. Ignorant, I thought, we all have to wait.

The young lady passed my bill back to me. "Nice to see you Mr Jackson, is there anything else I can do for you?"

"No thank you," I said.

"Take care," I heard the young lady say as I made my way towards the door.

I made my way outside. Did I need to go anywhere else? I asked myself. The answer was no. I could get on and do what I had planned.

I looked up and down the street. It was further along the street I had stood on that cold December Friday thinking of Louise. The family had disappeared into the crowds on that day, and today the crowds were back.

I made my way down from the steps of the bank entrance and turned right; a few yards and I would be out of the way and free from all of these people. I moved quickly, trying to avoid as many mothers with pushchairs as I could. I made the right turn into the lane.

It was littered with other people's rubbish. I had just completed the obstacle course of broken bottles and tins and was approaching the wider part of the lane that leads into the car-park when someone came into the lane. A man in his twenties, about five foot ten in height and broad enough, if met at the start of the lane each of us would have to turn sideways to pass. Dressed in jeans and a black fleece jacket, zipped to the neck, his hands were stuffed into his pockets and he had a somewhat menacing appearance about him.

His fair hair had migrated to his face and he had a full beard. From behind I heard very heavy footsteps quicken, then a very familiar and unpleasant voice behind me which stopped me dead in my tracks.

"I want a fucking word with you!" It was Gary's voice.

I turned and in doing so saw Gary nod to the other man in the lane. Any hope I had of this other individual coming to my aid quickly disappeared.

"Look," I was about to say, but before any more words could come out I felt his right knee in my groin. The blow took the air out of my lungs and I started to fall to the floor with a numbness that made me feel sick. As I hit the ground my glasses came off and I just managed to gather them up and hold on to them in the way a rugby player hangs onto the ball in a maul. He was a big man and I was going to get to know his only way of reasoning things out.

I felt his large right foot bury itself into my stomach, knocking the remaining wind from my lungs. Struggling for breath, I felt it come down on my head. He repeatedly kicked me in the chest and stomach. I rolled myself up as tight as I could to lessen the surface area, but my head was still exposed. Several more stamps on my head and I could faintly hear someone saying, "That's enough now Gary, this could fuck everything up, don't kill him, its not worth it! Stop! Stop it now!" That was the other man's voice and it had slightly foreign accent to it, of Scandinavian origin I thought, but I couldn't be sure, for I was more concerned with the injuries I was receiving.

I could taste blood in my mouth and my fingers on my right hand were hurting. I think I'd put my hand out to break my fall and the back of it came into contact with the wall on the way to the floor. I looked up thinking it was all over, when the big man bent down and looked into my eyes at very close range.

"I told you I'd see you again Mate! Didn't I? She's got just the same as you!" He paused. "Have you got the fucking message now?" I tried to nod but every part of me was in agony.

I lay still on the ground in this filthy lane as the two of them made their way out of it and thought I heard Gary say to the other man, "He won't feel like using the phone for a little while, I'm bloody sure of that."

The aching in-between my legs sent pain to every other part of my body. I struggled to regain my breath, very slowly, and shallow to start with but the pain wouldn't go away.

As I'd stood in the queue in the bank I'd thought things couldn't get worse, and now I wished I was still in that queue.

Two people passed by without even attempting to offer any help; just went on their way making comments about being drunk at this time of the morning. I sure could have done with a drink!

It was a little old lady who came to my aid. With the help of her shopping trolley and a walking stick I was able to get up. I was covered in blood; it seemed to be coming out of every part of me.

"Been mugged have you love?" Her harsh words of kindness helped ease some of the pain. "Happens all the time here love, that's why I carry my stick everywhere with me." She finished with the words, "Bastards aren't they?"

She helped me to my car and offered to call the police. I said I would report it later but for now I just wanted to get back to the comfort and relative safety of my own home. It did cross my mind that they, or more like them, could be waiting for me at my house. When I eventually got back home I stayed in the car. It had been difficult to drive the damn thing, and now I was faced with getting out of it alone and making my way up the drive to the house. It was a bad time to be alone, and as I attempted to exit the car I fell. The knee in the groin had done more damage than I first thought. A group of kids going down the road made the same comments as the people in the lane, only not so politely. "Pissed again," I could hear them sneering, as they swaggered off down the road in a drunken manner. Laughing was something I wouldn't feel like doing for a few days at least.

I struggled to get myself indoors and in the process I set off the burglar alarm. Oh, I don't need this, I thought to myself. I reset it and hoped the police wouldn't be called. I also managed to make a cup of tea, and sat in the conservatory to drink it. My right hand had a vast amount of skin missing from the back, and that was only one of my injuries; my face felt like a football.

I couldn't get to the bathroom to see what I actually looked like, but I did manage to make it to the downstairs cloakroom. That journey took almost a quarter of an hour, and I wasn't pleased with what I saw in the small mirror. My right eye was beginning to close due to the deep cut above it, I had a massive wound to the other side of my face where it had come into contact with the ground and my left ear had a deep cut to it. I cleaned some of the blood off of my face, but my mouth started to bleed again. My cheek had been in collision with my teeth with the help of Gary's foot and they had cut the inside of my mouth. I knew Gary would be well pleased with his handy, or rather footwork.

By the time I returned to the conservatory the rest of the tea had gone cold, and the phone rang. He's ringing to see if I really got the message, I thought, or it might be Louise. I struggled to get to the phone in the kitchen, and this time before answering I checked the caller display. It wasn't Louise's number, in fact I didn't recognise the mobile number at all.

I answered with, "Hello", and then waited.

Silence, then the voice of a woman, "Andy, is that you?" I was so pleased to hear this woman's voice. It was Christine, the woman I referred to as 'my adopted sister'.

"Are you alright?" she continued, and once Christine starts very little will stop her.

"No, I'm bloody well not," I had to interrupt her. "I can't tell you what's wrong but I need your help," I finished.

"I'll call in on the way home from work," she said. "Anything you need?"

I wanted to say a surgeon, but the word wouldn't come out.

"You'll have to let yourself in," I managed to blurt out, then more blood.

Christine was the one woman, apart from Kate, I could trust with anything. We had become friends a long time ago. She had been a shoulder for me to cry on during a period of illness many years before my lifestyle had changed. An attractive blonde woman in her fifties with a heart of gold, only five foot tall, very slim she was a woman who had looked after herself over the years. In the time I had got to know her and Bryan, her husband, I'd found they were people I could trust and rely upon. Christine had looked after the house when I was in America, and was fully aware of my situation. Both of them had always been there for me.

Five thirty came and I could faintly hear a car pull onto the driveway. Within less than a minute Christine was at the back door. As she looked at me sitting in the same chair I had reached upon my return home she covered her mouth with her left hand, a look of horror on her face.

She opened the door with the spare keys she had and came in with the words, "Christ! What's happened to you? My god, what are we going to do?" she continued, with shock in her voice. "I'll have to get a doctor, your face is such a mess!"

"By the way, it bloody well hurts as well Chris!" I said. I was fortunate I could and often did say anything to Christine because I knew it would go no further and she wouldn't be offended.

"I bet it does, but you're covered in blood. Are you cut anywhere else?" By now her small frame was crouching at my feet and she put her hand up to mine. "When did this happen? Who did it? How did you get home? Did you call the police?"

"Stop," I said. "Too many questions Chris. Well, its 'no' to most of your questions, and 'I don't know' to the rest," I finished, deeply grateful she had now come to my aid.

"You need to get out of those clothes and have a bath. That'll bring the worst of the bruises out, I'll help you upstairs."

And that's what she did, got me up stairs, ran the bath and even helped me undress and get in the bath. I know for sure I couldn't have managed on my own, and as always I had complete trust in Christine and felt no shame in being naked in her presence.

"Jesus!" she said as she helped me into the bath, "you've got some awful bruises to your ribs and stomach, and it looks like you won't be using that for some time!" pointing at my private parts. I looked at them; they were blue.

"That's not so much of a problem anyway, they haven't had any use for some months now," I quipped, but as I tried to laugh my ribs hurt.

As I lay in the bath and Christine sat on the small stool by the side of it I told her about the last few months and how happy I'd been since I'd resumed contact with Louise. I told her in detail about my wonderful evening with her, how pretty she is, and as Chris sat by the side of the bath rubbing my back I began to cry.

"It's all gone now, back to being alone," I wept, broken and beaten. "I don't want this, I don't want to live in America. I know it seems like giving up. I just wanted to be her friend, this is so unfair," I sobbed. Christine cradled my aching head. I'd had my dignity kicked out of me for taking a woman to dinner, or so I thought.

"Don't cry," she told me in her warm womanly way, not like she was talking to one of her grandchildren who had just had a bump, but in a far deeper and more caring manner. "I'm sure something will work out, and you've got Bryan and myself - we'll help you as much as we can."

"I know you will. I just wanted this one chance to treat somebody special. I've got all this bloody money and nobody really close," I told her.

My tears had now stopped. Christine helped me out of the bath and I dried myself while she found some loose fitting clothes for me to put on.

"I'd be much happier if you'd see the doctor," she told me. "If not the doctor," she paused, "Tell you what, I'll have a word with my friend, she's a nurse. If she says you need to see the doctor, will you?"

"Ok" I said, "It's a good compromise."

The diagnosis of the nurse was in my favour. If it gets any worse call for an ambulance but I should be all right. She also said she would call back on Saturday morning.

"I'll have to go soon," Chris said, "but first I'll fix you something to eat. Do you want me to put your car away for you?"

"Oh, yes please," I said.

This she did and by seven thirty I was alone. Chris said she would call on her way to work in the morning.

I called Phillip late in the evening and again my tears came pouring out. I hadn't had the chance to tell him about our dinner together, and now it was bitter sweet to relay it to him. I'm not sure what hurt the most, coming so close or the beating; I certainly looked the worse for the beating. I spent over an hour on the phone to him and we discussed how Gary could have found out. I said it might have been the chap I'd seen in the car park. "Did she see him?" Phillip asked.

"I don't know," was my reply. "I thought she was looking at me. Oh shit, she is so beautiful Phillip, I thought I had it made this time."

"Is there anything I can do?" Phillip asked. "Do you want me to come up for a few days? I've never had a beating over a woman, but as you know I was alone for a long time, something will come from this!"

"No don't come up, I'll not be much company for a few days. I think I need to be alone to get over this," I finished.

"Take care then," he said, and then he was gone.

I made my very slow way to bed, and was almost glad to get in a horizontal position. Most of the pain was on my side, so I lay flat and still and went to sleep. I dreamt of her, sitting opposite me again in that restaurant in the pale evening light. I would relive that dream all night.

Friday

I was awoken by the voice of Christine and looked at the bedside clock. It was seven, and as promised she had let herself in.

"I'll make you some tea," she called up the stairs, and in what seemed like no time she was sitting on the edge of the bed having a cup with me. "The bruises are coming out now," she told me. "I wouldn't look, well not if you can help it. Do you want me to help you get up?"

"I'll be ok," I said, "just as long as I take it slowly! Chris," I started "I'm sorry about last night and crying in the bath. I really do appreciate what you've done for me and I didn't mean to start blubbering to you."

"Don't be daft," was her reply. "That's what friends are for. Bryan and I will have you up and about in a few days. Look, I've got to go now or I'll be late for work. We'll call in with some fish and chips this evening, will that be alright?"

With that she finished her tea and was out of the bedroom, popping her head back round the door to remind me to take it easy.

I managed to get myself up at about ten, had a wash and struggled down stairs. I'll watch some box, I thought. I put it on but couldn't be bothered to pay much attention to what was going on in the rest of the world, mine had just come apart. The news didn't contain anything good.

There was still a scandal going with at least three government ministers and another motorway crash had claimed six lives. Well, things aren't so bad for me, I thought, I've still got my life, unlike those poor families, and so near to Easter. The closing segment caught my attention; investigations were still continuing into suspected fraud within the Post Office in Scotland. It went on to say that the police were reluctant at this stage to release too many details. It's going on everywhere, I thought, but then my thoughts went back to the headlines I'd seen on the front page of The Times just before Christmas. I hadn't taken much notice then; at the time I took it as a reference to post early, but as I recall that article was to do with fraud. I racked my brain trying to remember what it was about, but it wouldn't come back and the paper was long gone. Anyway, I was in no fit state to go looking for it even if I had kept it.

I whiled away the hours of the afternoon waiting for Christine and Bryan to call, and when they did at six o'clock they brought with them the promised fish and chips.

I was sitting out the back in the conservatory. Bryan greeted me with his usual sharp wit. "Don't you lot shake hands over this neck of the woods, then. Fuck! You look more of a mess than usual, and you aren't very pretty at the best of times. I think I'd rather see Chris in the morning than look at you now."

"And its nice to see you as well Bryan," I replied, "you don't mind if I don't get up do you?"

"You always were a lazy bastard," Bryan retorted, then his tone changed, "Do you know who did this to you Andy?"

I shook my head, "No," I said, looking at Chris.

"He was mugged," was her quick answer to the question, "now lets eat the fish and chips before they get cold."

"Up in that lane by the bank, Chris told me. Here, you'll have to get up there in the morning love, that'll put a few of them bastards off doing a mugging if they come face to face with you at six o'clock in the morning. Well it would me, anyway," he laughed.

Then he lent across and whispered in my ear, "If you do know, just let me know, I can get it fixed. You know what I mean!"

But that would be all too easy I thought. Yes, I knew what Bryan meant. He had a good sense of humour and a wonderful relationship with Chris, but you cross him at your peril.

I'd first got to know Chris when I was a logistics operative, that's a van driver, for the company I left a year ago; the same company Louise had worked for. Chris was a receptionist at one of the sites I made regular drops to. Over the years our friendship had developed to what it is now.

Bryan runs his own company delivering building materials, and what he really meant was he had one or two boys he could call on if a touch of muscle was required.

"I sometimes wonder if you can ever be sensible," Chris said to Bryan.

"Yes of course I can," was Bryan's reply. "Let's get home before it gets dark, we don't want to frighten any small kids do we?"

This type of conversation was to be expected whenever they were together at someone else's house. I knew he didn't mean it, as much as Chris knew he didn't; they were devoted to each other.

We finished our supper and they were on their way.

"Quick," Bryan shouted as he stood by the car. "It's still light. Let's go now or you'll have to fly home on your broomstick."

"I'll see you tomorrow afternoon, I've got the grandchildren in the morning," Chris called with a smile on her face and gesturing Bryan was mad. "About two. If you need anything give me a call and Ill get wise guy here to bring it over."

"I'm not giving him a bath," was Bryan's input to the conversation, "he can do it himself." He closed the door of the car, saying, "Take care of yourself, see you soon."

Weekend

Their company and the fish and chips had done me good, and restored a bit of faith in humanity. I felt more like getting about and would be able to make it with a little more ease to my bed. My mouth still hurt slightly but that was from the vinegar on the chips. Ten o'clock; I slowly made my way up to bed, and much to my surprise had another good night's rest, but I don't recommend getting a beating to help you sleep at night. It was seven when I awoke and I realised I hadn't dreamt of her; not that I'm over her I told myself, perhaps Phillip's words were right, and it will get better. I managed to have a shower, then stood to take a look at myself in the full-length mirror in the bedroom. I looked the way a punch bag must feel, but it was beginning to hurt a little less, so I put some of my usual clothes on and was just making my way down the stairs when the door bell rang.

"Hang on," I called, "I'm on my way." It was the nurse.

"I can tell you must be feeling better," she said to me as I let her in. She stepped inside the front door and looked at my face, "That's even looking better," she said, as she touched my head above my right eye. "The swelling is going down. Any other problems," she said, as she glanced down at my crotch.

"No, I think it's all working ok. It did hurt to have a pee but that was on Thursday, it's somewhat better now, thanks," I said.

"Chris was very worried you know," the nurse went on. "If anything happens, you know, if you pass any blood or anything like that, you must call the doctor."

"Yes I know," I replied.

"Ok, I'm off. Go and sit down, I'll let myself out," and she was gone, pulling the door hard behind her.

I made some tea and today had two boiled eggs, easy to eat. My eldest son rang and said I sounded awful. I told him I had a dose of the flu and had been in bed for a day, but I was feeling a bit better. Then he asked how my evening had gone. I stumbled for my words, managing to tell him all went well. I didn't want him of all people to know I'd had a beating at the hands, or rather feet, of Louise's husband. After all, he'd wished me luck when I'd told him the evening I was taking her out for dinner. I know the first thing he would have done is put Gary in Hospital, as big as Gary is.

Two o'clock and as promised Christine was with me, pleased that once again I'd managed to get myself up and was dressed. We sat in the conservatory having a cup of tea and a sandwich, just chatting in general about her grandchildren and what I would be doing for Easter. I told her that if I could manage to drive I thought I might go to the apartments, it depended how well I could get about by then, and her company was very much appreciated, for I had to admit to feeling a bit weepy. I was sitting in the chair nearest to the kitchen with Chris on the seat to my left, and she had just finished telling me about her drive home with Bryan when the doorbell rang.

"Would you mind, Chris," I asked.

"No problem," was her reply, and she got up and made her way through the kitchen and along the hall to the front door.

"If it's someone selling things tell them I'm not interested," I called out.

"This door is stiff," Chris shouted back at me.

"You've got your nurse friend to thank for that," I called back.

"Done it," I heard her say. Then her voice went very quiet and I couldn't pick up what she was saying. She was talking to another female, that much I could make out, and finally I heard her say, "Well, you'd better come in then, but I warn you he's not a pretty site. I thought I heard a reply of I'm sure he's not," but I couldn't be sure.

I thought it must be the police, perhaps someone had reported it or it had been filmed on close circuit TV. The last thing I needed now was to be asked lots of questions.

"It is someone to see you Andy," Chris said in soft tones. "I'll leave you to it!"

I looked round at the doorway into the kitchen, and standing wearing dark glasses, black trousers and her full-length coat was Louise. She looked down at me.

"I'm so sorry," she said, and began to cry. Chris put her arm on her shoulder and she almost jumped. "Can I come in and sit down?" she asked. As she passed my chair her hand brushed my right hand. "He did all this to you?" Louise finished.

"Sure did," was my reply, "and just for taking you out to dinner."

She took off her dark glasses. Her eyes were red, and it was obvious to me she had spent a lot of time crying.

"Christine, isn't it," Louise called, "can you come in, I want you to see this," and with those words she stood up and started to unbutton her long black coat.

Christine made her way to the kitchen doorway and with a comment I would have expected from Bryan, Chris replied, "He's in no fit state to do any of that my girl."

Louise slipped out of her coat and let it fall to ground. She then proceeded to undo her navy blue blouse from the bottom, and as she did so I could see she was revealing the extent of the injuries she had sustained at the hands of her husband. She continued to unbutton the blouse right to the top and pulled it open. Underneath it she was wearing a pretty white half-cupped lace bra, but my eyes were focused on the massive bruises she had to her flat tummy. Her rib cage had punch marks on, and the impression of knuckles was quite clear, the bruises went up past her perfectly formed breasts and her shoulders and forearms were covered with red and black punch marks. I looked at her face, she was crying harder now.

"Oh, he never hits my face Andy," she sobbed. "That wouldn't look too good at the football club. I'm sorry. I shouldn't have come to see you. That's where he is now, with his mates sorting out their Easter football trip to Belgium."

"Sit down my girl," Chris told her. "You mean that bastard did this just because Andy took you out for dinner?" She went on, "That's it, Bryan will sort this out. He'll put the bastard in hospital, he won't hit another woman, I tell you now." Chris was off and as I said, once she starts it's a job to stop her.

"No, wait a minute," Louise said though her tears. "This isn't about the dinner!"

"What?" I asked.

"He doesn't know about the dinner," Louise replied.

"Well, what the bloody hell was this beating for," Chris asked, "and please do cover yourself up love, I don't want him to get too excited."

"This was because you phoned me," she said, looking at me and starting to do the buttons up on her blouse.

"Jesus, there's something wrong with this bloke if he beats you up just for being on the phone to another man," Chris said. "Bryan can't get me off the bloody thing."

"Hang on," I said. "I'm lost. I always withhold my number," I added, and then my voice drifted away, the penny dropped: in my excitement of the morning after our dinner together I was in such a hurry to call Louise that I'd just dialled her number. Also, it made sense of what Gary said to the other man as they walked away together, "He won't feel like using the phone for a while."

"Oh, this is all my fault," I said. By now Louise was holding my left hand.

"It isn't your fault," she said, "I was just as exited as you. I enjoyed our evening together as well you know. I wanted it to last forever. No one has ever treated me in that way before, I told you it was wonderful." She paused. "Gary is very obsessive, he demands my one hundred per cent attention." She went on, "He comes home in the evening and always checks the phone to see who's called last, by dialling 1471. If there's a number he doesn't recognise he goes upstairs, looks on his computer to see if it's someone he knows, don't ask me why he does it because I don't know, but he's just the same over the phone bill. I can't make a call to anyone without him knowing," she finished.

"But how did you find out where I live," I asked.

"I knew there would be trouble when he stood listening to the phone on that Wednesday evening as I hadn't had any other calls after we were cut short, so I made a note of your number while he was upstairs checking it on the computer." She continued, "Then I cross-referenced it in the phone book the day after, you're not ex-directory you know. He came back down after doing his check and you know the rest, he beat me after ringing you."

The tears were pouring from her eyes again, I put out my left hand to offer some form of comfort, and she responded by coming closer to me.

"You two go on into the front room, where it's more comfortable," Christine said, "I'll make some fresh tea."

They both gave me a hand to get up. Louise and I took the slow walk to the lounge and we had just got inside the room when Louise put her arms around me, the same way as on the platform of the station. Very gently she hugged me and kissed my left cheek and for the time she held me, I felt like that schoolboy again. If it had just been a slapping it wouldn't have been so bad, almost worth it.

We moved toward the window and I was about to lower myself into the settee when I glanced out of the window. On the drive behind Chris's Toyota was Louise's green Fiat, but what caught my eye was a car moving slowly up the road, I thought with two occupants. I thought they were looking in, but couldn't be sure, so I passed it off as someone pulling away from my neighbours'; it often happens.

We sat together on the settee, Louise by my left side. I touched her leg and she winced, moving away slightly.

"Oh yes, my legs have bruises as well," she said.

Chris came in with some tea on a tray and Louise's coat over her arm. She put the tray on a small table.

"Has he done this to you before?" she asked Louise.

"Yes, it's not the first time," she replied, "and I don't expect it will be the last."

"What was it for on the other occasions?" I asked.

"All sorts of things." she said. "His tea not being ready, losing a football match," she paused and then continued, "it doesn't take much for him to loose his temper. On one occasion when Sarah was a baby, she'd been ill most of the night and the following day he beat me for not having his football kit ready for him. It was his training night and the fact I'd been up most of the night and had been clearing up sick all day didn't come into it; he always says I spent too much time with the kids."

"Why do you stay with him?" Christine enquired.

"I've got nowhere else I can go. Not only that, but afterwards he comes back crying, and I mean really crying tears like a baby, telling me how sorry he is and he won't ever do it again. Then yes, things are fine for a few months until something upsets him and off he goes again, into one of his tantrums and I'm on the receiving end."

"Of his fists," I added.

"Yes, and after a time you begin to think it's your place to be treated like this. You don't trust people, particularly men, and when they pay you a compliment you think they're after something. You get used to being treated badly. That day in December, when I was in Smiths, do you remember he slapped my bottom," Louise said looking at me, "well, two days before he'd given me beating, Just because the car wouldn't start. It was hardly my fault was it, but he went into a rage and I came off the worst for it," she finished.

"What about the kiddies," Chris asked.

"No, he never lays a finger on them. I'd find some way of killing him if he did." She was by now talking to Chris as if they had been long-time friends. I had, during our telephone calls, mentioned to Louise about Christine and Bryan and the great support they had given me upon my return to this Country and in the years before my change in fortune.

"Where are they now Louise?" I asked.

"They're staying with my mother and father for a few days," she replied. "I'll have them back after he's done his apologising bit, I don't want them to have to live in that atmosphere for too long."

Her words brought back memories of my own childhood and how unhappy my mother had been. She'd suffered at the hands of a bully, only he was a little man who hit out when he couldn't get his own way and thought nothing of transferring his aggression towards his children. I often suffered at his hands and could recall hearing my mother cry out in the night, and as a result of his actions all those years ago I had an abhorrent hatred for violence, in particular towards women.

"Do your parents know he ill-treats you?" Chris asked.

"I'm sure they've got an idea something goes on, but I've never actually sat down and told them. I'm not sure what they could do anyway," she said as she drank her tea. "He even brags at the football club that he hits me," she continued. "Of course they don't believe him, his mates I mean, as I never show any bruises or marks, so they think he makes it all up." She finished her tea and put the mug back on the table, and continued, "My friend in the village knows what goes on, she saw some marks on my back one day when I was trying some clothes on at her house. Jill's very kind and a good support, she keeps my confidences for me. She knew you'd taken me out to dinner, I told her I'd met you after all those years, and about our phone calls. I told her you were still as kind and thoughtful now as you were when I first met you, and when you asked me to go out for a meal she helped me chose the right outfit. In fact it was her jacket I was wearing, as I didn't have one to match my skirt." She took hold of my hand, "But worst of all you've now got involved, and you've paid the price. I shouldn't think you'd want to be ringing me any more will you? Well, you can't anyway, he ripped the phone off the wall that evening he rang you, then he jumped up and down on it, just like a child." As she finished talking she squeezed my hand.

"I'd love to ring you." I hesitated, "I've always had a fear of getting you into a problem situation with Gary, I remember years ago you said he could be very jealous, but it seems this jealousy has now turned to obsession." Now I was looking into her eyes.

Yes I remember seeing the pain and unhappiness in them on that day in December and it was back now, but the night we went out for dinner they were filled with a sparkle and I wished so much I could restore that glow.

"You say he's arranging a football excursion for the Easter break. Will you be going with him?" I asked.

"Me! Go with the football club! You must be joking! It's men only. Really it's an excuse for them all to get pissed. I'm sorry Chris, I shouldn't have said that," was her reply as she looked at Christine.

"Don't worry Louise, I've heard much worse, even from Andy," she replied.

"Thanks Chris," I said.

"Well, what will you be doing?" I asked Louise, looking into her red eyes.

"I expect I'll stay with Mummy and Daddy for few days, they like to spoil the children and it will give me a chance to have a bit of a rest; or I may go to my sister, it's only two weeks away isn't it? What about you?"

"Well, I was talking to Chris about Easter before you arrived. I may go to Cornwall if I'm mobile enough, just to have a few days away, I'm not really sure," I said.

Louise stood up and picked up her coat.

"I'd better be going now," she said, as she started to wipe away more tears. "It's been lovely to meet you Christine, please look after Andy for me," she sobbed. "And Andy, don't worry, I'll be ok. Honestly I will. I know where you live now, I'll write to you in a few months, you know, when things have settled down a bit." She bent down and kissed me on the cheek, stood up straight, and then headed towards the lounge door where she stopped, turned and looked back at me. "Goodbye," she said as she slipped her dark glasses back on.

My heart stopped. Something inside of me wanted to take hold of her and keep her with me, but I also thought it might be best if we went our own ways. One day she may feel strong enough to walk away from Gary, or just learn to live with it as my mother had.

Christine jumped up. "I'll show Louise out and help her off the drive, you stay Andy," she said with an air of determination about her. "Stay!" she said again pointing at me, then made her way out behind Louise with her handbag over her shoulder.

But I didn't do as I was told. I pulled myself up from the settee and stood at the window, I watched Christine give Louise a hug, and saw them kiss each other on the cheek; all the time they were talking but I couldn't make out what either of them were saying. Louise got into her car, Chris watched for a space in the traffic and directed her out and onto the road and then she was gone, she didn't even wave. My heart sank, I was destined to be alone or go back to the States.

As Christine came back into the lounge again my own tears were beginning to fall and she came straight to my aid.

"I can see why you're upset Andy," she said as she helped me to sit down. "She is so pretty and her warmth towards you is so obvious."

"Then why can't I have what I want," I said through my tears. "I'd do anything to make it right. If she was happy with him, I'd be only to willing to walk away, but the bastard only mistreats her. It's so unfair; I could give her everything. Maybe I could pay him to go away and leave her, I've got the money."

"Now Andy, you're not making sense," Chris said. "Come on, you'll come and stay with Bryan and myself for a few days. Believe it or not Bryan will understand, and if the kids come over they will take your mind off her. Something will work out, believe me."

So that's what I did, as requested. No, as ordered by Christine. I went and stayed for a few days. Bryan, as always, had plenty of quick comments with regards to giving me a bath and helping me in and out of bed. He drove me everywhere, like a lunatic I must add, took me to the pub Sunday lunchtime and treated me to a wicked game of snooker, then made an absolute pig of himself at the dinner table, but that's Bryan for you.

For the first time in months my mind was occupied with thoughts of things other than Louise.

Christine was herself, and never stopped talking; Bryan even said she talks in her sleep, and that I can well believe. The grandchildren came over on the Sunday evening and you would have thought Bryan was five, not a man in his fifties. It all helped to ease my pain, both the physical and emotional.

Monday

By the Monday I was feeling much better. It had been a long time since I had more than one person for company and I was feeling stronger and more able to get about. I went out with Bryan for the day. No heavy lifting, Christine said. Bryan passed a comment about leaving my wallet at home so I wouldn't strain myself, and the day passed well.

I thought I'd go home on the Tuesday but Christine had other plans. She'd taken the day off from work and offered to take us all out to lunch, this would involve lots of drinking and as Bryan put it a "bloody great curry". By the time we got back to their house none of us were in a fit state to walk let alone drive, so it was decided that it would be in my own interest for me to stay over another night.

Wednesday came and of course my thoughts were on my usual Wednesday phone call. When Chris brought me a cup of tea in the morning I asked, "Can I stay with you today?"

"Of course you can," she said. "I'll ring in sick, I can blame it on the curry. I know how difficult it's going to be for you to go into that house alone after what happened at the weekend. We'll go for walk, if you feel up to it. Bryan can go off to work. Just let me make some phone calls and get dressed; you go and have your shower first and you can fix yourself something to eat. I think there's some bacon in the fridge, go and help yourself and can you fix something for Bryan."

And that's what I did: after I'd showered and shaved I fixed Bryan and myself some bacon sandwiches.

"Here Andy she's a long time on that phone," Bryan said. "I think the bloody thing must be welded in place, I've never known anyone talk as much as our Chris, she could set a world record," he said as he set of to work. "It's been a really good laugh having you to stay for the past few days and its not often I get Christine to pay for a curry, you'll have to come and stay more often. Whatever you do don't let her talk you to death. See you," and he was out of the door and in no time I heard his car pull away.

I finished my sandwich and we did as Christine had suggested and took a walk along the river. This helped to clear my thoughts and made me feel better, and by mid-afternoon I was back in my own home. Christine and I had some tea and then she set off home leaving me to my own thoughts and feelings. As she left she said, "Call me on the landline if you need anything. I've managed to loose my mobile phone; I expect it's deep in one of my handbags somewhere, God knows I've got enough of them. I'll have to find it when I get home." She kissed me and gave me a Christine hug that told me she loved me, and I had to force her to go.

I spent my evening sorting the post that had built up over the four days I'd been away, looked to see who had called and to my surprise found no one had. I fixed myself some supper and had a long in-depth conversation with Phillip.

"You do sound better," he said, "but are you feeling any better?"

"Yes, I do feel better," I replied.

"You're very lucky to have Christine, she gives you a lot of support," Phillip told me.

"You do as well," I replied. "I can't imagine what I'd do if you weren't on the end of the phone to listen to my moaning and complaining. Do you fancy coming down to the apartment for Easter?"

"It works both ways Andy. I do have my grumbles to you, or have you forgotten," he said and continued, "I'd love to but I'm sure I've got to work, I'll have to get back to you on that."

"Yes, that'll be alright," I said, and then went on, "You know, maybe there's some truth to that old saying."

"What saying's that?" Phillip asked.

"You know. It's better to have loved and lost rather than never to have loved at all," I said, but the thought of the truth behind the words still brought a lump to my throat.

"You must be feeling better my friend," Phillip replied. "You wouldn't have been able to understand that statement last week, let alone say it. You know you'll never forget her, I'll tell you that now, but you got closer than many men could dream of. She'll always be under your skin, just under the surface; she won't go away. I'm so glad you've been able to share that experience with me, and Andy," he paused, "it will get better. Now go and have a drop of scotch and relax before you go to bed."

"That's a damn fine idea," I said, still fighting back some tears. "I'll talk to you tomorrow, goodnight, and thanks my friend."

And a good night's sleep is what I got; not that I didn't think of Louise as I lay in my bed, but I'd come to the conclusion I could not change the laws of physics. I hadn't gone chasing after her, a little bit of the opposite: she'd asked me to ring her and it gave me the greatest pleasure to do so. If it had been destined then it would have happened, so I consoled myself with that thought as I went to sleep.

Chapter Six

Thursday

The morning came and as I got up I felt much better in myself. I would make some changes. First my daily routine would have to change. No more walks to get my paper, I could bloody well afford to have it hand delivered and ironed if I wanted, so I rang the newsagent and made the necessary arrangements.

"From tomorrow sir?" the newsagent asked.

"Well, I wouldn't mind one today if you could manage it," I replied.

"Not a problem, I'll drop one round in half an hour."

Time for me to have a shower and get dressed. This I did and was on my second cup of coffee when the paper came through the letterbox. I had a brief read while I finished my coffee. The Post Office issue wouldn't seem to go away, it had made its way to the inside pages of The Times and was getting a lot of coverage, most of it speculation. Well, I thought, it fills the space and gives people something to talk about.

After an hour reading the paper I decided it was time to move some of my furniture about. I hadn't been very happy about the position of my speakers and felt I could achieve a much better balance. The moving job was well under way and I had just gone out to the kitchen to make a fresh coffee when the phone rang. I looked at the caller display, a mobile number. "Oh, its Christine. She's found her phone," I said to myself as I picked up the receiver.

"You found it then," I said in a jovial manner. "And what handbag was it in?"

There was a long silence.

"Come on Chris, it's not like you to be stuck for words, can you hear me?" I asked.

"It's not Chris," the reply came back to me. I knew the voice in an instant but words stuck in my throat. I didn't know what I was to say; then, almost like being kicked started into life, I found the words I needed.

"Louise. Are you alright?" I asked.

"Yes," was the reply, and very gently she began to talk to me.

"Christine lent me her mobile phone, as you can tell. I was so worried about you, so was Christine. You sound so much better; are you?"

"I am, but it doesn't mean I've forgotten you, or will ever be able to forget you," I told her, in the calmest way I could. I felt ten feet tall again. With the help of my old friend, Louise had come to me.

"I've spoken to my mother and father. I've told them just how unhappy

I've been, and told them about you." She paused, "Mummy already knew. As I told you that night when we were out for dinner, she could see a change in me, more so when I got home that evening: she said I was brighter and far livelier than I'd been since a child," she finished.

"Well, where do we go from here?" I enquired, and continued, "I won't be able to ring again, even if I withhold the number."

"I've been thinking about that," Louise came in, "I could do with some time away myself. You know, to get things sorted in my head. I've made up my mind I'm not going to let him treat me like this anymore. My sister has said I can go and stay with her for the Easter holidays, but," with that she paused. She could always surprise me, as she had on the station platform that Tuesday night, and what she said next came as just as big a surprise, "I'd much rather come to Cornwall with you."

I held on to her words "Come to Cornwall with you."

"Andy, are you there?" she asked.

"Oh yes, I'm here alright," I replied, "I just wasn't expecting you to ask me that. I'm not sure if it would be safe. What if Gary was to find out?" I finished.

"I know it's a big decision to make," she said, and went on, "Mummy and Daddy are going to have Sarah and James for a few days whether I come with you or go to my sister, they feel I need to get this mess sorted. They have even said if I leave Gary I can go back home."

"But I feel that now I'm the cause of the problem, and would it help going away with the one person he must hate the most. What if he were to find out - he'd kill me next time," I said, but I felt excited at the prospect of spending more time in the company of this woman. "I need to think about it, well sleep on it, you know what I mean," I finished.

"I do know what you mean, but the chances of him finding out are small to nil. He's going away himself on Sunday on that football trip I told you about, and will be gone for almost two weeks. He never phones me when he's away and can't even remember much of what he's done either," she went on. "Last year, I think it was, he lost all of his kit and clothes and just had what he stood up in when he came home. We could be down and back and he'll never know," she finished.

"Has he been and apologised to you yet?" I asked.

"Oh, he started to try and break the ice, but I've spent a lot of time with Mummy and Daddy since I saw you and he won't stay there very long. He feels very insecure in their company. I expect he'll give it his best effort on Saturday before he goes away," she said.

"Can you call me tomorrow?" I asked. I really wasn't sure how to play this and I needed to think it over.

"Yes I will. About the same time?" Louise replied.

"Ok, I'll let you know my decision then, take care." I closed with, "Goodbye."

"Please Andy. Please think about it. Please!" she said, in the same way as she had asked me to call her back in December, when I'd met her in Smiths, only this time her arms weren't wrapped around me. If they had been I wouldn't have had any time to think about it, I would have just given in. "Goodbye," was her closing word, and she was gone.

And think about it I did, so many connotations and 'what ifs'. It's best I don't tell too many people, I thought, the fewer that know the better. I need to talk to Christine first, after all it was her tricks that had brought it to where we are now, I thought, but did she know Louise would ask to come away with me? Only one way to find out, phone her, but she wouldn't be home from work yet. I'll ring Phillip, he'll still be in the office at lunchtime.

He answered in his normal manner, was surprised by my unusual tone, and gave me questions in place of answers to my questions. I was in need of this type of conversation. It provoked some soul searching. I wasn't looking for quick approval of the relationship or a blessing from my best friend.

"If she came down with you how would you play it?" he asked. "Would you want to sleep with her?"

His question stirred deep emotions held back from long ago. I'd dreamt of her being in bed with me, but this was too far down a road I'd never travelled before for me to give an answer.

"No," came my reply, after some thought. "It hasn't been like that so far and I wouldn't want to spoil the friendship before it gets off the ground, it's had a big enough setback as it is. I'd want to take it steady," I continued. "She could come down as my guest, the apartments have two bedrooms, I wouldn't want her to be rushed into anything against her will."

"But Andy," he asked in a deep questioning tone, "what if she leads you by the hand to her bedroom? That changes everything doesn't it?" He went on, his tone firm and full of caution, "Believe me, you won't be friends any more, you'll be lovers and she will have made the move on you. Do you think you can be prepared for that? What if after a day or two she's not the woman you expected to have with you? Your dreams would be shattered. Could you handle that, or would you feel compelled to bring her home and end the friendship? Have you thought of all those scenarios?"

My reply wasn't clear for I hadn't thought that far ahead. "I don't know," was all I could say.

"Well, I think you've shown immense strength of character so far." He paused just long enough to draw breath before continuing, "It is possible for things to go wrong but it's more likely they'll go right. I'm sure you'll be able to deal with and handle any situation that occurs. Go for it, give it your best shot," he ended.

But before I could make any decision I would need to ask Christine what she thought, and she wouldn't be available for some time. I needed to clear my head and the only way I could do that was to go for a run. It had been a week since my hiding; I was feeling much better and the wounds were healing well. I changed into my running kit, after I'd restored some order in the lounge. The two-mile run didn't seem to take long and I arrived back home not too badly out of breath; my ribs and stomach still felt a bit tight, but as I got into the shower I told myself things would improve.

I fixed myself some supper before I rang Christine. She put on a surprised tone when Bryan passed the phone to her and I could hear him in the background telling her not to be on the phone too long as someone else might want to use it.

She answered with, "Hello Andy, are you ok?"

"I'm fine," I said. "You found that mobile phone of yours yet?" I enquired, almost trying to catch her out.

"No," she replied, "but," she hesitated and then went on, "I've got a good idea of where it might be."

"I bet you have," I said, with that we both started to laugh.

"I couldn't let it end like that Andy," Christine said, and continued, "A friendship with no romance, is better than no friendship at all."

I explained about the phone call I'd had and what I was asked.

"You enjoyed treating her as someone special, didn't you?" Christine said. "Just be yourself. If it starts to go wrong then you can always come back home. If there's anything I can do just let me know. By the way, I wouldn't mind having my phone back please," she finished.

Yes, I did enjoy treating her in a special way. She made me feel good, almost like a new man you could say, so with only a little persuading from Christine my mind was made up. I would take Louise to the Cornish apartment as my guest and expect only kind looks and her good company in return for my hospitality.

Friday

She phoned as arranged the following day and I could hear the delight in her voice when I said we would go away together. I explained it was my intention to leave on the Thursday morning and she would be my guest.

"That's Maundy Thursday, ok?" I said.

"I know when that is," was her cheeky reply.

"We'll come home on the Tuesday after Easter, will that be ok?" I asked.

"Yes, that'll be fine with me," was her reply.

We agreed to tell only three people maximum we were going away. I'd told Christine and also Phillip, Louise said she would tell Jill, her confidante in the village, and her Mother and Father. As they would be looking after the children they had to know, in fact they already knew, as it was their suggestion that she go away.

"I've told my father you're gay," she told me, and before I had a chance to question her reasoning behind the statement she explained, "Well, he asked why you hadn't made a move on me and it was easier to say you were gay. Not only that, it kind of puts his mind at rest. I think he watches too many TV soaps to be honest; everyone seems to be jumping in and out of bed with each other and he thinks it goes on in real life. Mummy knows you're not, but she won't let on, well, not yet." She paused before asking, "Will you help me sort things out while we're away, you know, help me get a solicitor and all those things."

"Yes of course I will, being gay has its advantages you know," I said as I started to laugh. "I've done and been some things over the years, you know, but never been gay before. Well, there's always a first time." I was unable to control my laughter by now and I could hear Louise laughing on the other end of the phone as well.

She thought it would be safer if she came to my house and we would leave from there. If she were to be followed then by going to the station it would appear she was going to her sister. In fact that was what she was going to tell Gary. She said she would get a taxi from the station but would get off at the next stop down the line "just to make sure that I'm not seen". I told her she wouldn't need a great deal in the way of clothes, just some walking shoes and something to wear when we went out for dinner in the evening.

So we made our plans to escape to Cornwall in the same way we'd arranged to go out for dinner, under a shroud of secrecy, and agreed she wouldn't call again unless there was a problem. She felt nothing could go wrong, and I shared that feeling.

I felt elated and excited at the thought of taking her away, but for some reason it didn't play on my mind and I was able to get on and complete all the tasks I set myself during the coming days. Yes, I often thought of her and was looking forward to our forthcoming adventure; for that was the best way for me to look at it, as an adventure.

I increased my running mileage and felt more relaxed; in fact the morning we were due to set off I went for a longer run, as I wouldn't be able to go while I was in Cornwall. I have in the past, but felt it would be rude of me to go out pounding the country lanes leaving Louise on her own.

Chapter Seven

Maundy Thursday

Ten o'clock and a taxi pulled up outside the house. I went out to greet Louise, my heart beating so fast I couldn't control it and my hands wet with perspiration. I paid the taxi driver and said thank you with a stammer in my voice, as I told him to keep the change from the twenty-pound note I'd given him. He winked in the same way the man had in the car park that evening in March. The taxi pulled away and I could hear the driver say, "Have a nice week-end."

I stood and looked at Louise, dressed in black trousers, white blouse and a black blazer-type jacket, and wearing just a small amount of make-up to highlight her eyes. Her hair was swept back into a ponytail and a small black bag hung from her shoulder. In each of her hands she was holding a zipped bag, containing her clothes I presumed. I took her two bags and she put her arms round me, and as she did my nervousness disappeared.

"Let's have a good time together," she said.

"I'm sure we will," I replied.

"Have you any idea what the weather is going to be like?" she asked, as she gave me her customary kiss on my cheek.

"The forecast is for a dry spell, up until Wednesday at least," I told her.

"Your injuries have healed well," she said, as she stroked my head above my right eye.

"Yes they have," I agreed, and then asked, "Have your bruises gone now?"

"Oh yes, all cleared up, and I'm feeling so much better, more so as Gary is away and out of the Country," she replied.

"I'll put these bags in the car," I said. "Do you want to go indoors before we leave?" I asked, adding, "Oh, I almost forgot, we need to leave Chris's phone behind. She'll come and collect it over the weekend."

"Yes please, could I use the bathroom before we set off? By the way, you haven't got much in the car, have you?" she asked.

"That's not a problem," I replied and went on, "I keep quite a few things in the apartment; you know, clothes and things. And the freezer is fairly well stocked, but we will need to get some fresh things for our supper, that is if we decide we want to stay in. There's a supermarket close by, we can stop there," I told her.

At ten thirty, after locking the house and saying goodbye to my immediate neighbours, we set off for our adventure in the warm April sunshine that I hoped would last for the period of our time together. The traffic was light as we headed for the motorway, and once we had joined the flow of traffic heading south Louise slipped out of her jacket. Her white blouse was short sleeved; she undid the top two buttons and took the hair band out of her hair, releasing the locks of auburn hair to cascade freely over her shoulders.

Her smooth white arms had no sign of the awful bruises of two weeks ago. She crossed her legs and as we travelled on she made herself comfortable, talking to me, asking how long it would take to get there, and what sort of facilities there were at the apartments. I teased her by saying we would have to fetch the water from a well at the bottom of the lane, and if she wanted a bath she would have to use the old trough in place for the cattle to drink from. "But it will be alright, I'll keep the cows away while you wash your hair," I told her. I'm afraid I couldn't keep the game up and a grin formed across my face and when she realised I'd been teasing her she gestured me to get away, and started to laugh.

She started to play word games with me. That didn't last long before we moved onto eye-spy. That also ran its course and we moved onto the interior of the car.

"What does this button do?" she asked me.

"Why don't you press it and find out," I said, and she did.

"Nothing's happened," she said.

"Not that you can see," I told her, "but you've just put all the lights on."

"Oh, then I'd better turn them off," she said as she flicked the switch back to its original position. "Now what does this one do?" as she turned the heater on. It didn't take long for the car to warm up, which answered her question. "I think I know what it does, I'd better turn it back. Now, what is this one for?" as she pressed the air- conditioning control.

"You'll find out in a few minutes!" I said, and sure enough she did, for in less time than I thought, cold air was pumping out of all the vents in the car.

"Oh gosh," she said as she rubbed her arms which by now had goose pimples. She reset the button and promptly crossed her arms so as to conceal her embarrassment at what was happening to other parts of her body, having had cold air blown against them.

"And this one?" she enquired again once she had warmed up. This was the CD player. She pushed the volume on/off switch and music came blasting from the all the speakers positioned around the car.

"That's nice, who is it?" she enquired.

"It's a band called Wood," I told her, adding, "The song is called Stay You."

She was having fun playing games with me, and it helped to make the journey much more pleasurable.

As she turned the volume down she asked, " What does that one do?" and promptly pressed the hazard warning light switch.

"That switch was put in the car especially for you; it's the hazard warning lights you've just put on," I said, looking in the mirror. She quickly turned them off, with a sorry and a grin on her lips.

About three cars behind us was a police car. The hazard lights flashing must have caught the driver's attention, for in an instant he pulled out into the fast lane and sharply accelerated to my side. I looked across at the officer in the passenger seat and he indicated he wished for me to pull over. I glanced at Louise.

"Have I done something wrong?" she asked, holding her bottom lip between her teeth, that little-girl-lost expression on her face.

"Its ok," I said. "You become fair game when you're in a car like this," I told her.

"Give him a race," was her reply, "I bet he couldn't catch us even if he tried."

"No, we mustn't draw any more attention to ourselves!" I told her, and with a wink, "Now, behave."

In return she poked her tongue at me.

I pulled over onto the hard shoulder of the motorway, got out of the car and walked towards the police officers, just as they were vacating their car and putting their hats on.

"Is everything alright sir?" the driver asked as he adjusted his hat. He actually beat me with the question; I was going to ask him if everything was ok.

"Yes, fine officer," I replied.

"Only we noticed your hazard lights flash and thought there may be a problem," the other officer explained, as they both stepped closer to me.

I went onto explain that my companion was just having some fun and got a little carried away. I was talking to the driver and the other officer went to see if Louise was alright. I looked round to see Louise getting out of the car, as she was unable to open the window to talk to the police officer. I watched as he held the door open while he was speaking to her, then, obviously satisfied with the answers he received, he closed it, and once she had resumed her seat he made his way back to where we stood.

"She says she was playing with the controls!" he said to both of us with a massive smile across his face. Then, "Seriously sir, you do need to take care, particularly with a car like yours." I thought he had finished when all of a sudden he said, "By the way sir, I hope you don't mind me saying so, your companion is very pretty."

"Yes I know, and thank you," was my reply.

With that they both touched their hats and made their way back to the police car, reminding me as they went to take care. I made my way back to my Porsche, to be met by questions from Louise.

"Are you in trouble?".

"No, its ok," I told her, and went on to explain where the switch for the windows was positioned. I didn't mention what the officer had said about her being pretty; that would keep, I thought. I pulled back on to the motorway and regained my original speed. The police car went by and gave us a courteous flash of the blue lights.

We travelled on our way making conversation as we went. She had seen the children before she left and they were happy and content to stay with Grandma and Gramps, as they call them.

By now I was seeing a different woman, different from all those years ago in the office, for this woman had suffered for years at the hands of a bully. Yes, she had two children, and it could be argued she was running away from them, but she needed to do this, be it with me or someone else, for this could be the saving grace she needed. It might possibly save the children as well, for one day he may even turn on them. For now she was relaxed, but at the same time excited, playful, a girl-like person that I hadn't seen before. I'd witnessed her jolly spontaneous manner in the office years ago, but this was now a mature woman rediscovering what it was like to have fun and also to have attention paid to her. She was good to be with, lively and sparkling, her smile pleased me, she made me feel good, and as a result I wanted to treat her well. I thought if I made her feel happy it would rub off on me.

We were travelling along the A30 when she asked, "How fast will your car go?"

"Well," I said, "I've taken it to 100 miles an hour, but it says 160 on the clock. I'm not sure I want to go that fast and there aren't many places you can even try it out," I went on.

"Go on then, give it a burn," she said.

"Where do you get these expressions from," I asked. "And what if we get caught? You won't want to pay the fine will you?"

But it was absolutely no use posing those questions to her. As I looked across at her and saw her face alight and her eyes burning into me, I was putty in her presence, and she was fully aware of the effect she had on me.

I looked in the rear view mirror: clear behind, and the road ahead was empty; what the hell, I thought, as I changed down a gear and pressed the throttle with my right foot. The engine growled and responded by providing the extra power that was required to take us from eighty miles an hour to one hundred. At that speed I changed back up into top gear, as we hurtled along the dual carriageway.

I glanced across at Louise. Her face was alight with the adrenalin rush that had come from being catapulted from a casual drive to racing car speed. Her hands were gripping the edges of the leather seat and I could see her nails slightly digging into the sides of the seat. At a hundred and twenty miles an hour I could see cars ahead. We passed them as though they were standing still. We were coming to the brow of a hill and I felt we had travelled at that speed for long enough, so I eased back with my right foot and we slowed down to a more comfortable ninety miles an hour.

"Now wasn't that good for you?" Louise asked. "I really did enjoy that, I've never been that fast in my entire life. Just how fast were we going?"

"Well, almost twice the legal speed limit, 120 mph," was my reply.

We drove on, still making good conversation. As we got nearer to our destination we got held up behind a farm tractor towing a muck spreader, and tailed it for several miles. As we came out of one of the villages I realised that unless I took a chance I would never get past the obstruction. My action was to take even myself a little by surprise. With the car in second gear I put the nose out just enough to see if the road was clear. It was, and in an instant as I pressed the accelerator we shot from twenty miles an hour to over sixty and passed the tractor and trailer. I pulled back onto the correct side of the road, looked in the mirror and saw nothing had attempted the same move.

"Are you ok," I asked Louise. I had to look at her to get any response. She was speechless, my actions had taken her completely by surprise. Yes, she was prepared for the first escape to high speed but this was totally unexpected, this time her face had lost its colour, and she looked almost frightened. I put my hand across and took hers. She was shaking, not rapidly, just a slight tremble.

"I'm sorry, I didn't mean to scare you," I said, gripping her small hand.

"Its ok," was her reply, as she squeezed my hand in return, "you just took me by surprise; you had to do that or we would have been behind the thing for ages. Honest, I'm ok." And she shook my hand, but didn't let go. I had to release my hold so I could change gear again and she put her hand out and laid it on top of mine over the gear stick. "Don't worry. I'm alright, it'll take more than going fast to frighten me, you should know that, particularly after what I told you about Gary." By now the smile had returned to her face, and as I looked across at her she shrugged her shoulders.

This was the first time that she had mentioned Gary, she looked relaxed, and I could feel the vibrant woman I had known six years ago was coming back to life. On the other occasions I had seen her she had seemed withdrawn, almost scared to relax. For years she had been trapped, not only in a house tucked away in a small village, but held prisoner by a man who didn't really care for her and was only happy if he was getting his own way. Her comment about Gary drew me to ask the question, "Have you heard from him since he left for Belgium?"

Her reply was to shake her head. "No, but then again I don't expect to. He came home doing his old trick, you know, crying, saying he was sorry and he'd never do it again. I'll get some help, he told me, but I know he won't change, and I'm not prepared to give him another chance; I've heard it so many times before." She wiped her eyes. "I do want to forget about him for now anyway, as I told you before we set off, let's just have a nice time. You did say you would help me find a solicitor to get this mess sorted out didn't you?"

"Yes," was my reply. "You can use the one I use if you like, or he may be able to put you in touch with one that deals in domestic cases like yours. I'll do whatever you want me to."

We were by now about ten miles from our destination and approaching the supermarket I'd told Louise about. I pulled off the main road and into the car park of the store. It was two fifteen when I stopped, and we both got out of the car into the warm April sunshine. The view from the car park was quite splendid: looking out towards the coast your eye followed the gentle rolling hills that lead to the sea; a shimmering heat haze was coming off the fields and the sea looked blue and inviting even from a distance. Inland wind turbines could be seen turning in the afternoon breeze, the wind was light and blew Louise's hair into her face as she turned and looked into the wind. She brushed her long wavy auburn hair behind her; off in the distance a tractor could be heard ploughing a field.

"You didn't wait for me to open the door for you," I said, as we came together.

"There's no need for you to do that all the time," was her reply, stating her independence. "Do we have to get much?" she asked as her hand slipped into mine. I have to say it felt right. I was becoming accustomed to holding it, I felt comfortable, and I reassured myself she must too or she wouldn't have taken the initiative.

"We need some fresh vegetables, bread and milk, just for the next few days," I replied, "and we could do with some chicken and other meat, and of course wine and beer. Oh by the way I actually like to open the door for you; remember you're my guest, which means I treat you as someone special."

We had by now made our way into the store and gained a trolley, the one with the wobbly wheel that has a mind of its own.

"I always get the one that goes where it wants to, not where I want it to," Louise said with a little frustration in her voice.

"Come on, I'll give you a hand," I said as I took hold of the handle. "We can do this together."

And so we did. Louse showed her keen eye for what must be considered the best, I put that down to the motherly instinct in her, and in no time we had completed our shopping and were making our way out of the store and back into the spring sunshine.

"Gosh," Louise said as we stepped out from under the canopy at the front of the store, "it's warmer out here than you think." With those words she undid another button on her blouse and looked at me. "You don't mind?" she asked.

"No, not at all," I said, relieved that she felt this relaxed with me. We made our way to the car, loaded the shopping and I opened the door for her to get in. She slid into the seat and looked up at me with a beaming smile. "There," she said, "I let you do it that time, are you happy now?"

"I think you're cheeky," was the only reply I could think of as I closed the car door for her. She still had that smile on her face when I got into the car. As I started the engine she asked me how much longer we would be.

"About fifteen minutes, as long as we don't come across anymore tractors," I said and with that we pulled away and headed back out onto the main road. Soon enough we were pulling off the busy trunk road and into the narrow country lane that leads to the converted barns. On either side of the lane the hedgerow had their new leaves open, fresh and green, showing them off like a child with some new clothes. They rocked in the gentle afternoon breeze, so different from when I'd been down in the winter. Louise again took my hand. "This is so different," she said. "Is it far now?"

"No, its not far," was my reply, "about three hundred yards and we pull off this lane and onto the track leading to the apartments."

No sooner had I said the words than we arrived at the opening to take us down to the apartments. I turned right and drove over the cattle grid, stopping the car on the other side by the sign built into the Cornish stonewall that reads 'Thornlee', just to take in the view.

The track is about two hundred yards long and straight. It has a slight slope to it, just enough to tire you and can take your breath away when you have to walk up it. At the end of the track is a small gravel courtyard, to the left a row of three two-storey apartments, carefully restored using the same Cornish stone as the wall at the top of the track, likewise the rest of the buildings.

Opposite the entrance to the courtyard is a similar row of four apartments, these being different in that they have a small porch to them and a tiny piece of garden under the window, also they are of a slightly bigger construction. Paving slabs lead from the courtyard to each of the dwellings and a small row of raised stones mark out parking places within the courtyard, adjacent to each of the properties.

Directly opposite this row of four apartments is a row of four smaller buildings, which are in fact the garages associated with the main building, one for each of the apartments. Behind them, open fields sweep up to a dis-used farmhouse on our right, about fifty yards away. To our left a low hedge, the other side of which is a field with cattle grazing. To the rear of the main buildings is more farmland. That in turn gives way to a valley leading to the coast.

Outside, the warm breeze carried a myriad of sounds: skylarks high in the air singing and calling to each other, a warning that someone is near and may disturb their nest; away in the distance the gravel croak of a pheasant, looking for its young. Way off in a remote meadow lambs can be heard bleating for their mothers.

"This is it!" I said, looking at Louise. She was spellbound and was gazing into the open view in front of us. "Are you ok?" I asked. It seemed like an age before she answered.

"Yes I'm fine," she said, her warm smile confirming what she continued to say. "This is such a beautiful view. I never thought I'd get to see this place, let alone stay here. Which one of the apartments is yours?"

"Well," I started, pausing, as I'd never told her that in fact I owned all of them, "actually I own all of this land and most of what's on it."

"All of it!" Louise said in a startled manner. "You own all of this? You must be rich! Which one will we be staying in?"

"It's the one in the main block facing us, the one on this end, number four," I said. "We're going to stay in number four, if that's alright with you."

I looked at her and she nodded her head in agreement. I started the car and drove carefully down the track and pulled up outside number four. The rest of the apartments looked as if they were empty; maybe people will be down during the weekend, I thought. We sat in the car for a few moments, taking in the stillness, with just the sound of the breeze washing round the courtyard.

"Come on," I said, "let's go and get settled and have a cup of tea." I got out of the car and made my way round to Louise's side and opened the door for her.

"Thank you," she said, surprise still in voice. "This is even better close up, it's so quiet and nobody else is about. I'm surprised you ever come home from here."

We walked across the few stone slabs that lead to the front door, and I took my keys, opened the door and held it open for Louise to go into the small porch. In front of her was another half-glazed door. She turned the handle and made her way into the lounge-dining room. This went the full length of the house and to the left was a flight of stairs with a handrail on the right side, leading to the first floor. At the top of the stairs on the left was a small picture window, which let additional daylight onto the landing.

In various locations around the lounge wall-lights were fitted and to the right was a doorway leading into the kitchen area. They were originally designed as holiday homes, but I'd had some heating put in so the winter months would be more bearable.

The other end of the room was set out as the lounge area, and had large sliding patio doors leading out onto the small paved area of about ten feet by twenty, the width of the apartment. A small fence separated the patio from a meadow that drifted away to farmland, in the left hand corner of the patio stood a bird table with two bird feeders hanging from it; blue tits and finches still busy feeding at the nuts.

"I'll put the kettle on for a cup of tea, and while it's coming to the boil we can get the things in from the car, and I'll show you to your bedroom," I said.

We brought the bags in from the car, put the shopping away, and in between made a pot of tea. I picked up Louise's bags and led the way up the wood-on-steel-supported stairs. At the top was a small landing, in the middle of which was a door leading to the master bedroom. At the end of the landing it turned right and headed back towards the front of the building and partway along was another door to the bathroom, which was positioned over the kitchen area. The other bedroom was at the front of the apartment and was only a single-sized room just big enough for a single bed and a small wardrobe.

"This is your room," I said as I opened the door to the master bedroom.

The light pouring through the windows seemed even brighter due to the white walls. The whole apartment had been aired and this bedroom smelt particularly fresh. The agent's wife had a set of keys and I'd been in touch with them to say I would be visiting for the Easter break. She'd given the place a spring clean, there was fresh bedding on the beds, and a small bunch of flowers stood in a vase on the dressing table.

The head of the double bed was against the dividing wall of the bathroom, to the left as you entered the room was the dressing table and a small wardrobe, directly opposite the door to the bedroom was large French widow which opened out onto a small veranda. Net curtains hung at the windows, and on either side of the bed was a small cabinet on which stood bedside lamps.

"Will this be alright for you?" I asked as I stepped inside the room.

With a sigh Louise replied, "It's lovely, so light and airy. But where are you going to sleep?" she enquired.

"In the room over there," I said, pointing to the front bedroom. "Oh, that's the bathroom on the left, it has a shower as well as a bath, so you have a choice. Just make yourself at home. Now, I think tea will be ready, don't you?"

I put her bags on the bed and we came out of the bedroom together, and as we did our bodies touched, the first time since our greeting in the morning. I wanted to take hold of her, almost force her to the bed, but common sense prevailed and I told myself not to spoil things. Louise just kissed me on the cheek which was all I needed to keep me going.

We came back down the stairs. I have to say I find it extremely difficult to descend them quietly. My shoes were clipping against the hard wood stairs all the way down, but not so Louise, for she was very light on her feet.

I poured the tea and we made our way to the lounge area by the patio doors. I opened them slightly, just enough to allow the warm breeze to enter the apartment. Just back from the doors was a sandalwood-coloured two-setter sofa, to the left a matching chair, and a small coffee table was positioned in between them - sparse but adequate for two people. The other part of the room was set out as the dinning area with a small oak table and four matching chairs, in line with the entrance to the kitchen.

Tucked away under the stairs was a small matching oak unit, on which sat a small music system and a television. The unit also contained the drinks' cabinet. Louise made herself comfortable on the sofa and I sat in the chair, relaxed and pleased to be back at my holiday home. Again we talked and passed the rest of the afternoon away.

The time had just slipped away, and by now it was gone five o'clock, time to prepare something to eat. We'd agreed on the way down it would be better if we had a meal in that evening, and had bought sufficient food from the supermarket.

"Have you got a phone here?" Louise asked, "Only I think I need to ring

Mummy to check that the children are ok, and let her know we arrived safely." There was some urgency in her voice.

"Yes of course," I replied as I made my way to kitchen, "it's over there on the unit under the stairs." I pointed to the phone. "And this line is ex-directory," I added.

Out in the kitchen I could hear Louise talking to her mother, explaining that we'd had a good journey to the apartment, and it was warm and very secluded. Then I noticed a change in her voice, and I heard her talking in motherly tones, "Hello darling, are you being good for Grandma? You've been helping her! That's good. And is James being a good boy? You say he's gone to bed, and you'll be going soon?" She closed with the words, "Good night, God bless, darling," a tremble in her voice. Then she was back to her Mother, with a final, "I will", and "Goodbye", and she hung up. She made her way into the kitchen. She came over to me with tears still in her eyes. I was standing by the sink unit, which is positioned under a small window, from which there is a good view of the patio. I had to put my arms around her to give her comfort.

"It's alright," I told her, "I do understand. It's always difficult on the end of a phone. You can ring any time you like and if you get worried we can always go home, is that ok?"

She wiped away her tears and nodded. "Mummy sends her regards. Is there anything I can do to help?" she asked, adding, "You seem to have everything under control cooking-wise."

"Well, it's only a chicken salad and a few potatoes but you can lay the table if you like," I said, releasing my arms from around her. As she turned I continued, "The cutlery is in the drawer next to the cooker and you'll find a tablecloth and napkins in the unit where the phone is, and that's where the wine glasses are as well. Oh, there's a bottle of Chardonnay in the fridge, would you like to open it?" I finished.

"Me! Open wine! You must be joking," she said, as she put her head back into the kitchen. "I'll get it out of the fridge, but I'm afraid you'll have to pop the cork, if you pardon the expression," she said.

Now the smile had returned to her lips and I felt comfortable in her company. It was if we were old friends, and as if we had never been apart, although in truth we had never been together. She was as relaxed as I was; she slipped her shoes off after setting the table and sat on the sofa with her feet tucked underneath her.

I opened the wine when the meal was ready. We sat and ate, talking all the time. Louise told me about her sister, she lived in Kent and was older than her. Jackie was her name and she, also, had two children, a boy and a girl, older than Sarah and James and the boy is the eldest.

The evening was drawing in and as the light began to fade we moved away from the table. We still had the wine to finish, so Louise resumed her position on the sofa and I relaxed into the chair, a small coffee table separated us and we duly put our wineglasses on it. From where I was sitting I could see the sun sinking into the western sky, a ball of red flame engulfing the horizon, and with the glow of the early night pouring into the apartment, it appeared as if the place was on fire. The still of the evening was disturbed only by the few birds remaining around the bird table, and crows could be heard as they made their way to roost for the night.

"Are you comfortable?" I asked.

"Oh yes thank you," Louise replied. "I did enjoy our meal, and this Chardonnay is very drinkable," she said as she placed her glass back on the coffee table. "I hope you don't mind, but I brought a book with me. Would you think me rude if I read for a little while before I go to bed?" she asked.

"Not at all, you can do whatever you want," I replied. "Anyway, I'd like to have a read of the paper."

Louise got up and made her way up the stairs to the master bedroom and in what seemed like no time she was back. I hadn't heard her come down the stairs, what signalled her return was the sweet smell of her perfume, confirmed by her hand running across the back of my neck and shoulders. I jumped, just a little.

"I didn't mean to startle you," she said.

"I didn't hear you come down the stairs; you're very dainty and light on your feet," I said in reply to her comment.

"Well, there's not a lot of me," she said, as she curled up on the sofa again.

The night had by now drawn in. I got up and closed and locked the patio doors, pulled the curtains together slightly and turned on the wall lights before returning to my seat with the copy of The Times. I glanced at the headlines; nothing dramatic had taken place other than the stock market had taken a bit of a dive. Well, it would recover, and with the money I had, in an arrogant way I didn't really care.

I glanced across at Louise, who was engrossed in the book she was reading, and to see her sitting comfortably reminded me of days when I was with my wife. She would sit in the same way and also loved reading, but we had never spent any time here together. I was still pondering the past as I was looking at Louise when she looked up from her book. Her face was a picture of surprise and in an instant a smile formed. She ran her right hand through her hair, pushing it back off of her face.

"If you're going to look at me like that I'm going to charge you!" she said, and the smile broadened.

"I'm sorry," I said, "I didn't mean to stare, but you looked so engrossed and yet relaxed at the same time. Every time I look at you I see a different woman."

"I am relaxed," was her response, "can I please get back to my book, or do you want to talk?"

"I'm ok with the paper," I said, and opened it out to the centre pages. Under the column entitled Home News there was a large article about the Royal Mail. It went into great detail about four men who had been arrested in the north of the country on suspicion of theft and fraud, and the closing statement said more arrests were expected within the next few days. It prompted me to ask Louise if Gary still worked for the Post Office.

"Yes he does," was her reply. "I'm never going to finish this book, am I?" She paused, put the bookmark in the place where she had stopped reading, then continued, "Why do you ask?"

I explained what I had been reading in the paper, inquisitive as to whether Gary ever spoke about work. Often things get blown out of all proportion in the press, and the truth bears no resemblance to what is written.

"He never says much about his job," she said, and continued, "He does the long distance runs from time to time, that's why he stays away for a couple days at a time. You know, when we had dinner out he was meant to be away for the week, but it was cut short and he came home early. But he tells me very little. I did ask him about that fraud thing; he got in a bit of huff and said he'd heard something was going on but that was all he said really."

I got up and made some coffee. The time had pleasantly slipped away and it was almost ten o'clock. Louise drank her coffee as I cleared the table and placed the dirty crockery in the sink. I made my way back into the lounge area just as Louise was getting up from the sofa with the book in her hand.

"I'll do the washing up in the morning," I said, looking at her as she stretched.

"If you don't mind I'll go on to bed," she said as she took a step closer to me.

"Yes that's fine," I replied. "You know where everything is, don't you?"

"Yes, and thank you for a lovely day," she said, as she gave me a hug and a kiss on the cheek.

As she got to the bottom of the stairs I asked, "What would you like for breakfast?"

She turned and looked back at me. "Well, we'd better have those hot cross buns, hadn't we?"

"Oh yes," I'd forgotten about those. See you in the morning. Goodnight."

She returned the "Goodnight" and also "God bless" and she was gone.

I was left alone but didn't feel alone. That's a strange thing to say, but I suppose all I felt was contentment. Louise was happy, and as a result so was I. She had shown me fondness I hadn't asked for, and that had brought about my contented state of mind. I had a change of plan; before going to bed I would wash up, so that's what I did. It must have been ten thirty by the time I climbed the stairs, after turning all the lights off and making sure everything was secure. As I passed Louise's door I softly said goodnight again, but there was no response and I took it she must be fast asleep and within a short space of time of getting into my bed I too was asleep.

Good Friday

It must have been five thirty when I awoke. I'd slept very well, not even waking during the night, and now as I lay in my bed with the early morning sun nursing its way though the light morning mist, I remembered that just across the landing my guest also lay in her bed. I got out of bed to the sound of two doves billing and cooing to each other on the electricity pole on the other side of the courtyard. I put on my dressing gown and made my way downstairs as quietly as I could, after paying a visit to the bathroom.

I pulled back the curtains on the front window after putting the kettle on, and the spring light flooded into the room highlighting the fine particles of dust that floated in the air. I went back into the kitchen and completed the task of making a pot of tea. I poured Louise and myself a cup, placing hers on a small tray along with a plate of biscuits. Carefully I made my way back up the stairs, and stood still outside her room, almost too frightened to knock. I gave two gentle knocks and I was relieved with the response.

"Come in," she said, still with sleep in her voice.

Slowly I opened the door and as I stepped inside the room I saw Louise stretch her whole body. Her arms went up to the top of the bed and held onto the headboard, her long auburn hair tumbled over the pillows, and as I stood and watched, her little feet wriggled at the foot of the bed. I could see she was wearing a white tee shirt, that had slipped off her right shoulder during the night. She sat up in the bed and my eyes looked at the outline of her small but curvaceous body. She beckoned me to the bedside, and slowly I made my way to the side by the French windows.

"Come on, sit here," she said, as she patted the edge of the bed, "but you've only brought one cup!"

"Yes, mine's downstairs," was my reply. "I wasn't sure if you would be awake. Did you sleep well?" I asked, my eyes transfixed on her bright early-morning smile.

"Oh yes thank you," she answered, "I didn't even hear you come up. What time did you go to bed?"

"I think it was about ten thirty," I said, and as those few words left my lips she took me by surprise and I was about to feel ten feet tall again. She lent across and kissed me on the cheek in her usual manner, but it was her words that lifted me. "Good morning my dear," she whispered in my ear.

Now normally any hot-blooded male would have felt a great arousal, sitting on the edge of a scantily dressed, beautiful woman's bed, but I had control of my own feelings. Sure I wanted her, and I felt very excited, but for the time being I was happy to savour the situation. I felt no need to rush anything. Things were perfect as they were, why spoil it at this early stage and possibly damage the trust she has in me, I told myself. I got up from the bed, leaving the tray on the bedside unit.

"I've embarrassed you," Louise quickly said, pulling the bedclothes up.

"No you haven't. My tea is downstairs getting cold, give me a call when you've finished and I'll bring you some more," I said as I made my way to the door.

I heard her say, "Ok" as I started to descend the stairs.

I stood in the kitchen drinking my tea, looking out of the small window and watching the birds eagerly feeding from the bird table. I'd finished my tea and was making my way to the doorway when Louise asked, "Is there any more tea in the pot?" I was dumbstruck, for she had made her way down the stairs with the same softness as last night, and was now positioned at an angle at the base of the stairs, looking towards me standing in the kitchen doorway. Her left leg was placed on the first step of the stairs and I'm sure she was totally unaware of the revealing way in which she was stood.

For as I have said the sun was cascading in through the window and half-glazed entrance door, and I could clearly see the fullness of her perfect body silhouetted through the transparency of the white tee shirt. Underneath she was wearing a small pair of white panties, hanging upon her hips. The sun cast a perfect image of her small but well-rounded breasts, and this in turn highlighted the flatness of her tummy. I looked now with a wanting deep inside of me, I felt sure would show if she stood there for any longer.

"Now you *are* embarrassing me," I said, and made a gesture to cover my eyes.

In an instant she realised what she had done. "Oh my goodness," she cried, and proceeded to skip back up the stairs, cupping her breasts with her hands as she went.

I took up another cup of tea for her and one for myself and by the time I got to the bedroom doorway Louise had reinstalled herself safely under the bedcovers.

"I think you're more embarrassed than I was," was my comment, for she still had the redness to her cheeks.

"I'm very sorry," she began, "I didn't realise the sun was that strong."

"You don't have to apologise to me," I said, and went on, "Don't be ashamed of the little bit of innocence still left in you." I brushed the edge of the bed. "Can I?" I asked, wanting to sit on the bed.

"Yes of course you can. But you saw everything," she said, as her face began to grow an even deeper red.

"Well I'm not complaining, anyway what have you got to worry about, Louise?" I asked. " I'm gay, or have you forgotten that?"

"You're not going to let me forget that, are you?" she said and put her right hand on top of mine.

"No, but I think I need to remind you from time to time just how safe you are with me," I said. What I really meant was I wanted her desperately, but I had learnt I'd have to be patient as I already knew it might prove to be nothing more than a good friendship, the kind of which I have with Christine.

We finished our tea and as I got up I asked, "Would you like to use the bathroom first or shall I go now?"

"You can go in first," Louise said, as she snuggled back down under the bedclothes. "I'd like to have five more minutes in bed if you don't mind."

"That'll be ok," I said as I left the bedroom. "I'll give a call when I'm finished."

"Would you mind if I had a bath?" I heard her ask as I made my way into the bathroom. I replied by telling her I would leave some towels out for her and she answered back with a "Thank you."

I was downstairs making a fresh pot of tea by the time Louise came out of the bathroom. I called up to enquire if she would be very long. The response I got was "Don't rush me."

Within ten minutes she had descended the stairs, this time fully dressed, with her hair still damp. She was wearing a pair of blue denim jeans, some flat shoes, and on top a light-blue tee shirt tucked into her jeans. Draped around her neck was a navy-coloured sweatshirt, the sleeves hanging in front. We sat and had our toasted hot cross buns together, with fresh tea.

As the morning began to unfold we made plans of what we would do with the day ahead of us. We agreed we would take a drive to the beach and have a long walk along it, maybe stop for some lunch in one of the local pubs, and would return by six o'clock at the latest for our supper in the apartment. Most of all we would relax.

It must have been nearly ten o'clock by the time we locked up and set of in the Porsche to take the five or maybe six-mile ride to the beach. As we walked along she took my hand. I looked around at the other people on the beach. There weren't many about, but it crossed my mind we could be considered to be lovers the way we were behaving with each in other in public.

Now this particular beach is about a mile long and the sand under our feet was quite warm. There were a few people in the water but it was to my mind too cold. By Sunday a lot more people would have arrived and if the weather kept up then some of the smaller beaches could be full. We walked the full length of the beach just a few steps from the water's edge, then returned via the sand dunes that offered some protection from the breeze that repeatedly whisked Louise's hair into her face.

We made our way to a pub, and managed to find a seat in the garden close to a wall that offered some shelter from the light wind. I had a pint of beer and Louise a glass of white wine and I ordered some sandwiches. It was very pleasant sitting in the afternoon sunshine just letting the day slip away. The sandwiches duly arrived. Neither of us appeared to have a care in the world as we sat talking and enjoying our lunch together.

Louise told me she had been to Cornwall in the past with Gary, when Sarah was a baby, but they hadn't stayed on this side of the coast, they'd rented a cottage in the Looe area for two weeks and she told me it was miles from anywhere. Gary was ok for a few days, then started going off in the evenings, not returning until late. I was somewhat surprised by this statement. Why should he want to stay out until all hours when he had this beautiful woman for his wife and company? It was beyond me. We finished our drinks and walked back to the car, and I asked if she would like to take a ride into the fishing village and a look round the shops. She replied she would prefer another walk along a beach, then she would be ready to go back to the apartment for supper.

I knew of just the place and it was only a short drive away, but we would have to walk from the car park, which is what we did, and much to my surprise we came across an ice cream van. Well, Louise's face was aglow, just as a child's would be. We walked along the shoreline, both of us enjoying the cold ice cream on this warm Good Friday afternoon.

We'd stopped by the edge of the beach, and I had just suggested if she wanted it would be possible for her to have a holiday with the children later in the year, maybe for a week in May, when a large wave broke behind her. She wasn't quick enough to escape the resulting splash and the cold Atlantic water washed over her feet. She ran as quickly as she could but unfortunately her shoes and jeans were well and truly soaked, her jeans up to knee height. We made our way as swiftly as possible back to the car.

She slipped her shoes off before she got into the car and I knocked the sand out off them as she slid into the seat.

"And these will have to come off as soon as we return to the apartment," she said, adding, "It's the only pair I brought with me."

"Don't worry," I told her, "we can give them a wash when we get back and I'm sure they'll dry very quickly in the late afternoon breeze."

As we drove back I could see as I looked down that Louise was wiggling her toes, and this prompted me to ask her if she was cold.

"No," she said, "But you'll have to carry me in from the car, unless you can dry my shoes out quickly."

I gave a little chuckle and more or less passed off the comment. As I pulled up outside the apartment four or five doves flew up into the air and made their way to the top of the apex roof on the other side of the courtyard. Another car was parked outside of the first row of buildings and as I turned off the engine we could see someone taking in bags. I got out of the car and made my way round to the passenger side of the car; as always I opened the door, and Louise sat there.

"Well, I wasn't joking," she said as she looked up at me. "I'm not walking barefoot on the gravel no matter how short a distance it is, so you'd better get the keys out and open up, you're going to have to carry me!"

I made my way to the front door and unlocked it, expecting her to follow me, but when I looked back she had remained in the car: she wasn't joking! I turned back and took the few short steps back to the car.

"Come on then," I said in a casual way as I crouched down and with those words Louise swung her legs out of the car. I put my left arm under them at the same time slipping my right arm behind her back and bringing a hand up and under her right arm, and as I did so she wrapped her left arm round my neck. With no effort I was able to lift her out of the car. She felt light, and as I stood up she tightened her grip around my neck and her warm face came even closer. Even after having the salty sea breeze in her hair and face she smelt good. I could feel her hair against my own skin, soft and gentle. I looked down at her and thought for one moment she was going to tell me something.

She felt so good and firm, cradled in my arms, as good as when we were wrapped together in our embraces. She closed the car door with her right hand as I stepped back and then I proceeded to walk along the slabs and into the porch.

"You can put me down now kind sir," she said, in a satirical way.

"And what if I don't want to, you're not heavy," was my reply.

"But we can't stand here all night, and I need to get out of these wet clothes," she came back with, and then as a sign of encouragement kissed me on the right cheek.

"Thank you," she said, as I gently lowered her, and she put her feet down.

"I'll put the kettle on, or would you prefer something stronger?" I asked as I made my way towards the kitchen.

"Tea will be fine," was her reply as she headed up the stairs, then she stopped. "Would it be alright for me to have a shower, just to wash the sand out of my hair?"

"Yes that'll be fine, just help yourself, you know where everything is, and by the way don't forget to bring your jeans down so they can be washed," I said.

I heard a muffled "Ok" in return.

After filling the kettle and switching it on I went back out to the car, as Louise had left her wet shoes in it. I had them in my hand and glanced back up to the top of the track. Pulling in from the lane was another car. I thought it must be some more visitors down for the weekend and I made my way back in to the apartment, closed the door and got on with the task of making a pot of tea.

I'd bent down to get the milk out of the fridge when there was knock at the front door, and as I walked from the kitchen across the dining area I could see through the window that the car I had just seen was now parked next to mine. It was a blue Ford. For some reason I thought I'd seen it before, but I couldn't recall where. Upon opening the front door I discovered two men were standing outside; a black man about five foot six tall and the other man white and about five ten. Both were dressed in suits; not holidaymakers, I instantly thought.

"Can I help you gentlemen?" I enquired. The reply was to take me by complete surprise.

"You are Mr Andrew Jackson, aren't you?" the black man asked. His accent told me he was from London.

"Yes I am," I answered.

"In that case may we come in please?" the other man said in a slight northern accent.

"First I think you need to tell me just who you gentlemen are," I answered. Now I was beginning to feel very uneasy. Gary may have had us followed and this could be a trap.

With this thought still in my head the black man put his hand into his inside jacket pocket and pulled out a small leather wallet, and the other man did the same. I could see from the first warrant card that it's owner was a policeman, and I automatically assumed the other gentleman was going to produce the same card. Not wanting my business discussed in the open, I invited them into the apartment.

Once inside the apartment, I stood with my back resting against one of the chairs, and they stood either side of the doorway.

"My name is Inspector Jones, and I'm with the fraud squad and this gentleman is Officer Rimes and he is a representative of the Post Office internal investigations board," the black officer said.

"Oh, haven't you lot finished with me," I said with anger in my raised voice. "You've had over three hundred thousand pounds out of me and you're still chasing me. The bloody money is mine." I stopped, interrupted by the Post Office official.

"We haven't come about your money Mr Jackson, in fact this is nothing to do with that at all," Jones told me.

"We're looking for a Mrs Louise Shaw. Have you any idea where she may be?" Rimes asked in a squeaky almost mouse-like voice.

"Why are you asking me?" I said, trying to look surprised.

"Well, we knew she was having some secret phone calls with someone, and we were a bit surprised to find out it was you," Rimes said. "You see, we had to do a bit of monitoring, well you know what its like, just to get one or two facts straight."

"No, I bloody well don't know what you mean," I said. Now I was beginning to loose my cool. I was just about to start asking questions when I noticed Rimes look up the stairs. I turned and could see Louise coming down the stairs still in her wet jeans, and she was full of her own questions.

"What the hell do you mean 'secret phone calls' and 'get the facts straight'?" she said, full of emotion. She was red with anger, almost to the point of shaking. I took her hand as she approached the bottom of the stairs. She stopped one step from the bottom.

"Oh, how very cosy!" Rimes butted in. "Just the two of you is it?" A smug grin had etched its way across his face, and he went on, "And what would Mr Shaw make of this then. I bet he'd give you another kicking, Mr Jackson, and I know you didn't come off too lightly either, did you Mrs Shaw?"

Louise's response was like I had never seen before and her words even took these so called gentlemen by surprise, as much as it did me, "You bastards must have had the phone bugged to know about Andy and me, and what for, we haven't done anything wrong, or illegal. And tell me, just how did you know I'd had a beating at the hands of my husband?"

"Come to that how did you know I got a kicking?" I asked, before they could answer Louise's question.

"Well it's like this," Rimes started, but before he had the chance to continue Jones interrupted him.

"As I said, Mr Jackson, its not you we're interested in, and to put your mind at rest we're not too bothered about you, Mrs Shaw. It's your husband we've been monitoring, for some time now, and the only way was to bug your house in one or two places. Believe me it was really necessary. We thought he might give something away during a conversation in the house. We couldn't get a tap on the phone, anyway it wouldn't have been any good after he jumped on it, would it?" His manner was almost condescending. And he went on, "Well, we've had an eye on you since the two of you made those secret arrangements to go out for dinner and the day afterwards when you got such a pasting we were watching. You must be quite a fit man to have survived that."

"But if you saw that happen then why the hell didn't you come to my aid?" I asked, still angry at the thought of being left on my own.

"We couldn't be sure it wouldn't jeopardises the operation that's been going on for some months now," Jones replied.

With those words Louise sprang back into the conversation. "But what has any of this got to do with my husband. I'm very confused by all of this. Me being with Andy has nothing to do with any of you, and why are you so concerned about Gary?"

"Mrs Shaw," Jones started in a slow and precise tone, "we have reason to believe your husband may have been involved with an incident in Holland last year, when unfortunately a Dutch customs officer was killed. That is the reason we have had him under close surveillance for a little while."

With his closing words, and much to Jones surprise, Rimes exclaimed, "And we at the Post Office have every reason to suspect him of fraud and theft." He paused to draw breath. I could see he was trembling with excitement, but his excitement and nervous shaking was in fact hiding a guilty secret.. "We raided his locker in the office yesterday afternoon, and you'll never guess what we uncovered?"

Now he was looking at me right in the eyes.

"No, I'll bet we'll never guess," I said, trying to kill his excitement, but in fact all I did was to fuel it.

"Well I'll tell you," he said as he wiped his lips. "We found all those letters and cards you sent Mrs Shaw."

Looking at Louise, I could see her face had dropped. I thought she was about to pass out.

"You'd better sit down," I said, and pulled the chair from behind me and helped her to sit.

But Rimes hadn't finished and was more than eager to carry on. "And that's not all," he started, but Jones demonstrated he was in fact the officer in charge and stopped Rimes by putting his hand on his shoulder.

Let me explain," Jones said. "Mr Jackson, Mrs Shaw, we - that is the fraud squad and the Post Office - have reason to believe Mr Shaw may have been, or may still be, involved in some form of drug smuggling or trafficking, but the investigations are still ongoing. Due to the nature of his work and some of the items recovered from that search on his locker we think he is still connected. You will understand that as a result of the death of the customs' official we need to rule out as many people as possible, and your husband was in the vicinity on the night of the incident. The customs man was working closely with us and had identified more than four known drug dealers who have been operating low-key in Britain. We think your husband may well have made contact with them with a view to carrying more of the illegal substances around England, and are sure these drugs have been coming into this country via Hull, a run your husband has regularly undertaken."

I looked again at Louise and saw the colour had drained from her: she was white and in a state of shock. I put my arm round her; she felt cold and almost lifeless.

"I don't understand," she muttered. "Gary doesn't use drugs, and he wouldn't sell them. For all his faults he wouldn't deal in death."

"But Mrs Shaw," Jones asked, "can you explain where he got thirty thousand pounds from?"

"What?" she replied, totally surprised by the Inspector's statement.

"Yes Mrs Shaw, that's how much money is in your joint bank account," Jones said, with an equally surprised look on his own face. "No, you didn't know." But he hadn't finished. "Now what we are concerned about is the type of people your husband has been dealing with in this Country. Some of them are not," Jones paused again before he went on, " well, not the sort you'd have round for dinner, let's say. It may be best if we have someone placed locally, to, you know, keep an eye out, kind of look out for you." He was stumbling for words.

"I know what you mean," I said, angry at what the inspector was going to suggest.

"You want to keep an eye on us, just to make sure we don't do a runner, is that it? Or is it the way he gets his kicks?" I said, looking at Rimes.

"No, that's not it Mr Jackson." Now Jones was the angry man. "Some of those people from Holland are now in this Country, and if they should get together with their associates in England they may come looking for you two. They may even try to use Mrs Shaw as a bargaining point just to persuade Mr Shaw to do a little more work for them. Do I make myself quite clear Mr Jackson?"

"So what do you propose?" I asked, still a little suspicious. By now Rimes had his hand in his pocket and looked like a little boy that had been told off.

"We plan to have an undercover man placed in the vicinity. He will report to me if he sees anything untoward. If there's a problem we can get backup in extremely quickly. By the way, he's a local officer but I doubt you'll ever see him and I'll give you my mobile number. If either of you should feel uneasy about anything just call me. Most of all we want you to carry on as normal," Jones finished.

I looked at Rimes; now he had a smutty grin about his face. I felt anger for Louise and myself. "Have you got a problem?" I asked, as I took a step closer to him.

"No" he said, as a frightened look replaced the grin.

With Rimes' answer still in the air Inspector Jones made a signal to Rimes to go out to the car. Rimes made his way, Jones started to follow him but stopped as he got to the outer door, then turned and said, "Think yourself lucky, I've got to put up with him all the time! Things will be ok, trust me!" then he added, "Don't worry about Mr Rimes, he's harmless, just not used to this sort of work. We're going back to Exeter for an overnight stop before going back to London tomorrow, but as I have just told you we're only a phone call away." But what none of us knew was Rimes had a dark and sinister secret that was to be revealed in the fullness of time.

I stood at the outer door and watched the two of them get into the car, with Jones in the driver's seat. He started the diesel engine and a puff of thick smoke hung in the air as they pulled away it slowly followed the car up the track. There was something very familiar about that car, and the way it was driven reminded me of something, as it had when they turned into the track, but for the moment I couldn't put my finger on it. Now my main concern was to tend to Louise.

As I turned and walked back into the apartment, she was standing by the inner door, holding onto the doorframe and running her right hand through her hair. She looked numbed, almost expressionless. All of this had drained her, and I feared this could spell the end of the weekend and, worse, the friendship I'd been working so hard at building. As I stepped closer I could see no smile. She was quiet, upset and disturbed by the intrusion of these two official strangers, and the news they had brought with them.

"Are you alright?" I asked, knowing as soon as I'd said the words it was the most stupid question to ask.

"No I'm bloody well not, I'm angry and very confused," she retorted. "I've lots of questions and I don't know who'll be able to answer them. For that matter I've a lot to ask you," she finished, releasing her hand from the doorframe.

"Well, before I can answer any of your questions I need a drink, how about you?" I asked.

"No I'm ok, I'll make do with a cup of tea, but you'd better make a fresh pot as that one will be cold by now," was her somewhat frustrated reply and she continued, "I'm going up to get out of these wet clothes and have that shower. I won't be long." She turned to make her way up the stairs and stopped, spun round, and looked me straight in the eyes.

"I don't blame you for this, it would have caught up with me sooner or later. Don't worry, I'm not going to beat you up, but I need to get some things clear," she said as she lent forward put her right hand on my left shoulder and kissed me on the right cheek. "You do understand, don't you?" she asked.

"Yes," I said, as she made her way up the stairs. I made my way to the small unit, opened the cupboard containing a bottle of malt whisky, and unscrewing the cap I realised I had a lot of my past to reveal. "Maybe it's best if I don't," I said out loud and put the top back on the bottle.

"Are you ok?" Louise called down as she came out of the bedroom and was heading for the bathroom.

"Yes, I'm fine, just talking to myself," I replied.

"Well don't! And how's that tea coming along?" she asked in a somewhat demanding voice.

"I'll see to it now," I said, as I made my way to the kitchen.

I made a fresh pot of tea and started on the supper; first the potatoes, then some boil-in-the-bag fish I found in the freezer. I thought that, together with some peas and bread, would be fine.

I'd just poured the tea when I heard Louise come down the stairs and looked out from the kitchen. This time I'd heard her because she'd put on a pair of black high-heeled leather shoes. She was wearing a blue, three-quarter length wrap-round skirt and a tight fitting white top that had thin straps over her shoulders. I could clearly see that she wasn't wearing a bra. In her right hand she was holding a cream cardigan, and in her other hand the damp clothes she had just taken off.

"Is that tea ready?" she asked, a little impatient with me.

"Yes I've just poured it," was my reply, thinking she had every reason to be somewhat edgy with me. "Do you want me to put those things in the washing machine?" I asked.

"No it's ok, just show me where it is and I'll do the rest, I've got a few other things if you don't mind," she told me.

I showed her the machine and, true to her word, she managed the rest as I set the table for dinner. We sat in the early evening sun, as it poured through the open patio doors, and for a time we sat in silence with only the sound of the washing machine going through its cycles for company, and the distant cries of some sheep looking for their lambs. When our supper was ready we ate sitting at opposite sides of the table, the sun highlighting the left side of Louise's face. Slowly the colour was beginning to return. I reassured myself if things were that bad or she felt so uncomfortable, then she would ask me to take her home to the children, so that was the first question I asked her.

"Look, if you're unhappy I'm quite willing to go home tomorrow," I said, looking into her eyes.

"No! I don't want to go home," she almost snapped back at me. "But I do need to ring Mummy and talk to the children, and as I have said I've lots of questions that need answers from you. Now lets finish our supper before it gets cold, it would be a shame to waste it," she finished.

After we'd finished eating, I cleared the table and got on with the washing up, as Louise made her nightly call to her Mother. She may not be too happy with the answers I give to her questions and it's a possibility she could change her mind about going home.

All the time I was at the sink I could hear her soft warm motherly tones, talking to first Sarah and then to James, a few more words with her mother and she closed with, "Good night, God bless, I'll talk to you tomorrow." I felt her presence behind me. She picked up the tea towel and completed the wiping up. The job was finished and everything put away and we headed for the lounge. Louise made herself comfortable on the sofa, her cardigan slung over her and I sat in the chair, feeling as if I was about to be interrogated. The sun was now sinking in the western sky, and looked like a ball of red flame on the horizon.

"You didn't have that drink?" Louise said, as she pulled her feet up onto the sofa and curled into the corner of it.

"No, but I may want it later, you know, to help me sleep," I replied.

"What did you mean all those years ago, when you said you were fond of me?" Louise asked, and immediately took me by surprise. And she hadn't finished, she had a very determined look on her face, wanting to get to the truth. "I'm also very confused by this money you have. I heard you say it was all yours. But please forgive me, where did it come from and how much is it?" She was looking at me and running her right hand through her hair. She'd only paused to regain her thoughts. "And tell me, just how do you feel about me now?"

Now she had finished and it was my turn to give the answers. But I felt as if she had an emotional hold over me, two of the questions went straight to my heart.

"Where do you want me to start?" I asked, shrugging my shoulders, trying to pick my way to the easiest question first.

"Start where you like," Was Louise's casual reply.

"Well," I started, "what I meant when I said I was fond of you was just that, I wanted to be your friend." I stopped and hesitated, not at this moment did I feel ready to declare my love for her.

"But you had your own commitments and a new husband, you didn't need my friendship then, but you made me feel so alive; you were always bubbly, full of excitement, I wanted to share in that. Do you remember going to Kim's wedding party, you danced with me for most of the night. I felt so invigorated, and at the same time I was jealous, yes that's right, jealous. Gary had you and I could see then he didn't really care, he just spent his time alone at the bar drinking. That's no way to treat a new young wife." I paused before continuing with, "You must also remember I am somewhat older than you and Gary, as a result, I see the things a younger man wouldn't, so when I told you I was fond of you that was exactly what I meant. I would always be waiting for you, if only to be your friend." I stopped again and Louise was still looking at me, waiting, maybe, to hear those words, but still I wasn't prepared to say them, but I did have more to tell her.

"When Kate was ill you showed me consideration and kindness, you thanked me for even the smallest things I did for you, then when we fell out, over what now seems like nothing, I was hurt. You wouldn't talk to me, and I felt very isolated, but I still felt the same fondness for you. I stopped ringing you because of my own feelings and the fear of showing them. The time will come when I'll need to ask you some questions, you know, after all of this is done and dusted." I'd finished. I still wanted to say those words, but had put the ball back in her court by saying I was going to need some answers to my questions.

"Ok," Louise said, "I now understand a lot more, and maybe time has taught me even more than I could have expected, but you haven't explained about this wealth of yours."

Well, I thought to myself, that won't be quite so heart-rending, after all it's only money.

"This is a very long and somewhat complicated story," I started, "and I'm not too sure I'll be able to explain it that well, but first of all let me say, all of the money I have is quite legal, all of it is mine. Oh, would you mind if I closed the doors?"

"No, please do, it's turned a bit chilly," Louise said as I got up and headed for the doors.

I looked at her as I passed by and in the dim light I could see the cool evening air had had the same effect on her body as when she'd turned the air conditioning on in the car. Now I could see Louise's nipples were pronounced and erect, and as I pulled the doors together she pulled her cardigan over herself. I made my way to the other end of the building and flicked the light switch. All of the wall lamps came on, and as I made my way back to my seat I turned the ones nearest to us off one by one, leaving only the glow of the lights in the dining area to illuminate the ground floor.

"Well, when I was a young man," I started, and I looked across at Louise to see her eyes fixed on me, "I can remember my Mother and a Great Uncle telling me about farmland in Somerset that had been in the family for centuries. Some of the land should have rightfully been ours. The difficult part to understand and explain is that during the last century a very distant relative managed to sell off the land and the farm buildings and moved to America with the proceeds. Sure, he made lots of promises about coming back when times were better, but of course he never did, nor did he send any money back. What he had done was to sell everyone's inheritance in any land or property in this Country. When things started to go wrong in the farming industry and the remaining relatives tried to call on the banks for help, they discovered everything was already mortgaged. Of course things went from bad to worse, then the first war came and most of the men went away to fight, very few came back, and those that did return came back to nothing. No land, no property, it had all been sold. I can recall being told that several of the men even took their own lives. That's how bad they felt, let down and penniless. Sadly, my Mother was the last true blood relative, and now she's gone, so that left just myself. I did have a sister, but she was killed in a car accident some years ago."

"But you haven't told me how you came into all of this," Louise asked.

"Well I'm trying to but, as I've said, it's very complicated. I left the firm we had worked for just before the operations centre was closed. It was moved to the other side of the country. I went to work in a solicitor's office, just as the office assistant, you know, doing the post and running errands. I quite enjoyed it, not too many responsibilities, I suppose I wanted an easy life. Then one day I came across a letter from America, the standard type checking for surviving family members in this Country. It was from a big law firm in the States, they'd put notices on the web sites and some people had come forward, but on checking them they proved not to be connected in anyway. By a strange coincidence the name they were looking for was 'Bush'. I did some research and found this was in fact the person that went to America from our side of the family all those years ago. Now it turns out he did very well for himself in the new country. He met up with some other like-minded rogues, and got involved in the oil business. At the time it was very small and nobody thought it was going to go anywhere. By now he had a family of his own, I think he had two sons and a daughter, and he went on to make a considerable sum of money. But as the saying goes, what goes around comes around, and the eldest son turned out to be just the same as his father, and he managed to squander the entire fortune, or so it was thought. After his father had passed away, the rest of the family all went to their graves as paupers. But they needn't have, because old man Bush was a little shrewder than he was given credit for. Once the business got off the ground, so to speak, he started to invest the income in various banks all over America. Some banks he paid money into, but that was soon found by the son and he managed to waste that as well, but what he didn't find was a sort of trust fund the old chap had set up in a very obscure bank in the back of beyond. I suppose he had an idea he would use it as a retirement fund if you like." I paused, Louise was transfixed and almost hanging on my every word. "Are you ok?" I had to ask.

"Yes I'm fine, I'm following, just carry on." she said, as she wriggled into the sofa.

"You see, for years this money was being paid into this bank from the oil rights that were coming from an oil well in some place or other, I'm not even sure where it is. But nobody even knew it was there in the bank until about four years ago. At that time an audit was carried out at the bank. They seem to have different laws to us out in the States, and this considerable fortune was uncovered, but there was no one to claim it, so that's where I fit in. I had to go out to the States and prove my identity to claim my inheritance. The firm of solicitors I was working for gave me a great deal of help in obtaining all of the necessary copies of birth and death certificates so I could prove my bloodline and the family tree.

Then I had the job of convincing the English authorities, and that's where I spent that sum of money you heard me mention. The Americans were relatively easy by comparison, they'd accepted the evidence, and because I'd gone out in person it was all done and dusted within a few months, but when I got home I had to fight all sorts of accusations and miles of red tape. Things were complicated because my wife didn't return with me. I still can't believe she enjoys living in the States, but she took to it so easily. A lot of the money is still in America."

"But you still haven't told me how much it is," Louise said. "What is it; a few hundred thousand, or a million?"

"Are you really sure you want to know?" I had to ask. I also knew it would be more of a shock than a surprise when I told her.

"I would like to know." She confirmed, as she pulled her cardigan tighter round herself.

"We're talking about two hundred and fifty." Even I had to pause to draw breath. "That's millions." I knew she would be shocked, and her mouth had dropped open.

"How much? No, don't tell me again, I can't take this in. All that money and you're stuck here," she said, and I almost knew what she was going to say next, "but you could have anything!" she finished.

"I know I could, but all of this money hasn't made me happy, in fact quite the opposite. Until I met you again, that is," I replied, and continued, "and the amount of the fortune was the reason I didn't tell you. The last thing I wanted to do was put you off; you may have thought I was trying to buy you into my life. It goes back to being fond of you, then and now."

"And what are your feelings now?" Louise asked the question, as she did so she changed position on the sofa. "Come and sit next to me, I need some warmth from you." I wondered whether she knew what I was going to say to her, and needed me close to hear the words.

I got up and took the two steps required to get to the sofa, and as I sat down I felt Louise draw in close to me and her left arm went round my back.

"You feel so warm," she said as she cuddled up to me.

"I'm not sure you're going to like what I'm about to tell you," I said, as I slipped my right arm behind her and felt her smooth bra-less back. She drew in even closer.

This was more intimate than at any time we'd been together, even more so than this morning. If there had to be a time, then it had to be now I told myself.

"I'm going to tell you that," I paused, hoping she knew what was about to be said, "I love you." With those words she gave a sigh, but didn't move away. "But I also think I need to quantify that love I have for you." I felt as if I was about to unload a heavy weight I'd been carrying for years. In reality I had, I'd longed to tell her that I was more than fond of her, my love was all consuming, even those years ago.

"Look," I continued, "it's like I've had a little box just for you. All those years ago when I realised I loved you I opened it up, and I put a small deposit of my love into it, then I closed it. That little box will never go away, it never gets filled with too much love and as a result every day I've put more love into it. So I love you more today than yesterday and that little box tells you. So, I wasn't just fond of you. I've always wanted to say 'I love you'."

I'd done it, told her my feelings and she'd stayed. This felt right, her arms wrapped around me and mine around her. Not only did I love her, I wanted to make her feel secure and to be loved by her. She must have felt secure, for now as I looked at this tiny, beautiful woman, she had fallen fast asleep in my arms, her head resting against my chest. It crossed my mind that she may not even have heard my words of love, but as I moved to get up she said she'd taken everything in, but now she was in need of sleep, for it had been a long and tiring day. I wasn't to get the answers to my questions tonight, I told myself as Louise got up. Maybe tomorrow. As she stood up she stretched, and shook her hair to make it cascade down her back. She came to me; not a peck on the cheek tonight, but a long, deeply thoughtful kiss on my lips, and the familiar words, "Good night, God bless," as she ascended the stairs.

"Good night and God bless you," was my reply. I wanted to add, "I love you" but I'd said enough.

I made my own way to bed after making sure everything was ok downstairs, and as I passed Louise's room I stopped, but tonight I stood in silence, frightened to even say any more. I got into my own bed thinking of our days together so far and hoping I hadn't spoilt everything. It took a long time for me to go off to sleep and it couldn't have been a very deep sleep, because at about one o'clock I was awoken by the call of an owl. Far off in the distance I could hear the mate hooting a reply, but in the softness of the night I made out the sound of a female sobbing.

It's Louise, I told myself, as I got out of bed, opened my bedroom door and quietly made my way to her room. Not only was she sobbing but she was also calling Gary's name. As I stood and listened I was unsure of what I should do, but I couldn't leave her like that. I knocked very gently and was surprised but warmed by her reaction, as she called very softly through her tears, "Please come in." I opened the door and stepped inside. "Come over here, to this side of the bed," Louise directed.

I could see in the moonlight shining through the French windows she was on her side facing towards them, and she beckoned me over with her hand. "Please come and lie with me," she almost begged me, and willingly I did as I was asked. As I lay on my back on the top of the bedclothes next to her Louise put her arms round me.

"I'm so sorry, I didn't mean to bring him with me! But all of these events have brought him to the front of my mind," she said and went on, "You do understand?"

"This is not what either of us had planned," I told her. "We came away together to relax and have a good time, but now we seem to have a whole load of problems to unravel, but we can sort things out you know."

"I'm sure we can," was her soft reply, "but for now, just stay with me until I go back to sleep. I do feel very secure lying here with you."

I stayed with her for almost an hour. I even nodded off myself and was awoken by her turning over. That was a cue for me to return to my own bed, somewhat happier now I'd got part of the answer I'd been looking for: she felt secure with me.

Easter Saturday

I awoke at six to the sound of a cow mooing close to the buildings, and as I got out of bed the events of last night came rushing back at me. I hadn't dreamt all of this, it was real and I'd been open and honest. I'd bared my soul, now I only had myself to give.

I got up and made my way downstairs, made some tea as I did yesterday and took the tray upstairs, this time with two cups. A knock at the door and I was beckoned in with the sweet sound of Louise's early morning voice, "Come in," and I did.

This morning she was sitting up in the bed wearing a pale blue nightdress and her face was beaming. Her big smile greeted me.

"Good morning," she said as I made my way round the bed. "Come and sit here. I see you've brought two cups today. I did hear you go down," she said as she took her cup.

"I slept better after you'd been lying with me, thank you for being so understanding. You seem a bit quiet this morning, is everything alright?" she asked in her caring way.

Her question stirred my thoughts to last night and what I'd told her, maybe she hadn't heard the things I'd said to her after all, or she may have just forgotten about the way I felt for her.

"I'm sorry, my mind was on last night and all of the events that went on," I said as I drank my tea.

"I did hear what you said to me," she said, as if she was reading my mind. "That hasn't disturbed me at all, I just need a little time before I can reply to you. I know you said you love me, and you've more than proved it." with those words she put her left arm out and rested her hand on my neck. "Please be patient with me. I promise I won't mess you around." She paused. "And if it's any help, I'm very fond of you as well."

And yes, that did help. It was part of what I wanted to hear, and gave me the encouragement I needed. I could have this woman, but only when she was ready, and I could wait.

"Well, it wasn't just the things I told you that have been on my mind," I said as her hand slipped away. "I've been thinking about Rimes and Jones."

Their names had just slipped off my tongue and Louise interrupted me with her own thoughts. "Something about them didn't add up!" she seemed in hurry to tell me. "But what Rimes had to say did clear away a lot of mystery, you know about those cards and letters. When did you write to me?"

"I used to send you a birthday card, also a Valentines card and occasionally a Christmas card, I also wrote to you on a few occasions." I added, "For days after I'd written to you I waited and waited for the postman to bring me a letter from you, but it never came, and as a result I thought you didn't want to communicate with me. The last time I wrote was just before I went to America."

"And what did you say in that letter?" she asked.

"I wrote to say I was going to America, and for all I knew at the time I may not have been coming back. I told you in the letter exactly what I told you last night," I told her, and a few more truths where out in the open.

That had taken her by surprise, and for a few moments she just looked at me, almost as if she had to regain her own thoughts, and that brought about a change of subject. "Do you remember when I came to your house, after we both got that beating," Louise asked, and then went on, "well, I think I remember seeing that car, you know the Blue Ford, the one Jones was driving. I'm sure I saw it pull away from outside your house when we'd made our way into the lounge."

"Yes you're right," I said, as excited as Louise. "That's where I've seen it before, I thought I recognised it last night when they were pulling away, but I couldn't place it."

"There's something not one hundred per cent about all of this," Louise said, "but they may well be right about Gary and the drugs, and I can check the bank account today. I've got a card, but I'm only meant to use it in emergencies. Come on, you said you would help me, can you think of anything we can do?"

She had stopped and was looking to me for inspiration, but my mind was a blank, transfixed by this excited little figure wriggling in the bed.

"We can't give up now," she said, taking my hand and giving it a squeeze. "We're far more resourceful than that. If we stop then they will have got us to believe them, and you know as well as I do that something wasn't right about what they were telling us."

"For the moment I can't think what to do next," I said in a confused state.

"Jump up," Louise ordered. "Come on, let me get out of bed, you need to think and I can help you."

I stood up and Louise swung her legs out of the bed and as she threw the bedclothes back she faced me and looked me directly in the eyes. Still bemused, I was unsure of what was to come next, as she stood in her short pale blue nightdress, her breasts heaving as she panted for breath due to the excited state she was in.

"I know," she said, "have you got any running kit here?"

"Yes," was my very puzzled reply and I went on, "I keep a pair of trainers and some running leggings in the wardrobe."

"Right then, you put them on and go for a nice run," Louise told me in a very forceful way. "And when you come back I'll have a nice surprise for you." She stopped, and I noticed her breasts heaving in front of her. "Not that type of surprise!" she said, as she pinched my cheek in a very playful manner.

"But I don't want to leave you on your own," I replied.

"I'll be ok," she retaliated, " I won't let anybody in and it will give you chance to think, clear your mind, and maybe come up with some ideas on what we can do."

Of course she was right. I'd told her in the past that I found running helped clear my head, and also I would have a surprise to look forward too upon my return.

I took my running kit and changed in my bedroom and after a kiss on the cheek I set off up the track. By the time I got to the lane my thoughts were much clearer. And as I plodded the Cornish country lanes, dodging the cowpats and trying to keep in close to the grass when I heard an approaching car, I began to think of what we could do.

After all of the years I'd been coming to Cornwall I had made many friends and maybe now was the time to call in a few favours. Most of the characters I'd met were straight, hard working people, but then there was one that might be able to help me. He was a Greek and he ran a second-hand business in Truro, along with his daughter and two sons and what seemed like ever-changing wives. He also had a habit of dealing in lots of other things, all of them quite legal, but he could be accused of sailing a bit close to the wind on occasions.

His name was Stavros. He was well past his fifties but had the energy of a twenty-year old. I hadn't seen him for a while but it would be worth a visit to renew this old acquaintance.

I must have been out running for almost three quarters of an hour, and I'd managed to hatch this plan. I arrived back at the apartment, and as I knocked on the door I could see Louise coming to open it. She was wearing the same skirt as last night, but had a jumper on in place of the white tee shirt. Her hair was still damp from the shower she had taken. I stepped inside the apartment and was greeted not only by her smiling face but also the aroma of fresh toast.

"There, I said I would have surprise for you," she said. "And did it help?"

"Yes it did, but before I can tell you what I've thought of, I need to take a shower and get dressed," I replied.

"Don't be long. I'm going to put some eggs on to boil," she told me as she pointed up the stairs. "Go on."

And I did as I was told. In less than twenty minutes I was back downstairs showered and dressed and sitting with a fresh cup of tea, two eggs in place in their cups and toast in the rack. She'd laid the table perfectly again, and now I felt as if it was me being spoilt.

"Right, before you tell me what you've come up with I must tell you what I've done," Louise went on. "I phoned Mummy and also Jill, just to make them aware." She paused, almost looking for approval. "You know, just in case Gary should turn up unexpectedly. I gave them Christine's mobile number and said she would know what to do, and also she would know how to get hold of us here, is that alright? And by the way, I put my washing out on that line. I almost filled it."

"Yes that's a good idea," I said, as I started on one of my eggs. "You've made a lovely surprise breakfast for me, but *I* was meant to be spoiling *you*."

"Just eat your breakfast," she replied. "And what did you think about while you were out running?"

I went on and explained about Stavros and what he got up to.

"He sounds a bit like old man Bush," was Louise's comment.

"I suppose you're right about that, but I'm sure you'll like him, and believe me if he can help, he will," I told her.

By now it was ten o'clock, and the sun was already up and burning down, with only the slightest breeze. We finished our breakfast, washed up together and each of us got a jacket to take in case the wind got any stronger. Ten thirty we stepped out into the courtyard and Louise made her own way to the car. I very cheekily asked if she wanted me to carry her, and her reply was to poke her tongue at me. I opened the door for her to slip into the car and as she did so she winced and I could see she wasn't wearing any tights and the warm seat had come as a shock to her bare flesh.

The traffic was quite heavy for this time of the morning, but then it was Easter Saturday and I had to expect more cars on the road. The weather was lovely. I told Louise I'd known colder summer days; it was in fact so warm I had the air conditioning on in the car. We pulled into Lemon Quay car park at eleven twenty, paid for a full days parking and made our way via the subway to the covered market.

"Where will we find Stavros?" Louise asked, as we made our way in through the arched entrance, hand in hand.

I told her that he used to have a small stall in the market but that he may have moved. It had been some time since I'd seen him and that was before I went to America. In fact he'd been talking about moving to newer and bigger premises, but we could look at the old place and if he wasn't there then the present owner might know where he was. We found Stavros's old market space.

The stand was now occupied by a young woman, who sold every variety of olive you could imagine. We took the opportunity to buy a mixed selection of her produce. A strong, pungent smell of garlic hung in the air. It wasn't unpleasant, in fact it simulated the taste buds and I suggested we could use the olives in a salad for our supper. Louise agreed and gave my hand a squeeze. I asked the young lady if she knew where we might find Stavros.

"Mr Stavros still owns this stand," she said, then went on, "He rents it out to me, and sometimes he even helps me sell my olives."

"Yes," I said, "that sounds like Stavros, always willing to help a pretty young lady."

"If you go out of the market and turn right, then head for Market square," she told us, giving hand directions, "its just up on the left. You can't miss it, he's got a big shop in the square. Well, in fact he's got two shops. When you find him could you tell him I could do with some more capers?" she finished.

"Yes we will," I replied, adding, "and thank you for the directions."

The short walk took about five minutes and we were soon standing outside of the twin shops. The entrance on the right of us had been blocked off and the windows of both shops were full of all sorts of things, mostly of an antique origin, but then you could never be sure with Stavros. We made our way in through the door and a bell rung above our head; he really had got into this business. From behind a large bookcase a woman appeared. She was in her late twenties, maybe early thirties, about five foot five in height, with very long dark brown hair that fell all the way down her back almost to her waist, and her complexion was of one from warmer climates.

"Can I help you?" she asked with a warm smile.

"Well actually I'm looking for Mr Stavros," I replied. "Is he about?"

"Yes he is. He's out the back, sorting some new stock" she answered.

No sooner had she said the words than from behind a curtain to her left I could hear his familiar voice. "Where have I put the invoice for the stuff that came in yesterday?" I heard him call. And with that the curtain flew back and standing there directly in front of us was Stavros. Louise pulled in close to my side, for he was a man who cast a powerful presence. He stood about five foot eight, of medium build, his big hands now out in front of him clutching bits of paper, his face grained with years of hard if not always honest work. He was still wearing the black moustache that matched his head of hair.

"Marie," he continued, "have you .." He stopped and the look of surprise on his face spoke a thousand words.

"My friend!" he said, dropping the paperwork on the floor and putting his arms out to greet me. "It's so good to see you, you are looking well. Are you back from America for good now?" Now he had his arms wrapped round me, almost pushing Louise aside.

"Excuse me," he said, looking at Louise, "I didn't mean to be so rude to you my dear." With those words he turned his attention to Louise and exchanged his grip on me for a hug on her.

"Hey my friend, you have a new wife, yes? Just like old Stavros." He gave me a wink and a dig in the ribs. "It's good to change them from time to time, yes?"

I looked at Louise and could see she was embarrassed. I needed to clear this up before it got out of hand.

"No Stavros, this is not my new wife, ok?" This was going to be difficult whatever way I put it. "This is Louise, and she's a friend of mine staying at the apartment for a few days." I stopped. He was looking into my eyes, as if he was reading my thoughts and had found the reason why we had come to see him.

He turned back to look at Louise and took her tiny hand in his vast open palm. "Louise, please forgive me, I didn't mean to be so presumptuous," he said, peering deep into Louise's eyes. "I know not every man is like me, and my friend, he is a good man, you can trust him. He will look after you, if not you come and see me and I will look after you." He finished talking with a raucous laugh, and now it was I that was embarrassed.

We need to talk? Yes?" he said, as he walked me through to the back of the shop. He stopped. "You have meet Marie, this is my new wife. Marie, this is my good friend Andy!" He paused. "Yes, I have known Andy for, how long? Oh, never mind, too long to remember. Why don't you close the shop, and then you and Louise go and do some shopping. You know, go and buy yourself a nice new dress. Take as long as you like, I think Andy and I have some business to discuss."

I looked at Louise. "Do you mind?" I asked.

"No, that's alright, I can check the bank details," was her reply.

With that Marie made her way to the front of the shop, put up the closed sign, then bent down and slid the bolt on the bottom of the door and reached up and did the same with the top bolt.

The two young women set off on their way via a back door. Stavros and I sat down in a small area made over for office work. He sat at a desk and I pulled up a chair. He poured some strong black coffee from a pot that was on the desk.

"You like some cream?" he asked. I nodded my reply and he went out into the kitchen and returned with a jug. "You help yourself," he said as he passed me the brown jug.

"Something is concerning you my friend, I am right? Yes, when I look in your eyes I see something that troubles you. Hey, it's not that beautiful woman, is it?"

"No, its not her, Stavros," I replied, but before I could say anymore this man read my inner thoughts and told me what I wanted to hear.

"I tell you something from this old man." he said, with his fist on his chest. "I tell you, she loves you with a hidden passion you have not yet found. I am right. Yes!" His index finger on his right hand was pointing at me, and his words and the pointing finger almost felt as if they were pushing me back into the seat.

"You are of course right," I replied. "I've told her I love her, Stavros, but I'm still waiting for her reply. Oh, by the way, the young lady in the market could do with some more capers."

"It will come, and believe me it will be worth it. I could see her love for you in her eyes," he told me, and then moved onto the other part of my comment.

"Oh, has she sold them all? It's one of the best lines we do. I'll get one of the boys to take some down this afternoon."

With those words the door opened, and in walked a dark-haired attractive young woman. It was Nana, Stavros's youngest child. I stood up to greet her and she came over to me, giving me a kiss on both cheeks and a warm hug.

"Its nice to see you Andy," she said. There was no hint of a Greek accent in her voice, but she did have a little of her father's complexion.

"And you," was my reply. "And you've grown even more since the last time we met."

"Father didn't say you were coming down," she said, looking at her father. "Ah, it's a bit of a surprise, I've just seen Marie, going into town with a young woman."

"My child, that's Andy's friend, Louise," her father told her. "Have you seen the boys on your travels?"

"Yes Father, they've just gone over to Falmouth to clear another house," she replied.

"Is there anything you need me to do?"

"Yes, could you go down to the market and take some more capers for Anne?" he asked. "She seems to sell out of them very quickly. Also could you remind her about the cheese I asked her to get for me."

"Yes, that's not a problem Father," she said. "Andy, are you and your friend staying for some supper with us? The boys would like to see you and maybe have a drink or two and a chat."

"Well, I'm not sure what Louise will want to do, and I need to have a chat with your father first," I said. Inside I was thinking it would be nice to stay. I'd always enjoyed the company of this man and his family: ever welcoming, warm and very hospitable.

"Tell you what, I'll ask Louise what she would like to do when she returns and I'll be guided by her wishes."

"That sounds good to me," was Nana's response. "See you later." And she made her way out of the door. I stood up as she left.

"Sit down my friend and tell me more of the way I can help you," Stavros said.

And I did as I was told. I explained about Rimes and Jones, and also gave a brief résumé of my own situation with regard to my money.

"I have some friends in Holland. We can get these stories checked out,"

Stavros said, determination in his voice. "I've never had any dealings with drugs, you know that. I've done a few dodgy deals over the years, cars and a bit of gold, some diamonds, but I wouldn't deal in death. I also know a few, how you say, bent coppers in this Country. I'll have a word with one of them and get this Jones identity proved. Did he say he was going to have a man about to look after you?" He paused. "Well, how about I put a man of my own to look after him and you?" He was looking into my eyes again. "You know you can trust me." His big hand came out and gripped mine, then he stood up, almost pulling me to my feet. His left arm wrapped itself round me, and I was entwined in the fatherly-type hug that makes you feel safe. I got from him the security I could pass on to Louise.

"Now we have a drink." And with those words he made his way into the kitchen, returned with two large wineglasses and a bottle of red wine. After a few minutes of fiddling with the corkscrew he passed it to me.

"My friend, please do the honours, I can't get on with this damn thing," he said.

I did as requested, and we sat and chatted. Together we worked on a plan that would prove the integrity of this policeman, and the truth of what he had told Louise and myself. The Post Office official might prove to be a little more difficult, but as the wine flowed I thought of other people who would be willing to help me. For now I was relaxed, safe in the company of this man.

We had almost finished the bottle of wine when the door opened and the two ladies stepped back into the building. In Marie's right hand was a shopping bag, and on the bag was a motif of a local boutique.

"I see you found something to buy," Stavros said a smile on his face. "But Louise, you haven't got anything. You don't like our shops in Truro?" he asked, a surprised look now joining the smile on his face.

"No, it's not that," Louise replied, "I did see a lovely dress, but I'd like Andy to see it, if you don't mind."

"That's very good, young lady. I'm already beginning to like you. Get him to spend some of that money he has on you," he said. "Now you two go off and have a look round the shops. I've got some phone calls to make, and Andrew, my friend, remember about supper and what Nana asked you."

I got up and Louise and I walked to the small cobbled street where the boutique was situated. We stood outside looking at the most beautiful blue and gold coloured cotton dress. It buttoned at the front and had quite a deep bust line.

"I wonder if they have it in my size?" Louise asked.

"Well, we won't find out standing here will we?" I said, and took her by the arm and led her into the shop.

Inside I said to her, "Go on then, ask," and with my prompting she did.

"Size eight, is it madam?" Was the response from the assistant. "If you'll excuse me I'll just go and check," and she made her way to the back of the shop. She was gone for a few minutes, long enough for me to tell Louise that this would be my treat to her, and that she was not to worry about the cost. She knew that I could well afford to buy the entire stock many times over if I wanted to. She was concerned about taking it home, but I told her she could leave it in the apartment, so she would always have something special to wear if and when she came down again.

The young assistant returned with the dress draped across both her arms. "Would madam like to try in on?"

"Oh yes please," Louise said in a very surprised tone. I think she had been hoping they wouldn't have her size. She made her way to the changing room and that gave me the opportunity to have a discreet word with the assistant.

"Madam may require one or two other items of clothing," I whispered in the young lady's ear. "And no expense is to be spared. Do I make myself clear?" I added as I pushed a twenty-pound note into her hand.

"I understand perfectly sir," was her reply.

"I'll leave you to it," I said and added, "I need to go next door. I won't be long and I'm sure she is in safe hands."

"Indeed she is sir," the young lady said as I made my way out of the boutique.

I'd noticed when we were standing outside that the adjoining building was in fact a small jewellery shop. Looking through the window I could see the most exquisite diamond and gold necklace. What the hell, I thought to myself as I stepped inside. Maybe the wine had given me some Dutch courage. She knew I loved her and if I wanted to spoil her then I was going to do so. Anyway, if our friendship came to nothing and Stavros was wrong, then she could always sell it.

A middle-aged gentleman dressed in a pinstriped suit greeted me. "Can I help you sir?"

I indicated what I was interested in and he got the item from the display in the window. As I held the necklace in my hands I could see it was like Louise, perfectly formed in every way.

"Yes, that's it. I'll take it." And with that I produced my American Express card from my wallet.

"That's two thousand five hundred pounds sir," the man said. "You will forgive me sir, but I'll have to ring this transaction through."

"That's not a problem," was my casual reply.

He was only gone a few minutes, returning with the words, "That's fine Mr Jackson, I'm so sorry to have kept you waiting. Would you like it gifted wrapped?"

"Yes please," I confirmed, as I signed the credit slip.

I made my way out of the jewellers and slipped the gift-wrapped box into my jacket pocket.

As I walked back into the boutique Louise was just coming out of the changing room. She made her way over to me, pulled in close and whispered in my ear, "You left instructions for me to be spoilt didn't you?"

"Yes, someone has to, don't they?" I told her and went on, "Just stay there and I'll settle the bill." I made my way to where the assistant was placing the new items of underwear, as well as two more dresses, into bags.

The young lady looked at me. "You did say .." I stopped her by putting my index finger over my lips.

Very quietly she whispered the total was eight hundred and fifty pounds, again I handed over my card, and the response was the same as in the jewellers. She also returned after a few minutes with almost the same words. I signed the slip, picked up the bags and made my way to Louise. I'd just spent over three thousand pounds and it felt wonderful, the best I'd felt for a long time.

Louise took some of the bags from me, and then held my left arm. Looking up at me she didn't have to say thank you, it was written across her entire face, but she did anyway, and gave my arm a squeeze.

"Did you check your bank account details?" I asked.

"Oh yes I did, and Jones was right, there's over thirty thousand pounds in it," she said with nervousness in her voice. "But I'd better not touch any of it, after all, I'm not supposed to know about it."

"Did you sort anything out with Stavros?" she asked me, looking up into my eyes.

"Yes I did," I told her, "he's going to do a few checks with some of his friends and also he said he'd put someone else to keep an eye on the man that's keeping an eye on us. I know it's a bit complicated but we have to trust him. He would like us to go back to his house for some supper with the rest of the family, how do you feel about that?" I finished, not sure of what her reaction would be.

"If you're going to be there, it will be fine," was her reply.

"I might ask you to drive home, would you mind doing that, if I have a few drinks with the boys? It's a bit of a tradition you see," I said.

"Are you sure you'd trust me with the Porsche?" she asked.

"Yes I would; it's just like any other car, only it goes faster. You'll be ok. I'm not going to get blind drunk, just a few glasses of wine. And by the way, we're going to use the Porsche as a bit of a trap, just to see how good this man keeping an eye on us is. We might have to lose it for a little while, do you know what I mean?" I asked.

"I think I know where you're coming from, but how will we get about if we haven't got the car?" Louise questioned me.

"Um, well," I paused, not sure of how to break the news to her, "I've got another car in one of the garages, back at the apartments, but it's not another Porsche, it's a Lotus. You see I like my sports cars!" I told her.

"You certainly do don't you? you're full of surprises," was her response, and she went on, "Ok, I'll drive the Porsche but you mustn't get too drunk. I couldn't manage to carry you out of the car." With those words we stood still, the memory of last night flooding back. We laughed, looking at each other as we stood with our arms entwined. Our laughter faded away and our lips came together into a perfect kiss. Long and meaningful, what I had been waiting for. We drew away from each other only slightly, and I was about to say the words 'I love you' but her finger covered my lips.

"I know!" she said, and her eyes showed she did know, and I could see what Stavros had seen, and I knew I wouldn't have to wait too long.

"I really like Marie. You know she's Stavros's third wife. She's only twenty- nine, and they've only been married for a few months. Did you know his eldest son is twenty-eight?" she told me as she stole the moment from me, and then continued, "I really could do with something to eat now, I'm getting very hungry, I don't know about you."

I, like Louise, was feeling a bit on the empty side and the wine had made me somewhat light-headed. We made our way back to the shop and arrangements followed for us to go to the Stavros' home for our supper.

Louise, as agreed, drove the Porsche and made an exceedingly good job of it, for it must be said that it's not one of the easiest cars to drive for the first time. We sat and relaxed with the warm and friendly Stavros family, comfortable in their company and they in ours. The two boys to arrived home - I say boys but I mean men, for I had seen them grow from tiny babies into fine upstanding men - just as supper was being placed on the table. Nana, Marie and Louise had together prepared a wonderful meal.

Both of the boys, as I still refer to them, were delighted to see me, and there was lots of hand shaking and hugs as only the Greeks can do. Andreas the eldest was full of questions about America, for he had a longing to go, and had been talking to his father about setting up a business there. Demetri the younger, from Stavros's second marriage as is Nana, was more reserved; a man of few words but powerful thoughts.

We sat and ate and drank as old friends do, and the meal went on and on, for what must have been more than two hours. The ladies left us alone to continue our conversation, and went to have their own girlie talk in the lounge while we stayed in the dinning room. By now the port was flowing and our laughter must have filled the whole house. Coffee was brought and consumed, and so with Stavros banging his hand on the table more was brought.

It must have been almost midnight when Louise came into the room. The boys stood up as she entered out of respect for her, my companion. She looked at me from across the room. She didn't need to speak, Stavros did it for her.

"My good friend, its time for you to go home for your bed," he said as he stood up and put that massive right arm round me.

The entire family accompanied us to the car, which was parked on the driveway. Louise pressed the button to unlock the doors of the car, Andreas opened the door for her to get in, and every one gave us a hug and wished us a safe journey. As Stavros opened the passenger door for me he whispered in my ear, "My friend, I have a volunteer that will be looking after this beautiful woman and you."

"Thank you," was my reply, "But who is it?"

"I'm afraid I can't tell you that," he said and tapped his nose with his finger. That information was for him and the other person only.

I'd fallen asleep before we got home, and was awoken by Louise giving me a kiss on the cheek, and her soft gentle voice asking me to wake up. As I came to I looked at the clock in the car; it was a quarter past one. Slowly I got my legs to move. I'd opened the door as Louise came round to my side of the car.

"Come on, I'll help you," she said as she took my arm. I wasn't drunk, but having been asleep had left me somewhat lifeless.

"Pass me the keys and I'll open up," was her next comment, forceful but not angry, and I did as I was told. Once inside I felt happy and a need to tell Louise how I felt, but before I could say anything, she told me to go to bed or I would feel worse in the morning.

"I'll lock up and make sure the curtains are drawn, after I've brought the bags in from the car," she said, pointing up the stairs.

I took hold of the stair rail on the right hand side and made my way up to my room, calling in the bathroom on the way. Once inside my bedroom I quickly changed into my bedclothes, conscious that if I made a wrong move now then I would spoil every thing. I got into bed and I think faintly heard Louise say the words, "Good night darling," but I may have been dreaming.

Easter Sunday

I awoke to the feeling of someone else in my bedroom. As I reached for my glasses from the bedside cabinet I heard the soft sound of Louise's voice.

"Good morning, and how's your head this bright morning?" she asked, and as I came to I could see her standing in the doorway with the tea tray in her hands.

"It's my turn to bring you some tea this morning," she said. "Can I sit on the edge of your bed?"

"Of course you can," I replied as I wriggled my way over to the side of the bed nearest to the window. She made herself comfortable on the edge of the bed and placed the tray on the bedside cabinet.

"This is very nice and unexpected," I said, and looking at her I could see she was wearing the same blue nightdress she'd had on yesterday. The bright sunshine streaming in through the window made it look even paler.

"You were fast asleep very quickly last night," she told me, looking into my eyes. "And when I got up, I came and had a look in. You looked so peaceful, I thought it was a shame to wake you, so I went and made the tea," she said, taking her cup in both hands.

By now the sleep was out of my eyes, and looking at Louise I felt there was something else she wanted to tell me.

Today we didn't have any plans; I think the previous day had all but drained us. Suddenly my memory of last night, or I should say early morning, came back to me and forced me to ask the question. "Did you say good night to me?" I waited for the reply.

"Yes." She hesitated. "But I thought you were asleep as you didn't reply." Her face began to colour up that deep red I'd seen on a few other occasions.

She then put her cup back on the tray, put her hand out and took mine, and I had an overwhelming feeling she was about to put me out of my misery.

"I think I need to tell you something." She paused, and of course my mind went into overdrive. It could be only one of two things she had to tell me.

"I said I wouldn't mess you about and now I need to clear up a few things between us." She stopped so as to make herself more comfortable on the bed. And just for a moment I thought she was about to leave, and tell me from the doorway that she wanted to go home, but as always full of surprises she leant forward, and came even closer. I could see her breasts were heaving as she struggled to find the words she was looking for.

It's now, I was telling myself, she is going to tell me now. Our eyes looked into each others, and our lips were only centimetres apart. I started to reach up with my right hand ready for the embrace I had longed for, and to gather her up and wrap her safely in my arms and keep her in my bed.

"I need to tell you .." she stopped as the telephone interrupted her words.

"Go on," I said, "the bloody phone can wait!" I felt cheated. Like a child promised something and at the last minute denied it.

"No! Go on, you answer it. What I have to say will keep," she said as I half-jumped, half-fell out of my bed, adding, "It may be someone for me."

In fact it was my eldest son. He was in the area after delivering a restored car and had been trying to locate me. He would call during the afternoon on his way home. He wanted to confirm I would be about. In the surprise of the moment I forgot to tell him that Louise was in fact staying at the apartment with me.

Louise had followed me down the stairs and had been in the kitchen. She'd poured another cup of tea, and as I replaced the receiver she was about to make her way back up the stairs with the tray.

When I asked her to continue her conversation she declined, saying it would keep. So I wasn't to be put out of my misery after all. She left my tea on the table and made her way to her own bedroom, leaving me with longing thoughts and a lasting desire. I drank my tea and made my way up the stairs to her room, where I stood in the doorway. Louise was sitting on the bed with her cup held tightly in both hands, and when I asked if everything was alright she told me she was fine, and became her bubbly self.

"What shall we do today?" she asked.

I replied I fancied a bit of a rest. "We could have a day here if you like and go out for dinner this evening."

"That sounds like a good idea to me," she replied and went on, "Could we go and get a paper? After all, it is Sunday!"

"Well, that's sorted then, a nice leisurely day," I replied. "Oh and I forgot to say that William and his girlfriend may be calling in this afternoon."

"That's ok, but what shall we have for breakfast?" Louise asked.

"I know, let's have a bit of a fry up. You know, bacon and eggs, but first would you like to have a shower first or shall I go in?"

"Can I go first?" she asked. "You need to book that table for this evening, if it isn't too early."

I looked at my watch and saw it was nine o'clock "I think it is a bit early. You have your shower and I'll make a start on the breakfast. You can take over when you come down if you don't mind," I said as I made my way back down the stairs.

"Yes, that's alright," she replied, and I could hear her make her way along the landing to the bathroom.

I have to say that all the time I was in the kitchen preparing our breakfast I had thoughts of Louise in the shower, her small well-formed body covered in shower foam. Maybe I would soon find out her true feelings for me.

In what seemed like no time at all she was back downstairs, wearing a long red and orange dress, with dark green piping around the sleeves and neckline. It was quite low cut, and as she stood closer to me to take over the job of cooking our breakfast I could see well into her cleavage and the tops of her white ample bosom.

"I'll go and have that shower," I said, trying to take my mind of the view I'd just had.

"Go on then and you'd better be quick," she told me in that forceful way.

And I did as I was told. When I returned it was as if she had put everything on hold: waiting for my last step into the dinning area she came in from the kitchen with the two plates. It was lovely, and we ate and talked about yesterday and what might happen today. It was just after ten before we set off to get the papers. I'd phoned the White Cross Restaurant and booked a table for seven thirty.

We stepped out into the courtyard. The sun was hotter than yesterday and there seemed to be no breeze at all. I was glad I only had jeans and a tee shirt on. As I opened the door for Louise to get into the car the heat rushed out to greet us. She slid in a little hesitantly, and I once again could see she wasn't wearing any tights. I walked round to my side of the car and got in, and from the door pocket I pulled out a bandanna and started to tie it round my neck.

"What are you doing?" Louise asked, but before I had a chance to reply she went on, "You poser!"

"Well," I started, a little surprised by her question and her other comment, "the seat belt in this car cuts into my neck if I wear something without a collar, so I have to wear this." My words drifted away as Louise interrupted me.

"I'm so sorry, Darling!" She stopped, surprised at what she had said.

I glanced across at her. Her bottom lip was held between her teeth, and her cheeks were beginning to colour up.

She reached down with her right hand and unbuckled her own seat belt. Her left hand was pulling on the interior door handle. "I have to go indoors now!" she said. With those words she was out of the car and almost ran the short distance to the front door. I was some way behind her, and by the time I got to her she was bright red and panting. I feared something terrible was wrong as I opened the door for us to go in.

Once inside of the apartment, Louise turned to look back at me. She took me by my right hand and pushed me against the wall between the door and the front window.

"Is everything alright?" I asked, still in a confused state. I hadn't heard properly what she had said. I was looking into her eyes, the light was streaming through the door and window on either side of us, my arms were out stretched and she fell into them. I slipped my hands onto her back, our lips came together as they should have earlier and now no phone was going to stop us.

Our kiss lasted for what seemed like an age, it was sweetness itself and I could taste her passion. We drew apart, for now words needed to be spoken and the time was right.

"I needed you to do that," she told me. Then the words I had longed to hear, "I love you."

I was speechless. I had wanted to hear those words from her, and now that I had I needed her to tell me again. I was looking deep into her blue eyes, the redness had all but gone from her cheeks, but she was still breathing very deeply.

"You heard what I said didn't you?" she asked.

"I think I did but I'm not sure what brought it on," I replied. "I didn't hear what you said in the car."

"I said I love you, but in the form of darling." She repeated the words and they almost hung in the air.

I felt as if I could have plucked them up and put them into my wallet. To me they were more valuable than money itself, for no amount of money could have bought these words, or this woman.

"I wanted to tell you last night," Louise started again. "Last night when you had got into bed, I said goodnight darling, but you were already fast asleep and you didn't hear me, then just now in the car I called you darling again and it came out with the same feeling. I just had to come indoors. I needed you to hold me. I love you so much, and with such strength, so different from the way I could ever have loved Gary, but" she paused, "that's in the past. Now I want to be with you."

My mind went back to last night. I hadn't dreamt those words after all. I had heard her say "Good night, Darling."

"I did hear you last night," I told her, "but what about this morning, when you were sitting on the bed? Were you going to tell me then? You know, when the phone rang."

"Yes I was, and I would have loved to have got in beside you, I feel so safe with you. But the moment was stolen, and it didn't seem right afterwards."

We kissed again, this time our tongues entwined and her right hand slid to the back of my head. I couldn't pull away even if I wanted to. I found myself running my own right hand up the outside of her left leg, over her hip and into the edge of her tight waist. My fingers felt a small strap and I took this to be the outline of her panties. As my hand traced its way up her body she forced her tummy against my own body. I felt excited, and a wanton need rushed through my very soul. Our lips parted and I started to kiss her neck moving slowly down to her shoulder. Her head was writhing with the pleasure.

"Stop! Please. Stop!" She was almost crying out, but her tone was telling me to continue, and as I pulled away she forced me back to carry on. I moved my attention further down her body and from the outside of her dress my hand had made its way to where I could feel her firm left breast cradled in a soft bra. Her excitement was now beginning to show as my thumb ran over the outline of her hard nipple. Her whole body was alive to the point of gyration. I wanted to continue and make her mine but something inside me also wanted me to wait. I wanted things to be perfect, and that would mean waiting until that night.

I pulled back to draw breath, and Louise also inhaled deeply. We eased our bodies apart and she rearranged her clothing. In my mind I knew I could have taken her upstairs there and then and we would have made the most wonderful love together, but I felt we needed to talk about our feelings before we resumed this most intimate of encounters.

"Let's sit and talk," I suggested.

"Oh yes. I need to sit down," she agreed. As she lead me towards the sofa, we sat together and she pulled in close, as we'd been on the Good Friday evening when I'd told her I loved her. With her arms wrapped around me and with her head against my chest, she looked into my eyes.

"You know that this will change everything between us," she told me, and now her words had a more passionate ring to them.

"Yes, I'm aware of that," I replied; they were the very words Phillip had said to me before we set off on this adventure. But we had both come to this stage without forcing ourselves on each other; it was a mutual thing we had embarked upon. Our love needed to be sealed, then it would change everything.

We sat together for almost three-quarters of an hour, for most of the time in silence, happy to be entwined together, our bodies relaxed and maybe preparing for the next stage of our lovemaking. We knew it would follow, smoothly and gently. We had got this far, and neither of us wanted to spoil what was to come.

"We could still go and get the paper!" Louise said, as she released her hold of me, but her eyes were telling me she would have been just as happy for us to go upstairs and complete our lovemaking. In my mind I knew that once we had committed ourselves to bed then it would be a long time before either of us would feel a need to leave the other's side.

"Yes," I said as I stood up and took her hand, "lets go and get the paper. I do love you and I want to make you feel so special. You won't forget it when we make love, I can assure you of that."

"Good. In that case I'm prepared to wait," was her reply, and she slipped her arms round me and kissed me and repeated the words "I love you."

I was now happier than I'd been in years. The woman I'd secretly loved for so many years had given me her love in word form and that, for the time being, was sufficient.

We made our way out of the apartment and again I opened the door for Louise to get into the car. This time she looked at me as her small body slid into the seat.

"Thank you," she said.

So we set off and got the Sunday newspapers. As it turned out Louise liked to read the Independent, myself I preferred The Times. It was gone noon by the time we returned to the apartment. The afternoon passed, and to help with the papers I opened a bottle of wine, and fixed a sandwich. Every time I made a move Louise would look at me, and her smile never faded - even when I glanced out from the kitchen she appeared to have a glow about her, and a new warmth had enveloped the apartment.

We had just finished our lunch and Louise had gone up to the bathroom, when there was a knock at the door. I could see it was William and Natasha so I opened the door and received my usual greeting from both of them: a big son-to-father hug from William and lots of kisses from Natasha. They stepped inside and in an instant William's keen eye had spotted I had a guest.

"You're not alone then Dad!" he said, for the two wineglasses and plates were still on the table. "Phillip's down for a few days, is he?"

"Um, well, it's like this," I began, unsure of how I was going to tell him that Louise was staying with me. I didn't have to have his approval and wasn't even looking for it, but he was well aware of the problem I'd had with Gary and might well be forgiven for thinking I was courting death, so to speak.

"No, actually it's a different guest I brought with me," I finished, and with that Louise started to descend the stairs. It was Natasha who spotted her first and she gave a welcoming smile.

"Hello," she said, as Louise reached the bottom stairs. Without any hesitation they embraced and kissed each other on the cheek as if they were old friends. "You must be Louise," Natasha said as they made their way towards the lounge. "I'm Natasha and it's so nice to meet you," she told Louise as they sat down together on the sofa.

"Some tea?" I asked. William's face was a picture, almost of disbelief. "This is William, my eldest son."

He walked across the room and took her hand and much to my surprise kissed the back of it.

"It's very nice to meet you," he told her. "I'm just going to help Dad make that tea. Please excuse me," he stammered.

He followed me into the kitchen and came over to me by the sink.

"Well, well, I don't know you at all, do I?" His words were spoken very softly and he went on, "Is this the lady you were talking about last time the three of us were here?"

"Yes," I confirmed.

"Dad, I thought she was a thirty-something with wrinkly tights and screaming kids, but she's beautiful," he said, and his words gave a massive boost to my confidence.

"I know," I said in reply to his comment. "And by the way, your mouth was wide open as Louise came down the stairs. So you thought the old man was past it, did you?"

"No, not at all." He turned towards the door. "Good for you, Dad, you deserve some happiness, you shouldn't be alone." With that comment he spun round and walked back to me and gave me a hug whispering in my ear, "I love you Dad."

"Thank you son," I said.

"How's that tea coming along?" It was Natasha.

"It's ready," I told her, and took some mugs off the shelf and placed them on the tray, which William picked up and took into the lounge, leaving Natasha and I alone in the kitchen.

"A penny for your thoughts?" I couldn't resist the question.

"She's lovely Andy," was all she could say.

We sat and talked the afternoon away; William on the floor, Louise and Natasha on the sofa, and me relaxed in the chair. William and Natasha had been to Penzance and delivered a Rover that had been restored, and they were on their way home having stayed the night in a hotel just outside Penzance. I asked if they fancied coming to dinner with us but they declined, saying that they were invited to a party later in the evening.

"Oh, I almost forgot!" William said as he got up from the floor. "I had two men in the garage on Thursday looking for you Dad."

"Did you? What did they want?"

"I don't know, they didn't say, they just asked if I'd seen you. One of them gave me the creeps; he had very shifty eyes, and seemed very interested in kids. He spent a lot of time watching the school kids go by. The other bloke told him to get in the car and wait and he did most of the talking."

"Did you get their names?" I asked.

"No," he said, "I didn't, I was getting ready to come away, you know finishing the car. I'll tell you what though, they had a smokey old diesel, a blue Ford."

"And the bloke that did the talking was black," I interrupted him.

"Yes, so you do know them," William replied, a little frustration in his voice.

I looked at Louise, she looked relaxed and composed and it was she who gave a reply to William.

"William," she paused and was about to be very precise, "your Father and I know of them now, as they paid us a visit here, on Good Friday."

"So you both know what they wanted?" he replied to Louise.

Louise willingly took up the task of telling William and Natasha the details of the Rimes and Jones visit. She explained the reasons and what Gary was suspected of doing. I took over to tell them about recruiting the help of Stavros. That met with William's approval.

"That's good Dad," he told me in a very excited way, "he won't let you down," and then went on to ask many question about Stavros and his family. I'm sure we could have sat for the rest of the evening just discussing them but time was rapidly moving on and I had to remind William that I had booked a table for seven-thirty and it was now five-thirty and both Louise and I had to change.

The four of us made our way out of the apartment and into the shadows of the afternoon. Our goodbyes were long. Natasha repeated in my ear that she thought Louise was lovely, and as my son and his companion drove away and Louise took my arm I felt complete. It had been a long time since I'd been able to watch either of my sons leave and not have to return indoors to an empty building. As they reached the top of the track he blew his horn, turned into the lane and was gone from our sight. As I turned to go back indoors Louise put her arms around me, pulled me close and kissed me. When she eased her grip she told me she had felt very nervous at the prospect of meeting William, but that feeling had disappeared as soon as she saw Natasha and the welcome she had given her. She also mentioned William's mouth was open. I said that was due to surprise.

We returned indoors. Louise said she would go and get ready first as it always takes her a long time. I told her I would clear things away and wash up while she was in the bathroom. I'd just finished the drying up when she called to say the bathroom was 'all mine'.

As I passed by her bedroom I could hear bags rustling and I knew she would be wearing one of the new dresses she had chosen yesterday. It reminded me to put the necklace that I'd bought for her into the pocket of my jacket. I seemed to be in and out of the bathroom in what must have been record time, back to my bedroom, into a light summer suit and I was ready. I asked if everything was ok on my way downstairs.

"Don't rush me," came back the reply, in the same tone as the other morning.

I closed and locked the patio doors, and as I passed the coffee table I looked towards the stairs. She was standing at the bottom of them, her left hand holding the rail, in her right hand that small black bag.

I couldn't believe my eyes. She looked gorgeous. Her hair was held up in place by a gold claw-type clip at the back and she was wearing the dress she had spotted in the window of the boutique yesterday. This was the first time I'd seen her wearing it, and it fitted perfectly.

Tight into that small waist and free-flowing over her hips, the button line ran evenly and without any sign of strain up and over her tummy. The top two buttons were undone and again exposed her cleavage and bare neckline. The sleeves came half way down her forearms and the cuffs fitted tightly around them. On her left wrist she was wearing a gold watch.

"How do I look?" she enquired, as she proceeded to give me a twirl, exposing the unfastened lower part of the dress as she turned round and revealing the lower parts of her legs. They had a sheen to them, indicating she was wearing tights, or so I thought.

"You look absolutely stunning," I said, as I stepped closer to her to get a better look at her immaculately made up face. A small pair of gold stud earrings matched well with the gold hair clip and watch. Her red lip-gloss was complimented by the same colour nail varnish she had taken the time to apply the same to her petite toe nails and these were exposed through the black high heeled sandals she was wearing.

Once again it was to be my pleasure to take her out for dinner. I took her hand and lead her to the patio doors. With the early evening light pouring through them I looked again into her deep blue eyes, made up to perfection with mascara and eyeliner. My right hand slipped into my inside pocket and I pulled out the gift-wrapped box, laying it across both of my hands. I had to give her the present now.

"This is for you," I said, adding, "You know I really do love you."

Her face lit up once she had unwrapped the case and had it lying opened in her small hands, and her eyes sparkled like the diamonds she was holding.

"It's lovely," she said, and I could see a small tear in her eyes. "Thank you," she continued.

"Don't cry," I said, as I beckoned her close to me. "Let me put it on for you." And as I took the necklace out of the case the smell of her perfume filled my every sense with desire. Louise bent forward and put her head onto my shoulder as I fixed the clasp at the back of her neck. Bringing her head up she stood back from me, the sun caught the diamonds and together with the gold it appeared as if she had a ring of fire around her neck. It was an exact match to the gold in the dress.

"That's the final and finishing touch," I told her. "You look wonderful and it will be a pleasure to have you on my arm." I looked at my watch; it was six-forty. "We'll need to leave at seven," I said. "It will take about fifteen minutes to get to the restaurant. You may need a jacket in case it's chilly when we come out."

"Oh! I'd better ring Mummy before we go," Louise said. "Can you go and get my dark jacket from the bedroom please."

I willingly did as I was asked, and Louise made her way to the telephone. Her bedroom was full of that wonderful perfume, it engulfed me as I entered and lingered in my nostrils as I made my way back down the stairs. I stood in silence and tonight took in the warm and soft words spoken as only she could to her children. A final word with her father and she hung up, no tears this time and she came straight to my waiting arms.

"I'm ready if you are," were her words.

So at seven o'clock we set off for dinner. It was only a short drive and as I pulled off of the main road a powerful motorbike flew past us, hugging the white line as it roared off down the road towards the town. I'm sure that the pillion released one hand from the rear grip and gave me the thumbs up, but I was unsure of the reason for the signal, if it was a signal any way.

From the main road it was only a short drive to the entrance of the restaurant. I pulled into the drive and parked by the left side off the building, with the front of the car pointing in towards some bushes. There were only two other cars parked in the same way. I got out and came round and opened the door for Louise, and with her impeccable style she swung her legs out of the car. Her dress fell open and I thought I caught a glimpse of a stocking top before her hand quickly pulled the dress together and she stood up, her red lips smiling at me. I slipped her jacket over her shoulders and we took the short walk to the front of the restaurant, her right arm holding onto my left.

The agent who takes care of my apartments had recommended the restaurant to me, informing me it was a family concern. I was assured that attention was paid to every detail. Two small steps and we were at the front door, and a small sign to the right read 'Please ring'. I did so, and in what seemed like no time a man was opening the door for us and ushered us in.

"Good evening Sir, Madam." He looked into my eyes. "Have you booked?"

"Yes," I replied.

"And the name Sir?" he enquired.

"It's Jackson," I said, as he directed us towards a small room to the right of the entrance door.

"Yes of course Sir. Would you like to have a drink before dinner?" he said as he made his way to the small bar in the corner of the room.

I looked at Louise. She nodded and I ordered a glass of white wine for her and half of beer for myself. As he brought the drinks over he passed us the menus and went into detail about the day's specials, then we were left alone for a few minutes and that gave Louise the opportunity to decide what she would have. Funnily enough we agreed we would both have the same for our starters and main course.

The man returned and took our order and led us to a table tucked away in a small alcove. Wood panelling covered the walls and the place had a Victorian feel to it, and there were stuffed animals in glass cases on shelves and in little cubby-holes. I quipped to Louise about not wanting a fox for dinner and our joint laughter eased the small amount of nervousness we both felt. This was the first time we had been out together in an unknown area; before, when we had dinner, I was familiar with the surroundings and could pass on my confidence to her.

As a further token of my love for her I'd ordered a bottle of champagne. Deep inside of me I knew this would be a night to remember and I wanted Louise to feel very special. I already did by having her as my companion.

The champagne duly arrived and as the man poured a taster into my glass he explained that he was the owner, and his name was Tim. He mentioned he couldn't recall seeing us before at the restaurant. Louise told him we had come down for the weekend, and I added we had been recommended to come by the local estate agent. He said we had been very lucky with the weather, and his conversation relaxed us even more and before he left us he lit a candle in the centre of the table and hoped we wouldn't be disappointed.

Instinctively we picked up our wineglasses together, and made a toast to ourselves. In the flickering candlelight Louise looked across the table at me; her smile, her warmth, was everything I needed. She looked so beautiful, I felt as if I needed someone to pinch me to reassure myself I wasn't dreaming. Then her words, again without any prompting, "I love you. I've had the most wonderful time so far." She stopped and her eyes were like the diamonds she was wearing round her neck. Now it was my turn to put my finger on her lips.

"You don't need to say any more," I said as I held my finger in place. "I know you do, and believe me the pleasure is all mine. After tonight our entire world will change."

I felt the presence of Tim at the table. In his hands he was holding our starters. He placed Louise's down first, and I looked across and eagerly awaited mine. He left us with the words 'enjoy your meal'.

Mushrooms cooked in a butter and parsley sauce, with melted Stilton cheese drizzled over the mushrooms, served with fresh hot bread. It was delicious, as was the main course. Medallions of pork cooked in cider and apple, served with new potatoes, green beans, carrots and broccoli. We had almost finished our main course when Tim appeared at my side.

"Mr Jackson, there's a telephone call for you," he said.

My look of surprise prompted him to add, "It's a gentleman."

I took out my mobile phone from my pocket. It was switched on and we had a good signal. I looked across at Louise; she had a somewhat wry smile about her, as if she knew who was on the other end of the phone.

"It's this way," Tim, said as I got up and followed him. Just for a moment my mind dreamt up all sorts of things that could have happened: maybe one of the boys had had an accident, but that could only be William, Peter was at home. The worse situation then flashed into my mind: something could have happened to Louise's children, what was I to do if that was the case. We would have to go home.

But my mind was instantly put a rest as I held the receiver to my right ear.

"Hello," I said.

Without any hesitation the reply came back.

"My friend!" The voice of Stavros, and I breathed a huge sigh of relief. He continued, "I won't keep you long. Part one and two of our plan is now in place. Enjoy your meal." He paused, and knowing Stavros as I did I could tell he had more to say to me. "I've been reliably told, my friend, that she looks exceptional this evening."

"Thank you," was my reply and our plot came flooding back into my mind. I made my way back to the table, wondering just how he could have known Louise looked so lovely. As I sat down Louise's right hand came across the table and took hold of my left hand.

"Everything ok?" She asked, still wearing that grin. She went on "Was that who I thought it might be?"

"Yes it was." My reply was a bit short, for I was enjoying myself so much in this woman's company I had clean forgotten what we'd arranged with Stavros. "I'm sorry, I didn't mean to snap at you." I said as I gave her hand a gentle squeeze.

"Its ok darling, I'd almost forgotten myself, but then, I've begun to expect the unexpected now." Her words reassured me, and we continued with our dinner.

For dessert Louise had fresh Strawberries and Cornish cream, I chose the cheese board complemented by some strong coffee.

Tim asked if we had enjoyed our meal, and together we replied it had been lovely. I settled the bill. By now it was nine forty-five and as we stepped out of the main door and into the dusk of this April night my excitement returned. Louise took my arm and we walked round to where I had parked the car.

"It's gone," I said, looking into Louise's eyes.

"Remember?" she said, and that reminded me of my phone call.

There was a bigger look of surprise on Tim's face when he came to let us back in. When I explained my car had been stolen, he immediately went out of his way to do anything he could to correct the situation. He wanted to call the police; this had never happened to him before, and he even started to ask some of the other guests if they had seen anything. I told him not to worry, I would call the police when we got back to the apartment or in the morning. For the moment if he could arrange a taxi it would be sufficient. He did just that and told us it would take about half an hour for the taxi to arrive, and we were welcome to have a drink on the house while we waited. We took him up on the offer, to put his mind at rest and not raise any suspicions. Louise had a port and I managed a malt whisky.

I can never understand why it is that a taxi driver will always find a different way home each time you use one. It must have been ten-thirty by the time we got back to the apartment. The driver commented he hadn't been called to people at the apartments before and he passed me a card as I gave him a ten-pound note for the journey home. I told him to keep the change as I closed the door.

We stood in the courtyard and watched him drive up the track, the bright moonlight illuminating the surrounding area. The whiteness of the light had a fresh crispness to it. I opened the door for Louise and I followed her into the small porch, and as I closed the front door she turned and we came together in a kiss that was to be the start of a new and exciting experience for both of us. We drew apart long enough for her to tell me to leave everything.

"Come with me," she said, taking my hand and leading me through the inner door. She slipped off her jacket and placed it over the back of a chair, I managed to let mine fall to the floor, and that's where it was destined to stay for the night. I followed her up the stairs one step behind her. The landing was illuminated by the light of the moon pouring in through the window at the top of the stairs and Louise's open bedroom door. Her perfume hung in the air, as fresh as when I'd been in there more than three hours ago.

The whole room was alight with the white of the moonlight shining in though the windows. As we stepped inside I turned to close the door but was pulled by Louise into her waiting arms.

"Make me yours," she whispered. "I want you! I need you now!"

And with those words I started on the completion of the job I had carefully laid the foundations for that morning. I eagerly but carefully unbuttoned her dress, then slid both of my hands up from her waist and over her breasts, pushing the dress off her shoulders and allowing it to fall to the floor. I turned her slightly so that the light penetrating the French window would enhance the view of this exquisite body; not that I required any light to see what I was going to do.

Under her dress she was wearing matching light-blue and white lace-edged underwear. I hadn't been mistaken in the car park, for to my extreme pleasure she was wearing stockings, held up with a small suspender belt. I put my hands at the back of her head and started to kiss her cheeks, working my way down her small cheekbones to just below her ears. The sweet smell of her perfume was in every pore, the fine hair on her cheeks even tasted of it.

As I kissed her my hands wandered up and down her back, and as I moved them further down I could tell that in fact it was a very tiny string pantie she was wearing. Her sighs and moans told me what I was doing was right.

She lay on the bed, and with her aid I pulled my shirt over my head and our almost naked chests came together. I say almost, for Louise was still wearing the most daring half-cupped bra. Between our kissing she indicated that it fastened at the front, and without any trouble it came undone.

I cupped and caressed each breast in turn, paying particular attention to her nipples. Her hands were holding my head in place and I could hear her sobs of delight as I continued to heap pleasure upon her perfectly formed body. Slowly I made my way further down her torso returning from time to time to her breasts, so that I could delight to the sounds of her ecstasy. I wanted this to last forever, and now I felt that I had the energy to make it last. As I got to the most intimate area of her body she begged me to stop and I did as she asked.

"No one has ever done that to me before," she said, " and I'm not sure if I'll like it."

"My darling, you won't like it, you'll love it," I told her in the most reassuring of ways, and proceeded to use the most sensitive item of my body to give her pleasure. As I held her small panties aside my tongue delivered all the sensations that this woman had missed out on for years. I looked up to see her hands cupping each of her breasts, her thumbs rubbing her nipples franticly. Her face was crimson, she was panting as if she was running the race of a lifetime and her tiny tummy was heaving, up and down as it went in rhythm to the orgasms she was experiencing.

"No! No!" I could hear her crying. "Please don't stop!" And I couldn't, for this was the best way I had of showing her my love was real. I wanted to get to know every part of her anatomy and I had as much time as it required. I went on and on giving myself to Louise.

I felt her hands on the back of my head, and thought she was in need of a rest. As I stood up I slipped off my shoes, and undid my trousers, letting them fall to the floor. I looked down at her on the bed and saw she was covered in a dampness that reminded me of the early-morning dew. In truth it was perspiration that had come from the exhilaration of the acts I had performed upon her.

"Come and lay down," she said, her voice oozing passion as she spoke the words. She pulled me onto the bed next to her, but a rest was the last thing she wanted, for no sooner was I by her side than she had removed the tiny string from around her waist, and my own underwear. She slipped her naked body on top of mine. Now I had double the pleasure. She leant forward and her breasts fell into my hands, then her lips came to mine, a long and passionate kiss that went on and on.

Then I could feel her breasts against my chest. I diverted my attention to them, kissing and sucking on them, before moving my hands to her bottom. There I cradled each of her buttocks as she rose and fell on top of me, until a joint orgasm arrived that sent a shiver running through our bodies and we both cried out in sheer ecstasy. We lay together wrapped in happiness, our bodies hot and exhausted, too tired to talk and too tired to sleep.

Easter Monday/Tuesday

But we did sleep, and together. Sunday drifted into Monday. In the early hours we both awoke, and we lay in the silence and stillness of the night. With Louise by my side I needed nothing else, and she told me the same, then to my surprise she sat up.

"I must tell you that," she paused, slipping her hand under the duvet, "I've laid in this bed at night waiting and wanting you."

I looked down at the bedclothes. Her hand was rubbing her tummy and a smile had formed on her face.

"Why didn't you try to make a move on me before?" she asked, and continued, "I wouldn't have put up much of a fight, you could have had my love much sooner."

"I wanted it to be right," was the start of my reply. "If I'd barged straight in the first night, you would have thought that was all I'd brought you here for, and then we would not have been able to withstand the trauma of the following evening. We would have had to go home, not that I knew those things were going to happen, but they did bring us together, didn't they?"

"Yes they did darling." Now the word had slid from her tongue with ease, and I could see she felt no embarrassment when she said it. She went on, "That was so good, nobody has ever made love to me like that, it was wonderful, wasn't it?" She stopped and I could see the outline of her hand moving between her own legs.

"Could we do it again?" she asked, as she pushed the duvet back and forced herself upon me, not that I was going to complain.

"Not bad for a gay boy!" I couldn't resist the chance to get the comment in as she rode me again into her own delight.

"I said you wouldn't let me forget that, didn't I?" She screamed with the utmost of pleasure as she reached another orgasm.

And so we made love long into the night and the early morning, only stopping to get up for the bathroom and later, when the sun was alive, to make tea.

Late on the Monday morning Louise held my head in her hands and I knew a question was on is way.

"I know you said we would go home on Tuesday, but could we stay just one more day?" Her eyes peering into mine, she already knew the answer. I had no need to go home and it may be a long time before we could share a bed together again.

"Will your Mother and Father mind if you don't go back tomorrow?" was my response.

"I'll ring them now," she said as she jumped out of bed, and together we made our way downstairs, naked, to the phone.

I faintly heard her mother say another day wouldn't make much difference. The children were out with gramps.

"Ok," Louise said. "We'll see you on Wednesday about lunch time," and I took 'we' to include me.

We spent the rest of Monday and Tuesday doing what new lovers do. We bathed and showered together, and it had been many years since I'd shared my bath with anything other than a rubber duck. We cooked together and Louise showed me skills I didn't know she had, but most of all we showed our love to each other and built a stronger friendship with that commitment. On the Tuesday evening before we made for bed Louise took me to the sofa, there we sat together and she cuddled in close to my body.

"I've got to tell you something before we go home." She sat back and waited for my signal before she would continue.

"Go on then, tell me," I now felt relaxed and ready for anything.

"I've got a little box that I'm going to keep for you," she said, as she slipped off the sofa and onto the floor. Her eyes and smile told me everything. "And I think I've lost the lid for it, as it's overflowing with my love for you." She paused and brought her hands up to take mine and placed them on her breasts. "I want you now, just for the last time on this holiday."

And that's what we did; made love downstairs in the lounge before we made our way to bed, for who knew how long it would be before we could indulge ourselves again.

Chapter Eight

Wednesday

We awoke to the sound of rain falling on the patio. Unlike our love affair, the good weather had come to an end. It didn't make us feel any different towards each other, if anything we became closer, but we shared a sadness that we had to go home, and I was concerned for Louise's safety. If Gary should find out, then his reaction would more or less be predictable: he'd go mad. I put those thoughts to the back of my mind as we showered together for the last time.

Over breakfast we decided it was best if Louise left her new clothes at the apartment. I would keep the necklace and place it in my safe at home, until we could go to dinner again. I agreed to accompany Louise to my solicitors to start the ball rolling with regard to her getting a divorce. That, we knew, would be a painful experience in itself, let alone Gary's reaction.

We could make no plans for ourselves and where the relationship would go; our love was too young to plan the future, but it was strong, and would have to be in the coming days and weeks.

If our lovemaking was good then it only went to prove that my memory wasn't, for while in the raptures of the delight we had been experiencing over the last two days I'd forgotten to report my car stolen. It only occurred to me when I realised I had to get the Lotus out of the garage in the rain.

"Oh!" I said, angry with myself as I stood looking out at the wet courtyard from the small window.

"What is it my darling?" Louise asked as she came to my side.

"I haven't reported the Porsche missing," I told her.

"Don't worry, do it now, you were going to ring Jones, weren't you?" she said to me in very reassuring tones.

I found his card in my wallet and dialled the mobile number. It rang and rang and I thought it was about to trip into the answering service when a very out-of-breath man said "Hello."

"Is that inspector Jones?" I asked and I had to wait for the reply.

"No, who's that?" the voice said, and then I recognised the tone, it was Rimes.

"Ah, that's Mr Rimes isn't it?" I said, and instantly caught him on the hop.

"Yes," he stammered back at me, "but who's that?" frustration in his voice.

"It's Andy Jackson, Mr Rimes," I said, and went on, "I'd like a word with the Inspector please." There seemed to be a long silence before he came back to me, almost as if he had to gather his thoughts or even make something up. The silence made me even more suspicious of him. I'd had my doubts in the beginning and William's words came flooding back into my head: he gave him the creeps and had shifty eyes; a good description by anyone's standards.

"He's not here, what do you want?" Rimes eventually replied, and that confirmed to me a lack of tact and no diplomacy. "I'll give him a message if you want," he finished.

"Yes, if you wouldn't mind." I paused. I still felt uneasy about telling this individual anything. "Will you please tell the Inspector my Porsche has been stolen?" I tried to sound angry but it was wasted on Rimes.

"Yes," he replied, "I'll tell him."

"Aren't you going to ask me when it went missing?" Now I was frustrated as well as beginning to feel angry.

"When?" he replied.

"Just ask him to ring me," I said. No point in pursuing this conversation.

"Ok," and he was gone.

"That wasn't Jones was it?" Louise said, and we must have been sharing the same thoughts for her next words I could have spoken: "I don't trust him; you know, Rimes, there's something not right about him."

But neither of us could put our finger on what it was that made us feel uneasy. It would come to light eventually but we had no idea of the depth of his strangeness at that moment, he had to be trusted but at a distance.

So after getting the Lotus out of the garage in the rain, together we packed it with the belongings we were to take home. I think I left more behind than I'd brought as I seemed to only have one bag in the car, and after checking that the place was secure we stood in the rain. More like drizzle, that can only fall in Cornwall; not that it falls but hangs in the air and gets into every part of your body even if you just stand still.

"It's time for us to go," I gently said to Louise, and as I looked at her I could see she was crying. I pulled her in close to me. "Don't cry, we will come back, I promise you. You've made this place complete," I told her as I fought back my own tears.

I opened the door for her to get in and looking up at me through her tears she said, "Thank you so much for bringing me here. I really do love you." And with those words she looked back at the converted barns for the last time on that wet Easter Wednesday.

I got into the car and took off my glasses to wipe the dampness away, and as I was putting them on Louise took my hand.

"If, when we get home," she paused before choosing her words to carry on. "Please don't be put out, if I give the children a lot of my attention." She looked worried as I squeezed her hand to reassure her. "Gary used to get very jealous and that would upset the children."

"My love, they'll have their Mother no matter what happens. But I've got the woman." I told her, and with those words I started the car and we headed for home.

For most of the drive home we were in peaceful silence, extremely happy with the time we'd spent together. Louise slept for part of the way. That was just how secure she felt with me, she told me when she awoke and asked how far away we were.

"I'm assuming that you want me to take you to your parents," I nervously asked.

"Yes please." She added, "They won't bite!"

"But what about me being gay?" I enquired.

"I know you're not, you've certainly proved that to me." She said. "Not that I had any other notions."

"That does bring me to a very delicate subject," I said, and I felt I needed to pick my words very carefully, but once in my head I just had to say them. "I was a bit reckless, you know, during our love making, I should have taken some precautions." Louise stopped me by putting her hand up.

"You've no need to worry yourself about that," she said, putting her hands together as one would to pray. "Gary made sure I can't have any more babies, when he gave me a beating about twelve months ago. I won't go into the details."

"I'm sorry, I didn't mean to distress you," I said.

"It's ok, it's in the past and things are going to be better for me from now on," she said, taking my left hand and giving it a gentle squeeze.

We were nearing Chillingston, the village where Louise lived. She gave me perfect directions to her parents' house, which was about three-quarters of a mile away from her own home. As I pulled up outside the gates that led into the driveway I took the opportunity to look at Louise. Her face was aglow with happiness and thoughts of seeing her two children.

But this was a different woman now from the one I'd taken to Cornwall seven days ago, and I too must have had a somewhat smug, self-centred smile, for I had been the one to release her from her prison of unhappiness. Once again she was that free-spirited individual I'd known over six years ago, and now I had experienced her long-awaited love.

We drove in through the entrance gates and along the shrub-lined driveway that led to her parents' house, a detached double-bayed property, the driveway opening out to a large semi circle bay in front of the house. To the right stood a double garage, separated from the house by a path I assumed led to the back of the buildings and rear garden. To the left of the house was another path, also leading to the rear of the property. On the other side of this path was a line of carefully trimmed bushes.

I swung the car round so that Louise's door was opposite the front door, and as I turned the engine off I glanced up at the bedroom on the right, my attention being drawn to it by the curtain moving.

"What's their names?" I asked.

"Oh, Trevor and Diane," Louise replied, with almost a laugh about her.

"No, what's their surname, and what do they do for a living. I can't call them by their Christian names on this first meeting," I said.

"Of course, you're right, it's Morrison, but I thought you knew my maiden name," she said, looking at me a bit puzzled. With those words she took my hand. "Daddy was a bank manager and Mummy, well, she's always been Mummy. Don't worry, they'll be fine with you." Then her attention moved, for out of the corner of her eye she'd seen her mother appear from between the house and the garage. "Look, there's Mummy and James." The excitement in her voice was a marvel to hear. I looked at her and her face was aglow and a pleasure to see. I opened my door and walked round the rear of the car to open Louise's door.

"Thank you," she said, and squeezed my hand as she passed by and headed towards her mother and son, crouching down as she got closer for James to run into her arms. I stood and watched, holding onto the car door and listening to her tender words of love for her baby boy. Picking him up she walked towards her mother, and her mother's waiting arms wrapped around Louise.

"Darling, you're looking so much better," I heard her mother say, a very articulate and precisely spoken woman. "And have you had an enjoyable time?"

"I have Mummy," she replied. "And this is Andrew, Mummy, my friend I've been staying with."

By now I'd taken Louise's bags from the rear seat and closed the car door and I headed towards them. As I got closer I put my right hand out. Louise's mother was looking me straight in the eyes with a look that said a thousand words. I could see where Louise had inherited her looks; she was small woman in her late fifties, maybe sixty. She too had tight curly hair and I assumed that at one time it would have been like Louise's, auburn in colour.

"Mrs Morrison, it's so nice to meet you," I said as we came together, but this lady wasn't going to shake my hand, instead she put her arms out and gave me a hug and as she did so her words in my right ear rang for some considerable time.

"Thank you for bringing my baby back," she whispered in my ear. "She is so much better now."

"Mummy, where's Daddy?" I heard Louise ask.

Now, I'd always been of the opinion that, mature, grown up people who still call their parents 'mummy' and 'daddy', must be very insecure, but that notion was to very quickly disappear as I stood on the Morrison's driveway. It was natural, what they had always done, and who was I to argue with it.

"Daddy's in the conservatory with Sarah darling," her mother replied, and continued, "I think she's reading to her Grandfather. Go on round." She ushered Louise ahead with her hand.

"Now Andrew, you will of course be staying for lunch with us?" her mother asked me.

"Yes please, if it's not too much trouble Mrs Morrison," I said in reply.

"It's no trouble at all. And please, call me Diane," she said, taking one of

Louise's bags from me. "Trevor may seem a little frosty at first, but he will soon warm to you," she said, taking my arm. We followed Louise, who went on ahead carrying James.

We made our way through a side door into the kitchen. Off to the right was the entrance to the conservatory and sure enough Sarah was sitting in a wicker chair reading a book to her grandfather. As we approached, Sarah dropped the book to the floor, sprang from the chair and ran to Louise calling, "Mummy, you're home!"

Her father stood up, a small man who cast a powerful presence. His grey hair had all but receded and he was sporting a small moustache. He took off his glasses as he came to greet me, his right hand out straight in front of him. I took it in my hand; this man had a grip like a vice, almost to the point of causing pain.

"And you're Andrew Jackson," he said, as he looked me in the eyes. Releasing his grip he rubbed his tiny moustache, then he turned and outstretched his arms towards his daughter.

"And how's my Pudding been?" he asked as he embraced her. She flashed her eyes at me as his back was towards me.

"Andy, that's Daddy's nick name for me," she told me, a little embarrassed. I stood and watched this very tight family complete their greeting to each other.

"Daddy I'm fine, and I've had the most wonderful time; the weather was so good, that was until today; it was raining in Cornwall when we left but had stopped by the time we got to .." she stopped and was looking at me, "Where was it, Andy?"

"I think it was around Taunton," I said in reply to her question.

"Mr Jackson." Louise's father corrected, his tone firm and accurate. "Do you like fish?" he asked as he opened the door leading out of the conservatory and into the garden.

The question took me by surprise and normally I would have returned with a comment about batter and chips but on this occasion I thought better of it.

"Well yes," I replied, a little puzzled, but I could see he wanted a quiet word with me as he signalled for me to accompany him out onto the patio. I followed him out of the open door. The patio, which was surrounded by a low wall, had a gap in it leading down onto the lawn, striped from a recent cut and I have to say it appeared as if the lawn went on forever. At the end I could see trees and the outline of a river.

"I know about you," he said, once we were out of earshot, and continued "You're that fellow with that huge family fortune aren't you?" and before I had chance to say anything he continued. "Yes, I remember reading about you and all that money, before I retired from the bank. Do you know that brought some problems to us in the banking and finance business?"

"Yes, I do remember the press giving it a lot of coverage," I replied.

"Well I'm sure you do, I had a queue of little old ladies at my door wanting me to check the bank records for long lost relatives, and it took a long time for that to die away. You remember the press made a big thing of this and it even caused a stir in Whitehall. I can tell you now the Treasury ordered an immediate investigation; they didn't want that sort of thing to happen over here, in jolly old England. It's ok for them to cock-up, but hell, if someone from outside finds that there a big hole in the system then they go into overdrive to try and sort it out."

"It's brought some problems for me as well, you know," I said.

"Yes, I bet it has, but you seem like a sound sort of chap, I'm sure you've managed to take care of things. You have, haven't you?" He'd stopped and was again looking in my eyes. "You've taken good care of my Louise haven't you? No, you don't need to answer that question, I can see just by the way she is behaving. This is the best she's been for such a long time. She's not been right since she married that brute of a husband, not very sound, you know. She thinks her mother and I didn't know what was going on. I could tell she had been beaten in the past, I knew before she came and told us. I've a friend who works at the club, you know the football club, and he's told me about Gary's big talk, and once when I touched her she nearly jumped a mile. Mrs Morrison met her friend Jill in the village not so long ago and she asked if we knew about the bruises on her back. Of course Diane said no, you see, we can't interfere, we'll support her but she has to make the decision herself."

We had walked as far as the river at the end of the garden, and he was pointing to some large fish that could be clearly seen under the surface.

"Yes, of course you are right," I said and added, "I've said I will help her." I paused unsure of whether I should go into detail about our weekend, and I was to be saved the task by Diane calling to let us know that lunch would be ready in five minutes.

"I just want to say one more thing to you, Mr Jackson," he paused and scratched his head. "If you're queer, then I'm the Pope's brother in law!"

Now it was my turn to look this man in the eyes.

"There're no flies on you are there, and please call me Andy or Andrew, Mr Morrison," I said, smiling. That was it, and as he took my hand in both of his he said,

"Andy, I know she's safe with you, even though you must be at least twelve years older than her. Do you fancy a whisky before lunch?" he asked. "And by the way, it's Trevor."

"I wouldn't mind a glass of wine, or a beer," I replied.

"Sound. I've got a damn good claret in the rack. Come on, let's go back," he said as we turned, and he put his arm on my shoulder.

As we approached the patio Louise came out onto it, a smile from ear to ear.

"I can see you two have got off to a good start," she said as she came to greet us. She squeezed between us and took our arms, and gave me a kiss on the cheek and very quietly whispered, "There, it wasn't that bad, was it?"

And so I was introduced into this very middle-class family, and within no time I felt at home, comfortable and relaxed. We talked over lunch about the economy and world affairs. Diane liked my Lotus, saying she had always wanted to have a ride in one, the idea of her hair blowing back in gay abandon had always appealed to her.

Then Trevor caught Louise and I by surprise. He brought up the subject of the Post Office. We looked at each other before attempting to answer and said we hadn't been able to get the paper for the last couple of days due to a shortage locally in Cornwall. Well, as luck would have it he gave us a quick resumé of the situation, without asking for our opinions on things, but adding things didn't seem right about the whole affair.

Proceedings did come to a sudden halt, quite out of the blue. Sarah made a comment that really did take all of us by surprise.

"I remember seeing you before Christmas," she said in her very childlike manner. It would have been ok if she had stopped there, but as is often the case, small children have more to say. "Daddy says Mummy thinks of you a lot of the time, then he gets cross and," she paused and we were all hanging on her words, "then he hurts her, and he gets drunk. I don't like Daddy then, neither does James."

So the children, well at least one, were aware of what went on, and now it was in the open. Louise told Sarah that her daddy wouldn't be doing it any more, and things were going to be ok. Once again I was saved any embarrassment by virtue of the fact that my mobile phone rang.

"Please excuse me," I said as I stood up and made my way into the conservatory. My 'hello' was greeted with that familiar Greek voice.

"My friend, I trust it is safe for you to talk?" he asked.

"Yes its fine," I replied.

"Was I right about that woman? You didn't come out for two whole days I'm told," he said, and continued, "you know you can trust old Stavros. By the way, your car is quite safe. Now, as for the other part of our plan; that Jones chap, he's a very good policeman, but as for the other man I can't find out anything about him. I'll have to leave that to you, is that alright?" he finished.

"Yes that's great, I'll talk to you soon, thanks for what you've done," I replied, and he was gone. By now Louise had come out to the conservatory and was by my side.

"Was that Jones?" she asked.

"No, it was Stavros," I told her, and went on to explain what I'd just been told.

"You know I don't really want to, but I'll have to be making a move soon." I paused, looking at Louise. "Are you going to stay here with your mother and father?"

I waited for her reply. I would have loved to say that she and the children could come with me but I was poorly equipped to take on a family, not only that but there was still a hundred and one things to sort out when I got home.

"Yes I think I will. Gary will come here if he gets home and finds no one there," she said. "I'll feel safer here and if I have to tell him I'm leaving him, Daddy won't take any messing from him. But will you be alright?"

"Well, I'm not sure just how I'm going to manage on my own. I'll be very lonely in my big house tonight," I told her.

Then she led me out into the garden, gripping my left arm as we went. I knew this was going to be a goodbye of sorts, and neither of us wanted to say farewell. We made our way round to the front of the house where the car was.

"Look," I said, as I took my phone from my pocket, "have this and the charger from the bag in the back and I can call you without disturbing anyone else."

"But what will you do for a phone?" Louise asked.

"I can get a new one tomorrow, and when I see you next you can have it, and I'll have that one back. The boys and maybe Christine might call, but I'm sure you be able to deal with them, just don't let Chris talk for too long," I said.

"Ok, if your sure, but when will I see you again?" Now she had tears in her eyes and I was going to feel hopeless leaving her like this.

"I'll make some arrangements for us to see my solicitor, say for next week, and I'll call you tonight. When did you say Gary was due home?"

"He's meant to be back tomorrow, midday," she told me as I got into the car.

"Maybe at the weekend," I said as I started the car and wound down the window. Louise put her head in to tell me again that she loved me, and as she said the words I wiped away her tears with my thumbs.

"Go on to the children. I love you and we'll talk tonight," I told her, and I could see her mother holding James. Sarah was standing at her grampa's feet and all of them waved as I pulled away and drove down the driveway, with my own heart sinking like a stone, for now I was back to emptiness.

So I drove home to my empty house. As I approached it I could see there were road works going on outside, indeed to the edge of my drive entrance, which made it difficult for me to manoeuvre the car into the drive. The warning signs had been knocked over and the guards around the hole were worse than useless. A tatty board stood on one side of the gaping hole in the ground apologising for the inconvenience on behalf of British Gas, but as is often the case no sign of any workmen, but still, it was gone six o'clock.

Once indoors I had a look at the post which had accumulated over the seven days I'd been absent from home: there was nothing of importance, and no messages I needed to respond to urgently. Christine had been round and collected her phone, and it was her who had been in the house last and left some milk in the fridge for my return. I made up my mind I would go and see her, as I was in need of some company, and after all it was her doing which had brought Louise and me together for the weekend. First I made a pot of tea and opened some of the post: a few bills and a offer from a local shop on mobile phones, that will come in handy I said to myself and put it with my wallet. After two cups of tea I was ready for the short journey to Christine and Bryan's home.

I pulled up outside their house, and could see Christine's car on the drive. Casually I walked up to the front door, but I was conscious of the big smile I had on my face. I wanted Chris to answer the door, because then I wouldn't have to say a word, but it was Bryan who came to the door.

"Am I glad to see you!" he greeted me with. "Now she can ask you herself. She's been bending my ear since you went away, she never stops! Do you fancy a beer?"

With those words Christine was on her way to see me even before I'd got into the lounge, and as Bryan had said she didn't stop. I almost had to tell her to be quiet so I could get a word in edgeways. With a beer in my hand I sat and retold the weekend to her. Bryan was indeed pleased that someone else was there, it gave him the chance to go and watch some football and give his ears a rest.

Chris told me the hole in the pavement had only appeared that morning: something to do with the gas. After an hour Bryan came back in and said he was going to get a takeaway. I happily agreed to stay and have a curry with my two good friends. By now it was gone eight o'clock and I asked Christine if I could use the phone to call Louise. I was reminded that I knew where everything was and I could help myself.

I was greeted by the usual soft "Hello" and almost no other commitment.

"Hello darling," I responded and went on, "are you ok?"

"Oh it's you," Louise said, relaxed now that she knew who it was. "There's no number on the display of your phone."

"That's because I'm at Christine's," I told her. We talked for about half an hour, by which time Bryan had returned with the curry. We closed our call telling each other how much we loved each other and Louise sending love to Christine. "I will, and I'll call you tomorrow. Goodnight and God bless," and she was gone.

Over supper Chris asked where I thought the relationship was going. I couldn't answer her question, for all of the events had come the way I hadn't expected. True I'd wanted her, but never in my wildest dreams had I thought we would become lovers, and lovers we were. We shared so many things, even our thoughts, and our thoughts brought me to the subject of Rimes, and the uneasy feelings we shared about that individual.

"What does he do?" Bryan asked, taking a sudden interest.

"Something in the Post Office," I replied, surprised by him asking the question.

"Why don't you have a word with Alex?" he said, and that was enough to bring Christine back into the conversation.

"That's a good idea," she said, "he knows someone everywhere, he'll be able to help you."

Alex was a mutual friend we had known for years. How we got to know Alex I can't remember. He had been a civil servant, and as a result had contacts in all possible places; if he didn't know who to ask then he would find someone who did.

"I'll ring him tomorrow," Chris said. "Should I ask him to ring you?"

"Yes please, that'll be fine," I confirmed. "I've a lot to do tomorrow: get a new phone for Louise, sort a date out with the solicitor, and make arrangements to see Alex, so I think I'd better be making a move." I stood up and made my way towards the hall, where Chris came and gave me the hug I've so become accustomed to.

"Give me a call when you've sorted everything out, and take care," she said as she released her hold on me, adding, "I'm glad that things worked out as they have." And I could hear Bryan say he was too, as it would stop her going on at him.

And those words were still in my head as I climbed into my bed, alone, back at my house.

Chapter Nine

Thursday

I slept well. It must have been seven o'clock when I awoke, came down, picked the paper up from the porch, made some tea and planned the day ahead of me. It wasn't easy. It had been a week ago that I'd taken Louise to Cornwall, and at about ten I found myself in the lounge looking longingly out of the window. I would have loved to have that week all over again, although without the visit of those two characters. But still it couldn't be; now I had other things I had to do.

Before I set off into town I rang Louise. She was a little surprised by the call but could see my number on the display which put her mind at rest. We chatted for what seemed like an age, until I could hear the mobile bleeping indicating the battery was nearly flat. We closed the call with her saying she would charge the phone and I was to call her in the evening once I had made all the arrangements.

My next call had to be to Phillip. It had been over a week since I'd spoken to him and, just like Christine, he wanted to know all the details. It was good to talk about my feelings to a man who understood just how lonely I'd been for a considerable period of time, and I agreed to keep him up to date with developments.

I went and did my business. I purchased a new mobile phone, and seemed to spend hours in the solicitors office, maybe due to the fact everyone I bumped into wanted to know what I'd been doing and how were things working out. Some people were surprised I'd come home at all. I managed to drag myself away, having made an appointment for a week following the next Monday. The partner who handles the divorce side of things was on holiday until then. It was three o'clock by the time I returned home, and I saw a van was parked across the road. I assumed it was something to do with the hole by my driveway, and when I enquired I was informed the work was 'ongoing'. I made my way into my home, thinking what a wonderful expression that was, 'ongoing', and nobody doing a thing.

There was a message from Chris giving me Alex's telephone number. She went on to explain that he had moved just recently and would be about for a few weeks only, before setting off on a cruise.

After making a pot of tea I called him and was greeted by his usual tone and a saying he always had for me.

"Well, my son, and what can I do for you?" His voice sounded like a thirty-year-old but he was in fact in his seventies.

I explained my dilemma, and I could hear him making notes, as he repeated some of the things I'd told him.

"Leave it with me my boy," he said. "I'll have some answers for you by .." he paused. "How about we have lunch next Wednesday?" he finished.

"That sounds fine to me," I replied and continued, "At the White Hart on the common at one o'clock."

"Good, I look forward to it, anything different and I'll contact you," he closed, and was gone.

I was in the kitchen preparing my supper. It must have been five-thirty when the phone rang. Looking at the display I could see it was my own mobile, but it did take a time to register.

"Hello darling," I answered, and she was silent. I asked, "Is everything alright?"

"No, its not!" I could clearly hear she was upset.

"Tell me; what's the problem?" I was desperately concerned for her, and my mind was going into overdrive. I thought one of the children could be ill, or maybe it was her parents.

"What is it? Please tell me!" I begged.

"It's Gary," she started, and I could hear panic in her voice.

"What about him?" I asked.

"He's not come home," she said, and then went on, " I've been to the house and he hasn't been home, so I went to the football club and saw one of his mates, I think it was Tony. He said Gary didn't get on the ferry with the rest of the crowd, in fact he couldn't remember seeing him in the hotel last night. I'm very worried, I know it's over between him and myself, but I have the children to think of, and he's always come home." Now she was very distressed, and I was a long way from being able to comfort her.

"Look, don't worry," I said. "We can sort something out." I paused, for I didn't really know what to do. "I'll ring Jones, he still hasn't got back to me about my car. Maybe they've been following Gary in Belgium. We can get to the bottom of this," I told her in the most reassuring way I could. "Do you want me to come over?"

"No, I think I'll be alright, I'm going back to Mummy and Daddy's." she said, "Just ring me when you've spoken to Jones. Goodbye, speak soon," and she was gone, just a little more settled than when she'd started the phone call to me.

So that was the next person I rang, leaving my supper in a half prepared state, and this time it was Jones who answered the phone.

"Inspector Jones, it's Andrew Jackson," I said.

"Mr Jackson." A surprise tone was in his voice. "I trust you are well, and Mrs Shaw and yourself enjoyed your weekend away."

"Well, I would have enjoyed it more if my car hadn't been stolen," I said, emphasising the word stolen.

"I'm sorry Mr Jackson, I don't think I heard you correctly, did you say that your car was stolen?" he replied. The question indicated he hadn't got the message from the day before, and also confirmed the suspicions we had about the person who was meant to be keeping an eye on us.

"I did indeed say my Porsche was stolen, on Sunday evening while Mrs Shaw and I were having dinner at a local restaurant. Fortunately I do own more than one vehicle, but I rang you yesterday!" I stopped. It was Rimes I'd told about the theft and he obviously didn't tell the inspector. "Didn't you get the message I left with Mr Rimes; he answered your phone and said he would pass the message on to you."

"I'm very sorry Mr Jackson, he didn't, and between you and me," he hesitated before continuing, "he's more of a hindrance than a help, he has a habit of disappearing and I've no idea where he gets to. To tell you the truth I'm thinking about asking for a replacement. He's just not up to the job. This has only been a trial. Anyway, I'd be better off on my own," he finished.

"Well, I've some more news for you," I said, "I've just spoken to Louise, I mean Mrs Shaw, and she tells me her husband hasn't come home."

"Oh shit, no!" Jones said quickly, followed with an apology. "I'm very sorry Mr Jackson, I shouldn't have said that. I'll have a word right away about the situation, and I'll call my man in Cornwall to check if he saw anything on Sunday. About what time was it when you discovered your car had been stolen?"

I was able to answer quite confidently about the time, and I knew that it wasn't going to be found by the police, for someone far more clever and craftier than they had spirited my Porsche away, but he didn't need to know that. I was working on the principle of 'what he didn't know wouldn't harm him', and we could afford to let the man in Cornwall chase his tail for a few days anyway.

"Can you give me the number of this landline so I can call you back when I have some information for you and Mrs Shaw?" he asked.

I went on to explain that I would pass on any messages to Louise, as my mobile was, as I put it, temporarily out of action for the time being. I heard him repeat my number back to me.

"It may be in the morning when I ring you Mr Jackson, will that be alright?" Jones asked.

"Yes that will be fine. I'll stay in until I hear from you," I told him, and he was gone. I had faith in this man mainly due to the digging Stavros had done. And Jones came across as genuine; this being supported by the things he said with regard to Rimes, almost as if he himself didn't trust the man. I returned the call to Louise and this did set her mind a little more at rest, and I promised to call as soon as I had any more news. In any event I would call her in the morning.

Chapter Ten

Friday

And so the call came from Jones at about eleven o'clock, and it didn't contain the news I wanted to hear.

"I've heard from the Belgium authorities Mr Jackson," Jones began, "and I'm quite concerned, I must tell you." Now his tone had changed and I feared he had some bad news to break. "I've been reliably informed that Mr Shaw got on a later sailing, and is back in this Country." He paused again. "But that's where we have a problem. No one was at the port when the ferry docked and we're unsure where he might be now. We do have an unconfirmed report of him being picked up by someone in a dark green Renault, but it could have been blue. It was night when the ship came in, and it was only a deckhand who saw him. He remembered him because they had a bit of a fall out. Apparently Mr Shaw had had rather a lot to drink and barged into this other chap, almost knocking him over the side. As I say, that's all I have to work on at the moment, so you can understand why I'm so concerned."

"And so am I!" I said, wondering where the hell Shaw could be. "Did you have a word with Mr Rimes, you know, about that message he didn't pass onto you?"

"Well I would have done, but late last night when I got home I had a message on my answer machine. It was Rimes saying he was sick and had gone home, and that he will call me when he's feeling better. Mind, he didn't look too good when we were together on Wednesday; as I told you, he kept disappearing," he told me.

"So you're well and truly on your own then," I said.

"Yes, I am until they get me a replacement," he said, adding, "We haven't been able to find your Porsche either. Our man is still working on it, but so far he has drawn a blank, but leave it with me. Oh, I almost forgot, could you inform Mrs Shaw?" He paused before going on, "Maybe you can water it down a bit, you know, so as not to alarm her."

"And what about me being alarmed, you do remember the kicking I got from him; and what about the other bloke who was with him on that day, have you any idea of who he is?" I asked.

"No I'm afraid I haven't," he said. "I'll keep you informed as things move along, try not to panic, I'm sure he can't know that we're onto him. By the way, those people are still in this country - you remember the ones I told you and Mrs Shaw about, the people from Holland - so if he's going to meet up with them then we'll be able to pick up the lead from there."

"Thank you," was about the only repeatable thing I could say to him. I felt let down by the entire incompetence of the police force and the worse-than-useless Post Office official who couldn't even pass on a simple message. Jones was gone, and I had to break the news to Louise that her husband was on the loose, unchecked.

And break the news I did. She wasn't happy, but I had never expected her to be, but once over the shock she agreed it would be best if we carry on as normal. She said if he turned up and started to cause trouble then she would call the police, and I would do the same if he came to my house. Louise agreed to come to my house for dinner on Saturday evening. That would be as near to normal as we could get at this very delicate time, but within an hour that relative normality was to be thrown into complete disarray, for the phone call I received next was to cast suspicion on everyone we knew, from Christine, to my best friend Phillip and Louise's parents, even Stavros.

I'd just put the kettle on for a cup of tea when the phone rang. Looking at the display I could see it was my own mobile number, and I was very surprised when I answered.

"He's just bloody well phoned me!" Louise screamed down the phone, fear in her voice.

"Hold on," I said, "I'm not with you. Who do you mean?" I was completely confused and Louise was beside herself with terror and now she was crying.

"Gary's just phoned me. I don't know where he could have got your number from," she said through her sobs, almost catching her breath between the words.

"I looked at the phone as it was ringing and the number was withheld, and I thought it was you calling again from Christine's," she paused so as to try to contain herself. "I answered with, 'hello darling'," again she stopped, "then the words I'd heard before 'I bet he fucking is'." She cried again.

"What can I do?" I asked. "Do you want me to come to your parents?" The truth was I didn't know what to do. If Gary wanted to, he would find us anywhere. It did prompt me to ask if Louise had any idea where he may be, but her reply was what I should have expected "No."

Then it occurred to both of us almost instantaneously, if he didn't know where we were before he rang my mobile telephone then he bloody well would now. By now Louise had calmed enough and her tears had subsided.

"He won't come here, even if he's angry," she said, and continued, "You remember, I told you he feels very insecure here. I'll have a word with Daddy, he'll not take any messing. I should be alright, but will you?"

"Yes I will," I told her. Even though I was frightened for my own safety, I was more concerned for hers and the children, but I put my faith in her father.

"Look, why don't you come down tomorrow afternoon a bit earlier than planned, we mustn't let this spoil everything. He knows now, sure it's a lot sooner than we had planned, but we can't turn the clock back, can we?"

Louise agreed and it was her who said it might be best if we played it the same way as when we'd gone to Cornwall. I said I would call Jones and let him know about the phone call she had received, thinking that might help in the search for Gary.

I went into the lounge to make the call to Jones, and as I stood holding the receiver in my hand I looked out across the road and saw there was now a van on the other side. Two men were preparing to dig a hole on that side of the road. After leaving a message for Jones to call me I felt I needed to go out and investigate. My enquiry was met with a short sharp reply, which would not prove its worth for some considerable time.

"We're doing this for you," one of the men told me.

"But there's nothing wrong with my gas supply," I said, "and what about that hole over there," I continued, pointing across the road to my driveway.

"Like my mate told you yesterday, it's ongoing work and this hole has something to do with that one over there," he said, as he proceeded to mark out a white square on the ground where they were about to start digging.

"Well, I'll leave you to it," I said, as I made my way back across the road. I'd realised I was wasting my breath, and thought it was best left to the experts, and I made my way back indoors.

Saturday

I didn't sleep that well, even though I'd taken the precaution of bolting all of the external doors and having a large whisky before going to bed. I was glad when the sun had risen and I could get up. I made up mind a run would do me good, after all it had been a week since my last run, and that had proved to be helpful in clearing my mind. It didn't give me any ideas on just how Gary could have got my mobile number, but often the obvious is staring you in the face and it's so close you can't see it.

At two o'clock I saw a taxi outside. I made my way out and paid the driver and he sped off down the road. As always I received a big hug and kiss, this time not on the cheek but on the lips and she didn't care who was looking, it was almost as if she wanted to show the world she cared. She even glanced across at the van on the other side of the road, and I think she gave the occupants a wink. As we walked arm-in-arm up the drive Louise did ask what they were doing with two holes, one on each side of the road. She also made a comment about road works just down the road from her parents' house and her own home, the mess was everywhere. I said it all seemed too complicated for me to take in and explained the conversation I'd had with one of the men last night.

Once inside we discussed who we thought could have let my number slip. Then it occurred to me that it was in fact me Gary had wanted to talk to; he couldn't have known Louise would have had my phone, so that in effect ruled out a lot of people. But just how did he get my number?

The talk of the phone reminded me I had purchased a new one for Louise. We spent some of the afternoon programming numbers into it, and I have to say Louise was far more adept at that than I was. We had almost finished when the landline rang. I could tell from the display it was William, he seemed somewhat concerned, and went on to tell me that, as he put it, the shifty bloke had been back, but not to see him, he'd just sat outside looking at the kids. William said it appeared as if he was more interested in the small ones. He must have been there almost half an hour, William said. The very thought of Rimes sitting in his car looking at children made me feel very uncomfortable.

"William, what sort of car does he have?" I asked. His reply was to shake me even more.

"A blue Renault," was his reply.

"And what day was he outside?" I asked.

"Hang on, I think it was Thursday. Yes it was, because Pete came back with a Volvo to be worked on and blew his horn at him to get the car moved. Oh by the way we've so much work on I've had to take on a lad. You don't mind?"

"Are you absolutely sure about the car and the day?" I almost begged him to answer.

"Yes I'm positive," he said, and then, "What about this lad?"

"That's fine, you're running the business, I'm happy to leave things to you," I finished and we cleared down, leaving it that we may get together on Sunday evening, but I would let him know.

I sat down with Louise and explained that it was William on the phone, and related what he had told me. I didn't need to remind her about what Jones had said with regard to the ferry coming in and a green or blue Renault. The memory came flooding back to her.

"And you did speak to him on Wednesday, didn't you?" she asked.

"Yes I did, but it could be a coincidence," I replied. But it was no good, for the seeds of doubt were sown a long time ago, perhaps even on our first meeting with Rimes. I made a call to Jones, and once again left a message. Well, I thought, even the police have to have a weekend.

"I think I need a drink," was my next comment. "Would you like one?" I asked Louise.

"I'll have glass of wine if its not too much trouble," she replied, and she went on as I got up, "I'm afraid I can't stay this evening."

Her words took me by complete surprise. I hadn't been looking for an evening of lovemaking, I more than anything needed her company.

"Is it one of the children?" I asked, as I came back into the room with our glasses of wine.

"No, it's not the children." She hesitated, needing to pick her words. "You know me well enough by now and I hope you'll understand," again she stopped. I was now beginning to get a little worried, unsure of what she was about to say. "It's just one of those weeks, my private week, well, that's how Mummy used to put it," she said very quickly as I sat down beside her.

"That's ok, if that's what you want, if it's what you feel easiest with, it's ok by me, but remember, I told you before we became lovers, it'll take more than a bad week to put me off of you," I said, looking into her eyes.

"It's not that so much," she said, taking my hand. "Gary used to say if it was that private a week then I could go and sleep with children. And as I told you not so long ago, it becomes the normal. I thought that every man treats their wives like that. I do want to sleep with you and if you don't mind, then I'll stay. There will be other times when we can make love. I think I told you, nobody has ever done it like that to me before. Gary was always brutish; no tenderness about him, only a few times was he warm to my feelings. Most of the time he was an on-and-off man, and he hurt me on many occasions, even during my week. I'd only ever read about the lovemaking that we did in books and magazines."

So after our supper we made for bed. Louise first made that important call to home and her words sounded like an angel talking as she spoke to her mother and father.

As I drew the curtains I could see the workmen were still outside. What they were doing I hadn't a clue, but I was certain I wouldn't work all through the night. My night was to be spent in bed with the woman I loved.

Sunday

I awoke at six, Louise wrapped around me, naked apart from the intimate underwear she needed to wear.

I got up and made some tea, taking two cups up to the bedroom. It was lovely to see Louise wake in my bed. She stretched her entire body the full length of the bed, and cast the duvet back so she could sit and drink her tea, with just her waist and legs covered by the bedclothes, her breasts pert and firm.

"I hope you don't mind," she said, "I've really made myself at home, haven't I?"

"Well I'm glad you feel this relaxed," I said as we drank our tea together.

We agreed to have a relaxing morning, read the paper and enjoy a light breakfast. I would take her home to her parents and the children mid afternoon.

As we sat out in the conservatory I suggested it might be a good idea if Louise brought a change of clothes to the house, then if the occasion arose again for her to stay she would have something to wear the following day. She thought she would go to her own house on Wednesday and pick up some outfits to bring to her 'second home' as she put it. I presented her with the spare set of house keys and explained how the burglar alarm worked.

We set of towards Louise's parents at about two o'clock, a steady drive, and at two forty-five we had parked the car on the drive and made our way via the side into the kitchen. We were greeted by the smell of roast pork and freshly cooked apples, then Diane appeared from the dinning room.

"You two have timed that very well," she said with a big smile on her face, and moved forward to kiss her daughter on the cheek. I too was greeted in the same warm manner. "Dinner will be ready at five, and of course, Andrew, you will be staying."

I could tell by looking at Louise there was on point in arguing. I'd been accepted into the family. I didn't have a problem with the way they behaved; I felt comfortable. They took me for what I was. The money I had didn't come into the equation; the feeling of acceptance made me happy, happier than I'd been in a long time. We shared the same views on many things, and those we didn't caused no problem. I couldn't understand for a moment what made Gary feel so insecure in this most homely of homes.

"Trevor will be pleased to see you Andrew," Diane told me. I think he's still in the garden with the children. With those words Louise kissed me on the lips and made her way out onto the patio, and instantly I could hear the children's delight at seeing their mother.

"Louise told Trevor and I about the phone call she had from Gary," Diane said to me, looking me in the eyes. "She also mentioned the trouble he's in, or let's say suspected of being in. We think the children need to be protected, that is until something is sorted, do you agree?"

"Indeed I do," I replied

"I'm sure you can look after my baby, I'm sorry, Louise," Diane said, taking my hand, and added, "but you need to look after yourself as well. We heard from Louise about the beating you received."

"Hopefully that won't happen again," I told her.

Trevor came in from the garden, and fatherly words rolled off his tongue, confirming his approval of my being part of this family.

"Andrew, it's good to see you again, and now I think we can have a drink. Diane, a G and T, and Andrew, I think," he paused, "I think you're a beer man, am I right?"

Diane replied first with a, "Yes please."

"You're absolutely right, I'd love a beer," I said, adding, "Is there anything I can do to help?"

To which Trevor said, "You could open that bottle of wine in the fridge and pour a glass for Pudding, I mean, my Louise."

I did as I had been asked and felt even more part of the family. Trevor and I took our drinks into the lounge at the front of the house and I made myself comfortable in a leather winged-back chair. It gave me the feeling of being in one of those gentlemen's clubs you see on the television.

Trevor sat opposite me in an identical chair and I had a feeling that a question was on its way. "Diane and I are thinking of taking the children away for a few days. What do you think?" the question didn't really take me by surprise. I felt most flattered that he valued my opinion and had asked me what I thought.

"I think that would be a very good idea," I replied, going on, "Had you anywhere in particular in mind?"

"No just to give them a break, you know till that brute of a man Gary has calmed down. We don't want him to upset the little ones. I know he'll have every right to see them but he needs to sort himself out first, and I'm sure you're more than capable of looking after Louise."

"Have you ever been to Scotland?" I asked.

"Well yes I have, but it was a long time ago, and it used to take days to get there. Why do you ask?" he replied.

"Well apart from having the place in Cornwall, I also have a house in Scotland, and to tell you the truth you'd be doing me a favour if you and Diane would go and stay there. I haven't been able to go myself this year, you know, with setting up the business for the boys, and time just seems to disappear. Well, what do you think?"

"It sounds like a good idea to me, and Diane won't take any persuading, I'm sure of that," he said.

"Ok, that's it settled then. I'll give you the details before I leave this evening. Can you make your own arrangements to get there? Is that alright?" I said. "Or you can fly if you prefer, you tell me what suits you best."

"Drive will be fine," Trevor said, adding, "I think we'll leave tomorrow midday."

Over dinner we discussed the best route for them to take to get to Scotland. I explained and gave them the address of Mrs Baxter, the housekeeper I employed to look after the house. In between courses I rang her to inform her the house would be having some 'guests', as she liked to put it. She agreed she would go and air the whole house in the morning and also prepare the beds.

If Trevor and Diane needed anything, or wanted any shopping done, they were to ring her and she would make all the necessary arrangements. We also agreed if we got things sorted before the end of the week then Louise and myself would try to get up for a few days.

As I was about leave the Morrison's home, Louise told me she would feel safer staying with me, once her mother and father and the children had embarked upon the journey to Scotland. I agreed I would also feel happier, and it would also keep her parents' minds at rest if she were in my company, and not alone in the house. She had some clothes at their house and before leaving she gave me a bag containing enough to get her by for a few days, until she could go home and collect some more on the Wednesday, as we had agreed. She told me she would stay and see them off and then make her way to my house. Her father would run her to her own place in the morning so she could collect her car, ensuring she had transport of her own. She said the car would come in handy, as a visit to the school would be required to explain the reason for Sarah's absence. She wouldn't have long enough to pack clothes as that would take a lot of thinking about, as Louise put it, not only that, but she would have to pack some clothes for the children.

I left Louise stood on the doorstep, with her words of love still ringing in my ears and made my way home on that late April Sunday evening. My thoughts were still on her and the arrangements we'd made when I arrived home at ten o'clock. As I manoeuvred the car into the drive I knocked over some of the bollards. After parking the car I got out and proceeded to put them back in place. Looking into the gaping hole it seemed as if nothing had been done; in fact further down the road another hole had appeared. I was still looking into this open space of emptiness when one of the workmen came to my side. I was about to ask how much longer, when I looked in his eyes.

"Still ongoing," were his words before I had an opportunity to say anything.

There's no point, I told myself, as I made my way up the drive with Louise's bag in my hand. I hadn't done much all day but I felt shattered. I made my way to bed, and as I got under the duvet my thoughts went back to Louise and our night together. I went off to sleep thinking of the forthcoming nights we would be spending in this bed.

Monday

I awoke to the sound of the paper hitting the floor of the porch. I'd slept very well, not even waking during the night for the bathroom. Once awake I was up and out of bed, downstairs and making tea. I'm not someone who can stay in bed; unless I have good company to stay with that is. Today I needed to make contact with my sons. I felt as if I'd neglected them somewhat over the past week and a visit to the garage would do me good, as well to show I still had some interest in the business. Before that I needed to have something to eat. I fixed some boiled eggs and had just finished them and was about to settle down for a read of the paper when the phone rang. Looking at the caller display I didn't recognise the number, so answered with a tentative "Hello" and waited for the reply.

"Andrew, is that you?" A man's voice.

"Yes it is." And as I said the words I knew the voice, it was Trevor, Louise's Father.

"Are you ready to leave?" I asked.

"We are," he replied, then went on, somewhat hesitantly, "Diane tells me someone's been here looking for you. When I was taking Louise to get her car. A man. She said he made her feel very uncomfortable: she was giving the children a bath when he called, and he had the damn cheek to follow her up into the bathroom."

"Trevor," I cut in, for in my mind I felt I knew who this individual was "is Diane there?"

"Yes, shall I get her?" he came back to me.

"No, I don't want to alarm either of you, but just go and ask her if he took an unpleasant interest in the children."

"Andy," he started, and went on, "I don't need to ask her. She told me when I arrived back that she more or less had to push him out of our house. As I said, he followed her upstairs to the bathroom. Just stood in the doorway looking at the children in the bath. Diane said he reminded her of a weasel."

With that word I felt I knew the person she was talking about. Rimes. William's description came back to me - 'shifty'.

"Are the children and Diane ok?" I asked, concerned for their safety.

"Oh yes Andy, it'll take more than one strange man to upset Diane, believe me, she's sound," he said.

Now I'd noticed Trevor had a habit of using the word 'sound' often, one of those idiosyncrasies people pick up, but it makes you conscious of not using the word or saying it yourself.

"I think I know who it might be. It's best if we don't mention this to Louise, well not for the time being," I told him, and continued, "You have a good time in Scotland, have a safe journey, and give us a call when you arrive. I'll take care of things here."

"That's sound then," Trevor replied. "I think I can hear Louise's car now, everything will be fine, talk to you later, bye for now." And he was gone.

I rang inspector Jones again, as he hadn't returned my previous call, to share my concern about Rimes, and this time he did answer the phone.

"Yes," he said, "I can understand your concern. I'll make some of my own enquiries. I'm very sorry I didn't get back to you, but I've been working my way through so many messages. I still haven't had a replacement for him you know. You're sure it was him at your son's garage?"

"Yes I am," I said and then went on, "Mrs Morrison described him as weasel-like."

"I can't argue with that," he replied, "leave it with me. I haven't had a message to say he's back from sick leave."

And with that he was gone. I had a feeling of sorrow for Inspector Jones. He was obviously struggling to do the job on his own.

I hadn't long cleared down from the Inspector when the phone rang, and when I answered it I was greeted by the voice of Alex.

"We need to make that lunch tomorrow, my son." Concern in his voice.

"Alex, is there a problem I should know about?" I asked, knowing Alex doesn't change arrangements just for the sake of change.

"Well, let's just say there's something I'd rather be telling you face to face, and not over the phone." He had urgency in his voice that almost alarmed me.

"Same time same place, ok." And he hung up, before I had chance to argue.

My mind began to race, wondering what could be so important that he needed to see me a day sooner than we'd planned. I told myself I would find out when tomorrow came, for now I could see Louise pulling onto the drive, time for me to put the kettle on. I wasn't the only one to notice her. The men digging the third hole also saw her pull up and were taking a good view of her, as today she was wearing a short skirt and a loose-fitting top, her jacket draped over her arm. It was warm again, the spring-like weather had returned, along with my love.

We had some tea before we went to see the boys in the garage. I thought it best if I didn't tell Louise Alex seemed a little concerned when he rang. I did say I was going to meet him and she in return said she would go and collect her clothes a day sooner than planned, and maybe we could go to Scotland and join her parents with the children.

Just as on the first occasion when William met Louise, he made a fuss of her, taking her hand and kissing it. He then went on to introduce her to Peter, who had not been about when William had, but knew what was going on: William had kept him well informed.

We came back home and together we prepared our supper, all the time music playing in the background. I'd never been able to relax quite like this before, but sure enough just as we were about to eat the phone rang, and this time it was someone with good news, Louise's father. They'd arrived safely and had installed themselves in 'the big house' as he described it. He told me before I passed the phone to Louise that Diane was putting the children to bed. They couldn't get over how light it was and Trevor told me he'd forgotten just how splendid and "sound" the scenery was.

As always it was music to my ears to hear Louise talk to her children and she must have been on the phone for almost ten minutes, before she closed with the words "enjoy yourself and take care," then a final goodbye, and she had finished.

Over supper we talked about and I described the house in Scotland. It wasn't easy, as I'd only been to the place twice, once to view it prior to buying it and again upon my return from America, but that was during late part of the autumn early winter. It's a big house it has to be said, and even these days requires a great deal of heating, particularly during the winter months, and I found it too cold, and very dark during those long winter nights.

Chapter Eleven

Tuesday

We made for bed after the news, and it didn't bother me at all that we couldn't make love. It was, as I have said, enough to have Louise in bed with me, and a good test of my own self-control. We slept well, not unbroken, for I did wake in the night, and lay still just listening to Louise breathing and watching her breasts rise and fall in time with her gentle breathing.

When I did wake properly, it was to the sound of a motor bike outside. I got out of bed and looked out of the small gap in the curtains. Without having my glasses on I could just about make out the rider. He or she appeared to be asking for directions, and I could see one of the workmen pointing in the direction down the road. I say workmen, but I use the term loosely, as in all the time that I'd been back from Cornwall I'd only seen them dig holes in the road and pavement. Only the fact I had plenty of other things to occupy myself stopped me ringing the Gas Company to find out what was going on.

I did my usual thing when I had Louise as a guest in my home. I went down and made tea, bringing it back upstairs with some biscuits on a tray, and together we planned our day. First I would go for a run. I'd been on Saturday and I needed to get back into the routine of running. Louise was going to her own home to collect sufficient clothes to leave at my house, and I was going to meet Alex.

I would need to leave at about twelve fifteen and Louise said she would leave before me. She needed to do some shopping and would see me back here. She also asked again whether we would be able to travel to Scotland to stay with her mother and father and the children. I didn't see a problem, and to make it easier we could fly, then hire a car, but we would need to return home by Sunday as we had an appointment at the solicitors on Monday morning. What I didn't tell her was the urgency that seemed to be in Alex's voice when I'd spoken to him the day before.

After my run we had a light breakfast. Louise said she would have a meal in town when she was out, and as I was meeting Alex for lunch it was best I had something not too heavy.

It was about ten-thirty as I stood on the drive and watched Louise leave and at the same time observed the men over the road take some equipment out of the van. It looked like pipe cutting gear, but as I'm no gas engineer I couldn't be positive.

It was almost twelve thirty when I set off from home to meet Alex. I found him already installed at the bar of the White Hart, a gin and tonic in his hand

and a copy of the Guardian spread across the bar. He'd made himself at home, I thought to myself as I approached him.

"Well my son," he said, as he got off the stool he had been perched upon and shook my hand, "I trust you're keeping well?"

I nodded my reply, and then he continued: "We need to find a table out of the way," and he pointed to one positioned by a small window. I ordered a pint, and picking up a menu we made our way over to the table, Alex as always in front of me, his fawn mackintosh flowing like a cape as he walked towards the small table. We sat opposite one another, and before I had chance to look at the menu Alex had news for me.

"I've some bad news for you, my son," he said as I looked into his light brown eyes. He still had the features of the gentleman I'd met many years ago. His hair had receded long before I'd met him, but he still had a sharp manner to himself, a quick wit and the ability to tell a good story. Now his eyes were deadly serious, and so was the news he was about to relay to me, so much so I put the menu down in total disbelief.

"I must tell you, that young woman Louise and yourself are in what I would consider to be very grave danger!" He paused, looking at me. "I don't mean to alarm you Andrew, but you did ask me to find out what I could and, unsavoury as it may be, this is what I have uncovered." He stopped and picked up his gin and tonic, twirled it in his hand, the ice chinking against the glass, took a sip and put it down before continuing.

"What I think you do know is that Louise's husband has been doing a spot of drug trafficking, and that's what the police know about; and let's be fair, who would suspect a Post Office lorry, they are everywhere and go all over the place. What not too many people are aware of is this Rimes chap, and what he's been up to." He paused and took his coat off before he went on. "It would seem he, that is Rimes, is under investigation himself. This is very difficult to explain and I only have a brief outline of what's been going on, in fact that policeman he's been working with isn't even aware of Rimes' past and what he is still up to. Rimes is the master-mind behind a paedophile ring, and it would seem from the information I've been able to gain that he has been using Gary Shaw to bring into and move illicit material around this Country." Alex stopped and I was glad he had.

It was difficult to take in, but then things started to add up. William had said that he thought Rimes spent a long time looking at the small school children outside the garage. And even I had asked Trevor if the man had an unpleasant interest in the children when they were in the bath. I started to feel uncomfortable: a coldness came over me.

"This is indeed not the news I had expected," I said to Alex, who by now had picked up the menu.

"I think I'll have ham, egg and chips. Are you going to eat?" he asked in an almost casual way.

"Yes, I think I'll have fish and chips," I replied.

"Before I order," Alex paused, took another drink from his glass, then continued, "I'm afraid there's more unpleasant news I have to give you, but no, first let me order our lunch. Do you want another drink?"

"No, I'm ok for the minute," I said. As he got up and went to the bar, it occurred to me that Louise's children had had a close encounter with this monster.

Alex returned and in his hands he had two drinks.

"I think you'll need this," he said, as he put a large whisky on the table in front of me and had another gin and tonic for himself. Then he slipped his hand inside his jacket and pulled from the pocket a photograph. He passed it to me with his right hand, then said what he really didn't need to ask, as the look of surprise on my face must have told it all.

"Do you recognise this man?" Alex asked.

"You what? Yes I bloody well do. He was the other bloke in the lane on the day I got a beating," I said, as I picked up the whisky and emptied the entire glass into my mouth.

"Oh, I wondered if you'd come across him," Alex said. "Now he's a really nasty bit of work, in fact he makes Gary look like a pussycat. I mean nasty, and the twist in the tail is," he paused as the waitress brought our food. She was a big fat girl and seemed to hang around, taking an unnecessary interest in our conversation.

"Thank you!" Alex said somewhat abruptly, looking up at her over the top of his glasses, and she was on her way, with the cheap word "enjoy".

"Now, what was I saying?" Alex said, as he looked at his food and scratched his balding head. "Ah yes, I know, he makes Gary look like a nice guy, but what Gary doesn't know is, he's the brother of the chap Gary is suspected of killing in Holland last year. Now this blokes name is Jan Van-Elderman and it's Gary he wants to sort out, that is first, but he's got a reputation for trouble and I suspect he may well turn his attention on you and Louise afterwards. That's the way he operates. Of course Gary is under the impression he'd teamed up with him to find out about the drug smuggling, and there's a bit of truth in that, but the other interesting thing is that his brother, the customs chap, was in fact crooked, and was working with Rimes. They were both part of the same European ring, not that Jan is squeaky clean, for as I said he is quite heavily into the drug market, crime seems to run in the family. He has a nasty habit of disappearing, as he seems to have now, no one can find him. My son, you've not eaten your lunch."

"No," I said, "this is frightening news. I'm not sure what I should do next; you know for Louise's safety and of course my own."

"Well if you want my advice, I'd tell as few people as possible and bugger off out of the way, you know, try disappearing, like that Jan chap has," Alex said. "One other thing I didn't tell you, Gary was using Louise's name to receive instructions on where he had to pick up his next consignment, and of course deliver it to. He had a redirection put on any post addressed to Mrs L

Shaw, to a PO box, and he was able to pick it up, hence those letters Chris said you'd sent went straight to him. It couldn't have been better if you'd addressed them to him. Your feelings were in the open long before you met Louise again."

He finished and I felt a terrible sense of uselessness. I could take her to Scotland, but there was a chance we could be found, and from what Alex said it wasn't just Gary we had to fear, it was also this Jan.

Alex's comments prompted me to ask if any of the authorities were doing anything to try to find this individual. He went on to tell me that the serious crime squad was now involved, looking into Rime's background, and because Jan was in the country the drug squad had an interest, but they had also managed to lose him.

He also explained Jan wasn't working with the other drug dealers from Holland who were in this Country. Jan was freelance and a very loose cannon. I picked away at my lunch - this news had all but taken away my appetite. I couldn't even be bothered to finish my beer.

"I think the best thing I can do is take Louise to Scotland. It seems a bit like running away but for the time being it's probably the safest place, until this Jan is found," I said.

"Yes, I think that's a good idea," Alex replied and added, "I'm going to make a move now, I've got to meet my wife so we can go shopping."

We walked out of the pub together, made our way across the car park, and finished saying our farewells standing close to Alex's car. He said he would call me if he got any more news about these two sinister characters. I watched him pull out onto the road, and into the flow of traffic. I knew there was a lot of work to do before we could go to Scotland, I didn't keep any clothes there so I would need to pack a bag at minimum, and then I needed to book the flight. A whole host of other things were required before we even thought about going away.

I turned to head towards my own car, and as I did so from between two parked cars out stepped Gary. A shiver ran thought my entire body. Alex had gone and I was alone and, I admit, very frightened. This big man stood about six feet in front of me, blocking the route to my car, his hands down by his sides, his fingers forming into fists then relaxing. I could hear the traffic on the main road behind me, and between the pauses of vehicles tearing along the road I could faintly hear a motorbike's engine running. But my thoughts were on escaping what I feared would be more than a just another beating. That was to be confirmed when Gary spoke.

"I thought you'd got the message last time we met," he said, looking into my eyes, and went on, "And now a little bird tells me you've been shagging her, in that place of yours in Cornwall."

How did he know we'd been to Cornwall? Only a few people knew, then suddenly it dawned on me it must have been Rimes. If it had been Rimes who had picked Gary up at the ferry port then he would have gleefully sung his head off, reporting to Gary that Louise and I were together over the Easter break. At this moment though a discussion on our weekend was the last thing Gary wanted to talk about.

"I'm going to fucking kill you this time," he told me, his tone very soft but to the point. In fact this was the first time I'd heard him speak quietly, and he had a chilling stillness in his manner. His comment about killing me prompted me to make an observation.

"I see you're on your own today," I said, and his reply was even more chilling.

"I don't need any help. You're easy shit, I proved that last time, and when I'm finished with you I'm going to find that little tart and give her a beating she'll never forget. We'll see what 'mummy' and 'daddy' do for their little girl then. They'll be welcome to her."

So his anger wasn't only to be aimed at myself. Louise was to be his next target, and who knows what he would do after that? He may well turn on the children, or even her parents, he obviously had a deep-rooted hatred for them. What I'd found comfort and reassurance in, was to him reason for the most unpleasant thing he could ever do. But for the moment I feared for my own safety: what was I to do?

If I cried out for help then by the time someone arrived I could well be on the floor taking a kicking. It wasn't possible for me to turn and run, for that would only take me out onto the road and fast moving traffic. I couldn't allow that to happen to myself again. I was going to put up a fight, as feeble as it is may be; I had to attempt something.

Gary's hands came out in front of him as he took a step closer to me. I knew I had just one chance to avoid them and inflict a blow to his body. If I got it wrong, then I was dead for sure. As he raised his left leg to bring himself even closer I took my opportunity. Just as his foot was coming into contact with the ground I shot in with my right foot. The outer edge of my leather shoe came into contact with his shin, just below the knee.

I felt it dig in and slip down the lower part of his leg as his full body weight was coming onto it. He cried out with the pain as it buckled underneath him, and he was on his way to the floor, his arms flapping in desperation trying to steady himself as he crashed down. I stepped aside to avoid being caught by his hands, knowing that he would soon be up.

Changing position I prepared myself, slightly lowering my body almost into a crouching pose. I turned at a slight angle to him, my right arm went behind me at hip level and then with my whole body strength I hit him with my right fist, catching him square on the jaw. His head went back as he absorbed the blow and his look of anger was now replaced with one of total surprise. In came my left fist with uncontrolled aggression. It made contact on the right side of his face, he went down and I was making sure he wouldn't get up for some considerable time. I felt as if I'd rained blows onto him for minutes, when it was probably over in seconds.

This wasn't just my anger at having been beaten by him, it was the anger and hatred I felt towards my father, bottled up for years, when he used to beat my mother and then turn his aggression on me. It was also for Louise: no man should ever beat his wife, I was telling myself. I couldn't control my frenzy and he may well have been rendered useless after the first blow. I felt an adrenalin rush, the type I'd only felt before when completing a marathon, the release of energy saved up for that last mile. My last blow was to send his head crashing to the ground with an almighty thud.

I stood over him as a boxer does in the ring waiting for his opponent to get up. But he didn't. Now I didn't fear him; I pitied him. All he knew was to control people with fear and aggression, and I wasn't to be his victim this time. His face was a mess: a massive cut above his right eye, blood pouring from that and his nose. His bottom lip had a huge split in it, blood was coming out of there as well, and he was unconscious. I was sure he would have marks on the back of his head where it had come into contact with the ground with such force. His left leg was still crumpled under his massive frame.

The roar of a motorbike pulling out into the traffic snapped me out of my victorious stance over Gary's smashed and now disfigured face. I need to get home, I told myself and ran panting to my car. I'm not sure how I got home. I pulled onto the drive and Louise's car was already parked there.

Still in a state of shook I made my way to the front door. Louise came to it and let me in, a look of horror on her face.

"Oh my God! What's happened to you?" she gasped as she held the door open for me, looking down at my hands. I turned my attention to them myself. They were covered in blood, and now the effect of the adrenaline was starting to wear off, and my knuckles on both hands were hurting. I stepped inside and we made our way to the bathroom, and as I started to wash Gary's blood from my hands I explained I'd met him in the car park of the pub, where he'd made plain his intentions for me. And he had also told me he was looking forward to seeing Louise again - and not with a view to discussing what sort of Easter she'd had.

My blows to his head had removed a considerable amount of flesh from my knuckles on both hands, and also my wrists hurt from the impact of my fists coming into contact with his head. Louise's voice showed no sign of sympathy for him; her attentions were directed purely towards me. This told me in itself that their marriage was over. I hadn't set out to break up the union between them, it was already under a great deal of strain. Perhaps I'd applied the final pressure to take it to breaking point.

When I enquired as to why she was already home she said her car had broken down. She'd called William as she couldn't get hold of me due to my mobile phone being turned off. William had asked Peter to help her and he had managed to fix the car on the side of the road, but she'd come back home as it took some time for him to repair the car.

"I'll go and get my clothes in the morning," she told me. "For now we need to get your hands sorted. What state was Gary in when you left him?"

"On the floor and out for the count," I replied. "He won't be very happy when he comes round, that's one thing I'm sure of!"

I told Louise about my conversation with Alex and the warning he'd given me about this Jan, also what Rimes' involvement was in all of this. I mentioned he'd been to her parents' house. I felt now was the time to inform her, as the children were away and safe. We both thought it best if we went away and then tell the Inspector from a distance, and sure enough Scotland would for the time being be far enough away. Other than that we were very uncertain of what, if any, other way we should play things.

With some difficulty I rang the airport and booked two tickets for us to travel to Inverness. Our flight was at eleven and we needed to be at the airport an hour before departure. The young lady assured me we would be able to hire a car when we arrived at our destination; we thought it was best if we didn't ring to say anything to her parents.

"Let's just surprise them, and the children," Louise said.

We decided to go out for dinner, to the restaurant we'd been to on that first outing in March. We changed, and as promised I got the necklace out of the safe for her to wear. She looked as stunning as always, dressed in a long flowing navy blue and white skirt, a short-sleeved white blouse, her hair long and free. The food was, as on our previous visit, wonderful. The only thing that marred the evening was my difficulty in using a knife and fork, as I was unable to bend my fingers fully. Louise made a comment about mashing my dinner up in the way she does for James and the lightness of her tone eased the pain.

She drove home and told me she found the Lotus easier to drive. The workmen were still outside, and this evening they'd erected a tent type cover over one of the holes. I wondered just how much longer this work was going to continue. Once indoors we had a nightcap and we were in bed by eleven. She cuddled in close to me and told me she loved me. I went to sleep with her warm semi-naked body close to mine, and she was like that when I awoke at six the following morning.

Chapter Twelve

Wednesday

"We have a lot to do this morning," I told Louise as we sat in bed drinking our early morning cup of tea together.

"Then you go and have a shower first," she said and added, "but can I have another cup of tea in bed before you go?"

As always it was a pleasure to do anything for her. It must be the way she asked. While she was taking a shower I prepared a light breakfast; some boiled eggs and toast, the same she had done for me when we were in Cornwall. We sat in the conservatory and ate.

At seven-thirty Louise was heading out to her car and on her way to her own home to collect her clothes, just as the postman had pushed the mail through the letterbox. The airline tickets were mixed in with the post. I said she would need to be back at the house by nine o'clock, so we could leave for the airport by nine-thirty at the latest, and I would book a taxi for nine-fifteen.

I went indoors and packed my own bags. Perhaps I should ring Christine and let her know we are going away, I thought. She'll look after the house in my absence. I rang and she was pleased for me. What I didn't do was go into the details of why we were going away, as Alex had said it was best if few people knew. Not that Christine or Bryan would intentionally say anything, but it might slip out during a conversation to a neighbour and that in turn could be passed on to a stranger.

Nine o'clock came and there was no sign of Louise. I was beginning to wonder if her car had broken down again. That may seem as if I didn't have any faith in my son Peter's ability to do roadside repairs, but often when one problem is sorted it generates another. At nine-fifteen the taxi was outside. I went out to talk to the driver and had my head through the passenger window explaining she would be here shortly when the driver's acute hearing picked up that my phone indoors was ringing.

"Hang on," I shouted back to him as I raced up the drive. Once indoors I made a grab for the phone in the kitchen, at the same time looking at the display. It was Louise's mobile. Slightly out of breath I answered with the words, "Has the car broken down again?"

"Andy," her reply was slow and very quietly spoken. "Gary's kidnapped me," she paused, her voice controlled, but I could hear the fear in every word.

"What do you mean, 'kidnapped'?" I asked, shocked by her statement.

"Exactly what I said," she replied, and continued, "He came to the house when I was upstairs. I heard the front door close. I'm sure he didn't know I was there because the car was in the same place as when he left before Easter. I looked out of the bedroom window and it was Rimes' car I saw pulling away. I was going to hide but I couldn't get out of the bedroom and back downstairs without being seen. I think he only came home to get a change of clothes. His face is such a mess, and he was still covered in blood, what on earth did you hit him with?"

"I only used my fists," I said, and then asked, "Are you alright?"

"Well, apart from being dragged around by my hair, and being slapped a few times, I suppose I'm alright, but Andy, I'm bloody frightened. I don't know what he might do next," she told me, and I could hear her voice begin to waver. She continued, "He's mad with you, I've never ever seen him like this before."

"But where are you?" I asked.

"We've got as far as Exeter. I told him I needed the loo. I think he's going to take me to the apartment," she replied. "We're in my car. He keeps on saying about going to see our 'love nest', as he put its it." Now she was crying and from so far away I was unable to do anything for her.

"Is it possible for you to get out and away?" I asked.

"No, he's standing outside the entrance to the toilets. I don't know what he'll do next," she sobbed down the phone to me.

"Ok, this is what I want you to do," I started. "I want you to turn off the phone when I've finished talking to you. We don't want him to know you have it. I'll ring Inspector Jones and see if he can get that man in Cornwall to move himself, and I'll make my way down. If you're in Exeter it's only an hour and a half to the apartments. If I leave now I can get to them in about two hours."

"But what should I do when we get there," Louise asked.

"It's best if you try and pacify him; keep talking to him. Tell him about Rimes going to your parents' house, it may take his mind off doing anything to you and divert his anger towards someone else. I'll be on my way as soon as I hang up," I paused and then there was one other thing I need to tell her. "And darling, whatever happens, remember our little boxes."

"I will, and I love you so much," she replied.

"Now it's best you go. I love you, and I will see you soon," I told her.

"Ok, take care darling," and she was gone. Her tone was that of someone very frightened.

I rushed out of the house and stuffed a ten-pound note into the taxi driver's hand, apologising for his wasted journey. I quickly turned and made my way back indoors, grabbed the car keys and mobile phone. As I was running to the car I dialled the Inspector's number and just as I climbed into the car I heard the sound of the voice bank take the call. "Bugger!" I shouted out loud, enough for the men working over the road to look round, and I continued to talk to myself as the message was playing in my right ear.

"Inspector Jones, this is Andy Jackson, please call me as soon as possible,

I need your help. I can't go into a great deal of detail at the moment but needless to say it's very urgent that I talk to you."

I cleared down and put the phone on the passenger seat as I started the car. The Lotus roared into life and I was about to drive it like I had never driven a car before.

I glanced to my right and left as I put the front of the car out of my drive and over the pavement. The road was clear, my right foot went to the floor and I was away at lightning speed. When I looked in the rear view mirror I could see some of the bollards had fallen over and the workmen came running across the road to reposition them, or so I thought.

I drove, taking the car to its limit in each of the gears before changing up to the next. As I pulled onto the motorway I got that tremendous rush of adrenalin as I drifted across three lanes of carriageway to the outside lane, forcing the accelerator peddle down to the floor. Glancing down at the Speedo, I saw it was reading one hundred and twenty miles per hour. I was sure to get caught for speeding, I thought, as I shot along the motorway. What saved me from the speed cameras were some slow-moving lorries, and in the process of slowing down, my thoughts went to Louise. I could only imagine what she was going through as I sped on my way, and my fears for her were to be confirmed later, as the day unfolded.

Gary had indeed kidnapped her, grabbing her by her hair in their family bedroom where he had discovered her, then slapping her face several times, the first time he'd hit her above the body, before forcing her to lie on the floor as he changed. Then he dragged her out of the house and bundled her in the back of her car so she could not easily escape, and then he drove them in the direction of the motorway. He had been given all the information about the apartments from Rimes and he repeatedly told Louise that he knew every detail of our long weekend together. Some of what he was saying was a figment of his own imagination, but the crux of it was true.

"He's been shagging you!" he screamed at Louise, and as much as I hated the expression, when it was put to me I'd never denied it.

"Andy made love to me," she replied, "which is more that you ever did!"

"You're a whore! You might have a fancy mummy and daddy, but you let him shag you. Well, we'll go and have a look at this little love-nest of yours, maybe you can show me just how he made love to you, if that's the way you like to describe it. Then I'm going to beat the fuck out of you. See what he thinks of you then, shall we!"

Gary's attitude changed after they had stopped so Louise could use the loo. Upon her return she mentioned Rimes had been to her mother and father. She painted a more lurid picture of Rimes standing looking at the children in the bath, and it was enough for Gary to confess he had been transporting the drugs around the Country, and on a few occasions pornographic material he brought into the Country following his visits abroad. The photos of naked men and women didn't bother him. It was the images of the small defenceless children that really did upset him, so much so that he'd snapped the year before when he was in Holland. The result was he'd killed the crooked customs officer.

It also brought out the anger he felt towards Rimes, for he had been using Gary all along for his own devices. But it wasn't Rimes behind the drug smuggling, even Gary wasn't sure who could be, he'd just been the transportation behind the outfit, and as Alex had put it, what better way to move things around the Country than "Her Majesties Mail" and all for free. His task was to stop en route at various service stations, go and use the facilities and upon return to his truck the consignment of drugs would have been loaded or unloaded as the case may be. He seldom handled the stuff he was transporting.

As Alex had also pointed out, he received his instructions via the redirected mail. The reason he checked the phone numbers each night was that a confirmation was given in the coded telephone no.: if it ended in an odd number then the shipment was off, but if it ended in an even number then the job was on. Sometimes the telephone number was used as a location as well, so Gary had quite a complex task of sorting out his pick-up and drop-off point, but as he told Louise, it paid well.

It was twelve-thirty by the time Gary and Louise arrived at the apartments. Gary pulled her by a clump of hair and dragged her to the back of the buildings, climbed over the dividing fence, still holding onto her hair, forcing her to do the same, then broke into the apartment by breaking the lock on the patio door, leaving it open after his forced entry.

Once inside he started to subject Louise to a string of verbal and then physical abuse, forcing her into each room in the apartment, asking if she enjoyed having sex in this room or the other. Louise was crying. With tears of fear running down her face she begged him not to hurt her anymore, and fell to the floor.

"Please Gary, don't!" she pleaded. "No more. I can't take any more your hurting me."

"Well, you shouldn't have messed around with bastard, should you?" Gary shouted as he kicked Louise again, in so doing catching her handbag strap with his shoe. When he pulled his foot back the contents spilled across the floor of the lounge.

For a moment Gary stood looking at the mobile phone on the floor. Louise's sobs didn't mean anything to him, he was just focused on the item had been expelled from her bag.

"And what the fuck have we here?" he asked, picking up the phone. "I suppose lover-boy gave you this. Well, let's see if it works after this," he said as he threw it across the room and it disintegrated against the wall. "And what else has he bought you?"

With those words he again grabbed Louise's hair and pulled her to her feet, her tiny frame bruised and beaten again, as her father put it so eloquently, by a brute of a man. He was just about to make his way up the staircase again when he paused. Something caught his eye as he passed the front door, it was Andy's car entering the track from the lane.

***

I was approaching a slow moving vehicle on the A30 when I glanced in the mirror. I could see two burning headlights coming up from behind, too close together to be a police car, and instantly thought it was a police motorcyclist. They appeared to be flashing, so I slowed slightly after passing the obstruction and returned to the near-side lane. The motorbike went past me like a bullet leaving a gun. I could see it had two people on it, both dressed in full black leathers, the blacked-out visors obscuring my view of their faces. I gave chase thinking that if they were to get past any speed detecting equipment so would I, but my attempt to follow them was futile and fruitless. Whether they saw me and didn't want to take part in a chase I couldn't tell, for with just a puff of light blue smoke from the twin exhausts, they disappeared into the distance at what must have been breakneck speed.

With the bike still just in my sights the mobile rang. I hastily grabbed it and pressed the keypad to take the call.

"Mr Jackson." It was the voice of the Inspector. "Are you driving, Mr Jackson?"

"You fucking bet I am!" I replied.

"I hope I don't need to remind you of the dangers of talking on a phone while driving, Mr Jackson," the Inspector said.

"Listen, you can remind me all you fucking like but I'm afraid I won't be taking any notice, and for that matter neither would you if you were in my position," I told him.

"What seems to be the problem?" he asked, a little impatient with me.

"Well, the problem is Mr Shaw. He's kidnapped his wife and is taking her to my apartment. Now there is only one person he could have got the information from, that we had been away together, and as it wasn't you I'm sure I don't have to tell you who that person is," I screamed back at him.

"Oh shit!" he replied. "You mean Rimes?"

"Yes I do," I said, feeling a bit better as he had proved he was capable of grasping the plot. "I must tell you there are one or two other thing you don't know about Rimes, and our friend Gary." And I went on to relay the things Alex had told me yesterday, and also explained Gary and I had met in the car park.

"Listen," the Inspector started, and went on, "where are you, and how long before you get to your apartment?"

"I'm about fifty miles away. At this speed, I think forty-five minutes and I'll be there," I said.

"Ok, I'm on my way," Jones said. "I'll come under escort with some back up. You know we can really get a move on. Whatever you do don't get into any trouble with him; from what you've told me he sounds as if he could be very volatile. Just take it easy, I'll call on the local chap for back up."

"Well, I hope he'll be more use at this sort of thing than keeping an eye on us, or for that matter finding my bloody car," I said.

"Just keep calm," I could hear him saying to me. "Call me if there's a problem when you arrive."

I put the phone down on the seat and paid more attention to driving, for now I was coming to the end of the dual carriageway and I realised I needed to exercise a great deal more caution. I drove steadily for the remaining part of my journey, my mind in complete disarray, all the time hoping Louise would be alright, and that thought was at the forefront of my mind as I pulled off the lane and onto the track leading to the apartments.

I could see Louise's car parked outside the apartment number four. No other cars were in the courtyard and it appeared as if all the apartments were empty. I stopped at the same place I had with her in the car on that first occasion, just the other side of the cattle grid, only for a few seconds to gather my thoughts. I didn't know what I was going to discover, but then nor had I on that Maundy Thursday, but now I was fearful of what I may find. I opened the window of the car as I slowly drove towards the courtyard. Just to the right, before the entrance to the courtyard, is a passing space. I was approaching this when the door of the apartment opened. I could see Gary, his left hand firmly holding onto Louise's hair. I quickly pulled into the bay and turned the engine off.

The silence was as before, only now it was to be broken not by skylarks singing high above, nor by sheep off in a distant field, no, it was Gary that brought an end to this relative peace.

"Nice place you've got here," he shouted across the courtyard, his face bruised and battered from our encounter yesterday. "She's been telling me about the weekend you had here."

"Andy," Louise started, "I haven't told him anything. Look what he's done to me," she said as she put her hand to show her cut lip, tears running down her cheeks, her whole body shaking with fear.

I made my way a few yards at a time to get a little closer, and stood on the small ridge close to the garage block, mainly so I didn't have to shout.

"Gary," I said, trying to appease him, "we can sort this out." But before I had a chance to finish Gary cut me short.

"Sort it out? Like you brought her here and fucked her! You've got to be off your head. Do you think I'm stupid? I've been thinking about you two since we met yesterday. You just got lucky then, but now I'm going to kill the both of you; maybe her first or the other way round." His tone was as yesterday, quiet and calculated. He meant business, but just as he said the words I heard another car approaching from behind me. Looking at Gary I could see his attention was drawn to the sound, and I took the opportunity to glance behind.

That's all we need now, I thought. It was Rimes. He pulled his car in behind my Lotus, got out and made his way in my direction.

There was an unpleasantness about Rimes, even in the way he walked. His presence made me feel very uncomfortable, more so now that I knew about his past and what he was into. Gary was angry enough, without Rimes fuelling it even more.

"Gary, mate," he said as he walked towards me, a smug grin on his face. "I see you found their little love-spot then. I gave you good directions, didn't I?" He was looking at the two figures standing in the doorway.

"Don't fucking mate me, you perverted bastard," Gary shouted at him. "And stop where you are, that's it, next to him." He pointed at me. He then slid his right hand inside his jacket and to our terror produced a gun.

"Oh, no!" Rimes said, fear in his voice.

"Yes. I've brought my own present back from Belgium this time, just something for me," he said, pointing the weapon in our direction. I could see the terrified expression on Louise's face and I was powerless to do anything about it, unable to offer help in any form.

"Listen Rimes," Gary said, "It's bad enough finding someone's been fucking your Mrs, then I find some dirty little shit has been trying to get their hands on my kids."

"No, it wasn't like that," Rimes replied in his mouse-like way.

"Don't tell me what it was like," Gary responded. Now he was extremely upset and Rimes was to be on the receiving end of his anger. "I've seen some of that stuff you like to look at. I didn't realise it was for you when I was bringing it back into the Country. I thought you moved it, but no, I find you've been looking at my children in the bath at her parents' house. You're twisted; there's something wrong with you. Well, I'll put paid to your antics."

With those words he pulled the gun up to waist height and unloaded a single shot. The bullet hit Rimes in the centre of his crotch and blood flew in every direction, covering my legs and even my face. Louise let out a scream of fear as Rimes cried out, falling backwards to the ground. He must have been in uncontrollable pain. He was writhing in agony, so much that he was unable to utter a word, but just gasped for breath. His hands were covering the entry point of the bullet, blood pumping through his fingers.

I looked across at the two of them, and Gary was preparing to fire the gun again.

"Don't!" I screamed, fear in my voice. "I can help you! Gary, I can get the best lawyer money can buy. Don't kill him, he's not worth it."

"You help me?" he shouted back at me. "Like you've had my wife and you think you can buy me off. Well, don't you remember what I just told you? Now I've had a change of plans. I'm going to kill her first and then you, just so I can see you suffer as this little tart dies."

"Gary, please don't," Louise begged him. "Think of our babies, what will they do without us, they'll be alone."

"That's rich coming from you," Gary screamed, looking into her eyes.

"You left them with that wonderful 'mummy' and 'daddy' as you call them so you could come away with that bastard. Don't tell me about being alone." He paused, and some of his own unhappy past was to be revealed. "I spent my entire childhood left on my own. I had to look out for myself, and I've managed alright."

"But Gary, this isn't managing," I told him. I could see his weakness and thought I may be able to befriend him through it. "Killing Louise and me won't change the past; it's the future we all have to think about."

From down by my left side Rimes had now stopped his wriggling. I glanced down at him; he was motionless. I looked long and hard and could see his chest slowly raising and falling, blood still pumping from below his waist. He wasn't dead, but not far away from it. The pain he was in must have been so great he'd passed out. Now as I stood and looked at this pitiful sight on the ground I noticed the silence had returned, only broken by Rimes' shallow breathing, and off somewhere in the distance the sound of a motorbikes engine, just ticking over.

"Is he dead?" Gary asked, but without any concern for Rimes in his voice.

"No! Not yet, and there's still time to save him Gary," I said, desperately playing for time. Somewhere deep inside I thought I might be able to persuade him not to fire the gun again, but I was to be proved wrong, for as I looked across at the two of them he unloaded another single shot straight into Rimes. It hit him in the head, just below his nose. The sound was awful, as he drew his last breath a gurgling sound came from his throat and more blood pumped uncontrollably from a hole in his face. But Rimes didn't make another move; this time he *was* dead.

And my thoughts moved on to Louise and myself. I looked across at her. She was white with fear and shock. Gary looked as if he'd just come out to take in the view.

"That's fucking sorted him then," Gary said, in a somewhat casual tone, but with an arrogance in his manner. He fired another shot into the air, almost in a victorious style, and now he was preparing the gun again.

"Well, are you ready to be the first?" he said, taking the gun up to Louise's head.

"Gary, I can get you out of this mess, and believe me it's going to be a bigger mess when the police arrive," I said, adding, "They do know, I've been in touch with them."

"Yes, I bet you have. And I found the present you bought her: you know, that bloody phone. But it won't work now. And let me tell you something else, mister-know-it-all, they didn't do much in the way of finding me after I killed that bloke in Holland last year did they?"

Now was not the time to inform him that Jan was the brother of the customs man and was in fact after him, not at all interested in the drug running as Gary thought.

"Listen, I can give you a million pounds and get you to another Country," I shouted at him in desperation, as he took the gun closer towards Louise's head.

"Please! Please don't kill her! We both love her and this will be so wrong." I could clearly see her tears and now my own were welling up inside me. The thought of possibly being alone for the rest of my life was too much for me to bear.

"Gary, I gave up everything for you," Louise sobbed. "My friends and most of my family. Please don't." She was starting to fall to the ground, sobbing uncontrollably, begging him not to end her life. I was just about to make a rush on him when he pulled her up by her hair with his left hand. Her scream of pain sent a shiver running down my spine. If I were to make a move it would for certain finish Louise's life. He pulled her to her feet and now had the gun pressed against her temple, so hard I could see the flesh stretching around the muzzle. I felt sick, and my stomach was beginning to retch.

"You got anything to say to this tart before I finish her off?" Gary shouted at me.

"Please don't! Please, let me be first," I pleaded with him, but he just pressed the gun harder into her head.

"I'll always have the lid off the little box," Louise cried across to me, adding, "I do love you."

"And I'll always love you. Forever!" I replied to her. And now I could see that her eyes were in fact closed as she was trying to prepare herself for death. Now my tears could not be contained and I felt them running down my face. My future didn't matter, I was to be next and that would be a relief. Faintly I could hear the sound of sirens and just a glimmer of hope came to me. But Gary was to end that feeling of hope as he spoke.

"I don't know what the fuck you two are talking about but .." he was stopped.

From far behind me slightly to my left I heard a crack, like a stick that breaks under your foot, but this was way off in the distance. I wanted to look round to see what it was but I was transfixed by the horror which was unfolding in front of my eyes. The crack was actually the sound of a high velocity rifle being discharged. The bullet had made contact with Gary just below his chin. The resulting impact threw his head back as it passed through his throat, leaving the back of his neck with a shower of flesh and bones that sprayed blood onto the surrounding walls and partly open door behind him.

He was dead. In an instant, his right hand holding the gun fell lifelessly down to his side and his left hand released the hold on Louise's hair as he started to fall backwards, and as he did blood came spurting out of his now jaw-less face. His eyes were wide open in total surprise of what had hit him. He hit the ground, and Louise let out the most terrifying scream, for she thought it was herself who had been shot. It even appeared to me as if she had been, for she was covered in Gary's blood. Her screams seemed to go on forever as I made my way across to her and took her in my arms. Gary's body lay still and lifeless on the ground by our feet.

I walked Louise away from the porch, just into the courtyard, my arms still wrapped around her and she clinging to me. I was unable to control her nervous shaking, but her screaming had stopped, to be replaced by crying. The wail of the sirens came steadily closer, and the sound of a motorbike joined the other traffic noise, far away on the main road.

I glanced to my right as I felt a presence in the courtyard. There, standing at the far end of the garage block, was Stavros. He was putting a mobile phone back into his inner jacket pocket. He did appear a little paler, but as always had some reassuring words of comfort for Louise and myself.

"My two good friends," he said, as he slowly came towards us, his arms outstretched.

"I couldn't let that happen to you. He had to pay the price!" We both fell into his massive embrace. Louise still sobbing uncontrollably, and my tears of fear had now been replaced with tears of relief.

"But how long have you been here?" I asked, and went on, "How did you know?"

"You never told me to stop looking out for you both. I've been here long enough to see him kill the other chap," Stavros replied. "At least he didn't go through that pain, did he my dear?" he said looking at Louise.

"No," Louise softly replied through her tears, and tightened her grip on me.

"But it wasn't you who killed him," I said.

"Andrew, I told you I had a volunteer. You must trust me," he told me, with his hand on his chest. "I will have to go now," he said, continuing with, "That will be the police. They will think it's their man who put paid to your husband. I'm sure they won't keep you long. When they say you can go, you come to my place, you will need to bathe and rest. Perhaps you would like to stay a few days. I won't rush you. I will see you soon? Yes?"

Jointly we both agreed we *would* see him soon, and as we said our goodbyes he slipped away in the same direction he came from.

We were still in our embrace when Inspector Jones and a whole host of police cars and an ambulance came screaming down the track, lights flashing, sirens blaring.

Chapter Twelve

Jones got out of the first police car, and as he made his way towards us he looked down at the body of Rimes, a massive pool of blood around his head. For a moment he stood gazing down at him, little or no expression on his face. As he came over to us another officer quickly covered Rimes' body with a blanket.

By the time he reached us Louise had stopped crying, but was still trembling. Not that she wasn't still feeling pain, but the discomfort was slowly being replaced by a sense of relief, coupled with the freedom that comes from knowing she would not have to suffer any more pointless beatings.

Jones had just got to us when he turned to inspect the body of Gary. He too was surrounded by blood. It was covering the walls of the porch and inner entrance door. The gun was still in his hand. As he looked down, Jones' right hand came up and he gingerly rubbed his own chin, just momentarily holding it in his hand. He turned and looked at us, both a very pitiful sight, blood across Louise's face as if someone had thrown paint at her, and down the right side of her dress. She was gripping my right hand as Jones spoke.

"Are you two alright?" he asked, then continued, "I mean you haven't been injured. I can see you're both covered in blood, I just need to be sure you haven't been hurt."

"I," Louise started to speak very softly, "have some new bruises, but that's all."

"What about you Mr Jackson?" the Inspector asked.

"I'm ok. Well, apart from being very shocked. That goes for the both of us," I replied.

"I'm sure you are. I'm sorry we couldn't get here sooner, but from what you told me on the phone he was very determined," the Inspector replied.

"I hate these crimes," Jones started. I was very unsure of what he was about to say but as he prepared to carry on more police officers were now running everywhere.

"These are the worse sort, you know. It looks like one man kills his accomplice and then turns the gun on himself, but our man will confirm what went on." He paused, and was now looking me directly in the eyes. "I don't expect either of you to make a statement now, it can wait until tomorrow. Do you have somewhere else locally where you can stay?"

"Yes," I replied, somewhat surprised, but in my shocked and dazed state I felt in no mind to start giving an account of what went on.

"Well, you know you can't stay here, not for sometime anyway," Jones told me.

"I have," I hesitated before continuing, giving Louise's hand a gentle squeeze, "a friend in Truro. I'm sure he won't mind if we call on him." Stavros's words were still in my ears as fresh as when he'd said them a few minutes ago. "It may be best if I ring him just to make sure," I finished.

"Try not to tell him too many details," the Inspector told me, but in his eyes I'm sure he was looking for something else. Then he continued, "Of course I'll need his address, so I can take a statement tomorrow."

"Ok, do you mind if I call him from somewhere else?" I asked, looking towards the end of the garage block.

"That'll be fine," Jones said, and with his words a young police officer covered Gary's disfigured body. As the policeman walked away I thought he was going to be ill. Maybe not used to this side of the job, I thought.

Louise and I made our way to where Stavros had appeared. Standing just out of sight we were able to have our first words together without fear.

"Are you alright?" was all I could ask, as I wrapped my arms around her again.

"I am now but I was so frightened. I thought he was going to kill me. I told myself it was the end and I closed my eyes. I thought I'd never see you again," Louise told me, and her tears began to flow again, mixing with Gary's blood as they ran down her soft cheeks.

"I know my darling, but I couldn't do anything to help you. If I'd tried I felt sure he would have killed you," I said, and continued, "It's best we let Jones come to his own conclusions for the moment. We know we can go to stay with Stavros, so let him think that we've phoned."

After a few minutes we came out from behind the shelter of the garages and made our way back to the Inspector. By now police officers were erecting tents and putting a screen around the entire area. Jones walked across and met us halfway.

"Can you stay with your friend?" he asked.

"Yes, that will be ok," I said, holding onto Louise's hand.

"In that case I'll arrange for an escort to take you." He paused. "Where was it? Truro you said, didn't you?"

"Yes that's right. You don't need to worry about an escort, we'll be fine," I replied.

"No, it's ok, I'll have two cars go with you," he insisted, adding, "We need to look after you two, this could easily have been one of you laying on the floor dead."

He didn't know just how close to the truth he was.

Jones walked us to my car. I opened the door for Louise to get in and as I got to the driver's side Jones told me the Serious Crime Squad had raided Rimes' home and had uncovered piles of pornography, including a lot of images of small children. I felt sick. So the information Alex had given me was correct; but why had it taken the authorities so long to catch up with him? Now it was too late. He also informed me that my Porsche had been found, parked in a disused barn. I tried to look surprised, but all along I'd known it was perfectly safe.

We drove under police escort to Truro, and as we made our way Louise carefully rang ahead and informed Stavros we were on our way. I pulled up outside the entrance to Stavros's home and the police cars stopped as well. The officers from the lead car got out and came back to talk to me, asking if we would be alright. I explained we had reached our destination and wouldn't require them any longer, then they both wished us a good evening but waited for us to enter the driveway before they drove off.

We made our way up the driveway which just over a week ago we had left, happy at being new friends. Now we were returning as frightened, almost wounded, lovers. We'd been taken to the point of death that one can be taken to without dying, and survived. Now we needed some time to reflect on what had happened, and to see where we could go from there, with regard to our relationship and our future together. Yes, we had planned to sort things out with Gary, but never in our wildest dreams did we think he would be dead. But he lived by administering fear and now he was dead; he couldn't frighten anyone anymore. And as consolation we knew he hadn't feared death: to him it didn't exist. He was in charge in life; but he wasn't in control of the situation that had brought about his departure from this world.

Stavros was waiting on the porch to greet us as I pulled up outside the double oak doors. He was alone and beckoned us in, giving Louise the embrace he reserved for special friends. As she stepped from the drive onto the porch he held onto her, looking into my eyes as he ran is big right hand down her blood-stained hair.

"Louise," he paused, maybe to gather the words so she would understand, "it couldn't have been any other way. When you wake in the cold of the night and think it shouldn't have happened, remember there was no choice. I was not prepared to let you or Andrew die." He changed his tone as he ushered us into his home, and as I drew close he put his arms around me. "My good friend!" They were all the words I needed to hear. "Now come with me. You both need a drink." With that statement we made our way into the lounge we had been relaxing in with the rest of the family only a short while ago and he passed Louise a very large brandy glass which was half full. I'd never seen her drink spirits before and she took an enormous mouthful and swallowed it in one go, her eyes half closed as the drink went down. Stavros passed me a very large malt whisky. I did the same as Louise, almost emptying the glass. He took the glasses and refilled them, at the same time pouring a brandy for himself.

"You both need to go and get changed. I have prepared the front bedroom for you; as I told you, stay as long as you want. You are now my guests and my heart is in these words." He stopped and took our hands and brought them together in his massive clasp. "When you came to me at Easter and asked me to help, I did just that. I made some enquires and found there was danger round every corner and I kept my word to you, I looked out for both of you. It will become clearer as time moves on." He paused and we drew closer to him. "Andrew, you are like a son to me, because you are not so proud you won't ask for help. And you Louise," he stopped and then, looking directly into her eyes, smiled and continued. "I told you that my friend is a good man. Now you know the love in his heart is only for you. On the first occasion I met you I could see through these old Greek eyes that you loved him and I told him so, now he will love you forever. Now you take your drinks and go and have a bath. You will find some cloths to fit well enough for the time being. Most of all you need some time together. The rest of the family will be here soon enough," he finished, releasing his grip on our hands.

We made our way up the curved staircase and into the bedroom at the front of the house. It was well appointed, having it's own en-suite. A bath was what Louise required most of all, she told me, so I ran the bath for her and found two bathrobes. Sure enough in the wardrobes were some clothes that would fit us just to get by with. Louise made her way into the bathroom fully dressed and as I sat on the bed undoing my shoelaces, I heard her call me after she had got into the bath.

"Would you please come in Andy?" she asked.

I made my way to the door, my shirt undone to my waist. I'd already removed my shoes. I stood and looked at her small frame lying in the bath: she looked so beautiful, even though she had some new bruises on her body. The water was just covering her breasts and, now the blood was washed from her hair and face, once again I was unable to control my feelings and my tears started to flow; now I was sobbing without shame.

"I thought he was going to kill you. I couldn't have managed life without you," I told her through my tears. She beckoned me to her and I knelt at the side of the bath, her wet hands holding my head against her raised body.

"Come on, get in with me," Louise said. "Together we will wash the blood of this nightmare away."

So I slipped out of my blood-spattered clothing and got into the bath with the woman I love, our naked bodies reunited in water. But it would take some time to heal the injuries of that day and many more baths would be required before we could say we were over this most traumatic of days. We washed each others' bodies, which was the easy part, to wash the outer, but the inner soul would take longer to cleanse. It would require us to relive and talk about what had happened, and in the process discover new truths about some of the people who unknown to us had been close all along.

We finished drying ourselves and managed to find some underclothes, socks, and a pair of jeans, tee shirt and sweatshirt and a pair of trainers that almost fitted, and got myself dressed. Louise was more fortunate than I, for she was almost the same size as Nana, and in the wardrobe she had discovered a cream off-the-shoulder top, and a wrap-round red skirt.

I stood by the window that looked out onto the driveway, Louise behind me, with the clothes she was going to wear spread across the bed. I watched her pull the top over her head and saw she wasn't wearing a bra.

"I couldn't find a bra to fit me," she told me. She was somewhat fuller than Nana, but she had found the smallest of panties and as I watched her pull them up she said, "My private week is over now."

As she wrapped the skirt around herself I looked out of the window and removed my glasses to clean them - they were still dirty from the blood of Rimes - and as I stood and rubbed them to remove the marks I saw something approaching the house; a motorbike. I put my glasses back on. Now either my eyes were playing tricks with my senses or I'd had far more whisky than I thought, for on the bike were two people, both dressed in black leathers. They looked like the same people I'd seen outside my house the other morning, and more importantly it looked like the same bike which had passed me earlier in the day when I was on my way to the apartments. The riders were to be revealed to both Louise and myself before the day was out.

I looked at my now fully dressed Louise. She was sitting at the dressing table and was applying a small amount of makeup, just enough to cover the redness around her right eye. Her upper lip was slightly swollen but the bleeding had stopped.

"How do I look?" she asked, as she got up and came to me.

"Can I say," I paused. "You look remarkably beautiful, considering what we have been through today," I told her, as I gathered her into my arms. She smelt wonderful, a different perfume from her own. She must have sensed I had noticed, for she told me it was something she had found on the dressing table.

"Shall we go down?" I asked, wishing we didn't have to, but soon enough we would have to face the truth about what had gone on that day. I would rather have gone to bed and protected Louise from danger, with my arms wrapped around her under the cover of a duvet.

"Yes, we must," she replied, in a somewhat forceful way, she too knowing that sooner or later we would have to come face to face with the truth and more importantly the person who had put paid to her husband. All of us would need to get our stories straight, for later Louise and I would be required to give statements, but little did we know what was to unfold before the evening had given up the truth, expected or not. Much more was to be revealed and the only way to overcome the events of the day was to be together, and what better place to be with the woman I loved than in the safety of the home of my true and trusted friend Stavros.

So, as we made our way back down the staircase, the empty glasses in my hand, Stavros came out of the lounge to greet us, his hands stretched out in front of him.

"You both look better now." His words echoed our own feelings; some of this was due to the two very large drinks we had consumed before taking our bath, the rest was down to the comfort we felt in his presence.

"Come into the lounge," he said, beckoning us. "Soon we will have supper. Now you may require another drink?" he asked.

"Not so much for me please Stavros," Louise said, and with those words she made her way to him at the drinks cabinet. "And thank you for," she paused, and looking into his old eyes continued, "well, for being you and being here for us." She reached up and kissed him on he cheek, in the same way she used to kiss me, before we had become lovers.

"Louise," he said, taking her hand, "it had to be done and as the evening moves on you will understand more of the things I have told you about this danger that lurked in every corner."

Louise and I sat together on the large three-setter settee, her small body wrapped tightly against mine. Stavros made himself comfortable in a matching chair, and with his glass in his right hand he told us that friends in Holland had given him information which gave him great concern. His contacts were people he had conducted some business with many years ago when he had dealings with the motor industry. Not all of his dealings were above board, as I have said, but he never dealt in drugs.

I felt that he was just about to go into great detail when slowly the door from the dinning room opened. A figure stood dressed in a black leather motorcycle suit, and lifted a hand to undo the clasp of the crash helmet it was wearing. I glanced at Louise. Her eyes were transfixed on this individual, and as they proceeded to pull the helmet from the back of their head a mop of dark hair fell from the inside of the helmet and all was to be revealed.

The dark hair belonged to Marie. Her right hand was still holding the crash helmet as she came towards us. Louise was up and out of the settee to greet her; they embraced and I watched as Marie carefully kissed Louise on both cheeks. No words were exchanged, for no words were required. I also got up from the comfort of the settee and was treated to the same warmth.

Marie released her hold and made her way across to Stavros. He was now standing and they held onto each other. I'd never seen him display affection towards his wife before and this did seem somewhat strange, but at the same time necessary, and his big right arm wrapped around her.

Our attention was once again drawn to the doorway leading to the dinning room, for standing there was the other person from that motorbike. In the same manner as Marie the helmet was pulled off to reveal the shorter and not so dark hair of Nana. In her left hand she was holding a long black gun case. She propped it against the wall and came straight to us. Louise had a look of surprise about her, but as Nana put her arms around her the surprise turned to a look of relief. And for the first time the silence was broken by Nana's words to Louise.

"I had been watching Gary for a long time." She paused and took my hand. "I could see he was hurting you Louise, and after he killed the other man I knew it was only a matter of time before he took his anger out on the both of you." She stopped to look across at her Father.

Stavros nodded at her, giving the signal for her to continue.

"It took Father some time to get in place, but once there he was able to tell me just how much danger you both were in." She stopped to pull down the full-length zip on the leather suit and she then stepped out of it. "I do hope you aren't angry with me," she said as she shook her hair into place. I thought I could see a tear in her eyes but my mind was to be taken off that as Louise spoke.

"I'm not angry with you," she said, pulling Nana closer to her again. "You may have taken away the father of my children but you've released me from the prison I've been held in for years and you saved my life. I'm not sure what I feel," she finished.

"Andy," Nana said, "I couldn't see your face so I had no idea what you were going through. You've been Father's friend for so long, I can't remember when we first met. This must have been awful for you." With those words she came closer and embraced me. "You looked so happy together every time I saw you." She paused, and then continued to enlighten us in what she had seen going on, unbeknown to either Louise or myself.

"Yes, I was never far away from you. Marie made sure we got about safely and quickly on the motorbike." She looked across at Marie, who smiled and nodded in agreement.

With that Stavros put his hand up and spoke for the first time since the young ladies had come into the room.

"Andy, you come with me and we will let these ladies continue with their conversation. Marie and Nana will want to get changed, no doubt." He paused and looked at Louise. "I'm so sorry, my dear Louise, that was very inconsiderate of me."

"No, its ok Stavros," Louise replied, as she moved closer to him. "I do need to have a chat with the girls and I know Andrew will be safe with you." With those words she kissed him on his cheek and added, "Thank you once again."

Stavros ushered me out of the lounge and into the dinning room. On the table was a bottle of wine; he picked it up and went to the unit and got a corkscrew.

"Could you, please, my friend?" he asked, passing me the two items, "but only if you want to," he added.

"I do want to, but I'll need to have a clear head in the morning," I said, and continued, "We may have to see the police tomorrow."

As I was pushing the handles down on the corkscrew I heard what I presumed to be a car door close, so I made my way to the window that looked out at the rear of the house.

The house is built into the side of a hill and as a result the back of the property is higher than the front. Under the dining room and kitchen is a double garage, and the drive sweeps round to a large paved area. I looked down and in the courtyard was a white transit van. I could see two figures bending over in the back of the van, then one stood up straight and turned and looked up at Stavros and myself. It was one of the so-called workers from outside my house. I was lost for words and in my shocked and speechless state I looked at Stavros.

"Yes, I've had terrible trouble with the gas here as well, you know what I mean?" he said, and a wry old grin formed on his face. "I said I would keep an eye open for you and after I learnt some very worrying news from Holland I thought it best if some of the boys got involved."

With those words another van pulled up next to the first one and I could see the driver talking to the man who had been looking up at us.

"Those boys in the second van were not far from Louise's home and also kept a watch at her parents' house," Starvos told me. "I'm sorry to say they missed Louise being kidnapped, but as soon as you pulled out of your drive the others were not far behind you and that left someone to clear up and come on home later. The four of them work for me, it was a bit like a holiday for them, a chance for them to get away from working in the yard over at Falmouth," he said as I poured each of us a glass of wine. "There is of course a lot more I could tell you and you do need to know, but for now we need to be happy that you and the beautiful woman are safe: no harm can come to you here," he finished.

"But Stavros, they aren't your sons, Andreas and Demetri," I said.

"My friend, someone had to look after the business while we were otherwise engaged," he told me.

With that the door from the lounge opened and the three ladies stepped in, with smiles but no outright laughter, for this was still a somewhat sombre occasion. It would be some time before we could all share in humour of the sort we had only a short time ago.

Louise made her way to my side and instinctively we linked arms. "Can I use the phone please?" she asked, looking into my eyes, "I need to ring Mummy and Daddy."

"There is no need for you to ask, my dear," Stavros replied for me. "For as long as you are here treat this as your own home. The phone is in the hall."

"Thank you Stavros. Will you come with me please Andy?" Louise enquired.

"Yes of course I will," I told her, taking her hand, and together we made our way though the lounge and into the hall. Louise picked up the receiver but then promptly put it back down again. Then turning to face me she put her arms around my neck and planted her lips on mine, pulling me tightly against her in a way I hadn't experienced her doing before. The kiss seemed to last forever and I could feel her tongue forcing its way into my mouth. I could taste the brandy still fresh on her tongue. I have to say I was somewhat surprised by her actions, but didn't feel a need to complain. I could feel her hand on the back of my neck holding our lips together, and when her grip was released and we drew apart to draw breath, Louise looked into my eyes.

"I really do love you so much. When that gun was so tight against my head I thought I would never be able to hold you again, let alone kiss you," she told me in a very soft and quiet tone. "I'm not going to tell Mummy or Daddy that Gary is dead, it can wait until everything has been sorted out." With that she pulled me close again and she performed that same erotic act on me. "For now I want to be with you. Please say you'll never leave me," she asked, when we had parted for the second time.

"I'll never leave you, I love you too much. Now that I've got you I'm going to look after you and keep you," I told her. "I do need to ask you some questions, but my darling they will keep for later, for now I'm yours."

She picked up the receiver again and dialled the number of the big house in Scotland. As it rang she slipped her arm round me and again pulled me close to her. It took no encouragement for me to put my arm round her, and we stood locked together as she spoke to her mother and then the children. In between she kissed me very gently on my cheek, and as the children paused to reply to her questions she told me quietly that she loved me. We must have been on the phone for almost twenty minutes, until she concluded the conversation with her customary, "Goodnight and God bless," kissing me again as she replaced the receiver.

We made our way back into the dinning room and as on the last occasion when we had been gathered together supper was progressing well. I opened another bottle of wine and together Louise and I laid the table.

"Stavros," I asked, "will the boys be coming for dinner?"

"Yes my friend. The men from the yard have gone now and I'm sure Andreas and Demetri won't be very long. They'll be pleased to see you both again," he replied, adding, "They knew what was going on and won't break any confidences we share with them, but you already know that anyway."

So Stavros, Louise and myself sat at the dinning table as Nana and Marie prepared the dinner in the kitchen. After twenty minutes the meal was brought in and just as we were serving ourselves I heard a car pull up at the back of the house, then two doors slam, and within a few minutes Stavros's sons were in the room with us. They'd made their way in via the kitchen entrance at the back of the house.

Both Louise and myself stood to greet them and, as on the last occasion we had been together, they made a considerable fuss of both of us. Then we were invited to resume our places at the table. I was about to propose a toast when I noticed Demetri talk to his father in fluent Greek, and heard Stavros reply in his native tongue; just what he said and what his father's reply was I'd have to wait to discover.

We sat and ate together and each of us relived the events of the afternoon as seen through our own eyes. Nana talked of her concern of missing with that shot, as she told us she had only one chance. Louise cried as she retold her fear of dying when the gun was held to her head, but now I was able to comfort her. I drew great comfort from being part of this very close family, for that was what we were, indeed closer than many people can ever get even in their own families.

"But where did you learn to shoot with such accuracy?" I asked Nana.

"My friend," Stavros replied for her, "its amazing what they teach these young women at private schools these days!"

"Father is right," Nana said, and went on to tell us in great detail how she had taken up her role of protecting us from day one and, with the skilful driving of Marie on the motorbike, had managed to keep a very close eye on us. She had indeed given me the thumbs up signal on the Easter Sunday night when they sped past us, as we were en-route to the restaurant. It was Marie I'd seen outside my house on that morning, and her motorbike I'd heard in the car park of the pub yesterday when Gary and I had a confrontation. But more importantly it was Marie and Nana who had raced past me when I was driving so urgently to the apartments. She told us they needed to be in place before I arrived. It had never been her intention to kill Gary. She was hoping that either the Inspector would arrive first, or the local man would be able to take care of things. As it happened the local officer was at the scene but was fast asleep, for this man had a terrible drink problem and spent a considerable amount of his time in the pub. In fact Nana was able to inform us she had overheard a conversation he was having on the Easter Monday saying he had been assigned to look after "some rich bastard", as he'd put it.

She explained to us he wasn't difficult to keep an eye on, as he was never far away from the local. Nana then told us that she met her father at the top of the track. He'd brought the gun with him from the family home and when he got himself in position was able to give instructions to Marie over the mobile telephone, and she in turn passed the information onto Nana. And it was Nana who had taken the decision to end Gary's reign of terror but only when it was obvious he would not back down.

"So you both see now there was no other way we could have saved you," Stavros said, standing up with his wine glass in his hand.

"Stavros, the Inspector thinks it was a suicide," I said, for his words had just come back to me.

"Yes that's right," Louise added. "He said these are the worse sort of crimes; one man kills his accomplice and then turns the gun on himself."

"Those were his very words," I said.

"Then we must let the Inspector lead the way," Stavros said. "For now I propose a toast," he continued, "to my new family members."

And the rest of the family toasted us with our names, "Louise, Andrew and the family!"

We both stood and thanked them for saving our lives, each and every one of them had done something to help protect us. We had tears in our eyes, but they were tears of joy.

"Now, Andrew," Stavros began, "there is one very big danger I am sure you are very aware of." He paused and poured himself another glass of wine and passed the bottle across to me, then turned to indicate to Andreas that more was required and Andreas got up and left us. "His name is Jan, and as your friend Alex told you in the pub, he is," he paused, "well, I think the best way to describe him is unstable. Now you know he is very good at disappearing, but we are very good at finding lost items." He stopped and emptied his glass into his mouth, swallowed hard and then continued. "The boys were coming by your apartments and just happened to find Jan. It would seem that he had been following Rimes, and it was his intention for Gary to have a little accident in repayment for his brother being killed by Gary last year. Oh yes, my friends in Holland were able to give me a full outline of what has been happening in the last year. The Dutch authorities were somewhat puzzled, but also relieved that he was out of the Country. He's wanted for one or two crimes in Holland you know." He stopped as Andreas came back into the room with two more bottles of wine.

Andreas passed the wine to Demetri, who opened both bottles and refilled our glasses.

"What I think Father is concerned about telling you, Andy and Louise, is," Demetri began, he turned and looked at his Father and then at Andreas and both signalled for him to continue. "We have Jan, as you might say, as our guest. He's something of a reluctant guest and so you see we are all now involved."

"And this brings us to the subject of what are we going to do with him," Stavros said. He looked at Louise and myself and our faces prompted him to add, "You've no need to worry, he is quite secure. He can't cause any harm to you, but should we turn him over to the police in this Country, or arrange for him to be sent back to Holland? I'm sure the authorities there would welcome him with open arms." He paused and put his elbows on the table bring his hands together, interleaving his fingers. "Of course," he said, "we may be able to use him as the assassin if the police start to make things difficult; after all he had every reason to want your husband out of the way Louise."

"But Stavros, maybe it's best if we sleep on this decision," Louise said, adding, "well, at least wait until we've been interviewed by the police."

"Yes, that's very good. Another day won't make that much difference," Stavros said, and then emptying his wineglass he gestured for all of our glasses to be refilled. Louise put her right hand over the top of her glass indicating that she'd had sufficient.

"If you will please excuse me," Louise said, standing up, for now it was ten o'clock. She looked at me. "I feel in need of my bed."

With those words the boys were up and I too stood.

"Will you please excuse both of us?" I asked, taking Louise's hand.

"That will be fine, you've both had the most trying of days," Nana said.

One by one they wished us a goodnight and we made our way out of the dining room through the lounge, into the hall and up the stairs, Louise in front of me with my hands wrapped around her waist. As we reached the landing at the top my hands slipped up over her tummy and came up to cup her breasts. She spun round and looked me directly in the eyes.

"You said you had some questions you wanted to ask me," she said, putting her hands behind me and pulling her body close to mine.

"Yes I have, but if you like they can wait until the morning," I replied.

"No, I'm ready to answer you tonight," she told me as we made our way into the bedroom and I closed the door behind me.

Louise sat on the edge of the bed and I positioned myself on the stool by the dressing table with my back to the mirror. Looking straight into her blue eyes I felt compelled to tell her I loved her. I would repeat it all night long.

"Well?" Louise asked. "If the answers to your questions aren't what you expect will it change the way you feel about me?"

"No, my darling. I loved you for so long secretly and now that it's in the open nothing will change the way I feel about you," I told her.

"Where do you intend to start, the beginning of our relationship or where we go from here?" she asked me.

"I know you love me, so I've no questions about now, also I feel we have plenty of time for the future," I said. "I wondered if you had ever thought about me. You were on my mind many times after I'd stopped phoning you. I wanted to call you, but" I stopped. I was about to reveal feelings I had been able to control, but now I just needed some assurance that I had done the right thing. I regained my thoughts and continued, "I stopped ringing you because I was upsetting myself, not because I was getting in the way. I'd wanted to ask you out long before I'd seen you in Smiths. I told you at Easter that I'd loved you for a long time, but if you'd never thought of me, then that Friday in December really was a chance meeting."

Louise leant across and took my hands. "Well, if it's the truth you want!" She paused and kissed me on my lips, not forcefully, just a touch, and then pulled back. "No, after you stopped phoning I didn't think of you, but when we met again before Christmas those calls came back to me. I felt so lonely, being on my own all the time, then when you rang me a week later and I felt lifted, you gave me something to look forward to, a hope to escape from my nightmare life. You showed me you still cared and you'd kept your promise. I hadn't been able to see that all those years ago, but then I remembered you had tried to show me when we worked together. I put you off, thinking things would be ok and I'd be happy. But all that time with Gary had left me very downtrodden, and your call each week after we'd met kept me going. He could tell and said I seemed more cheery, then he got very suspicious as every Wednesday there was a withheld number on the phone. He even said one time there was someone on my mind and it was you. But I didn't love you." She still had hold of my hands and squeezed them.

"On one occasion a long time ago you said you were frightened." I had to ask her, as it had played on my mind for a long time after the initial friendship had become dormant.

"I wasn't frightened of you." She paused, still looking into my eyes. "No, I was frightened by the feelings I found I had for you. I thought I shouldn't feel them for anyone else. If Gary hadn't come along and I'd met you we could have probably been together sooner," she told me.

I didn't feel let down by her words. I'd asked for the truth and that was what I had received. Then came her words of reassurance, "That was then, but now I love you with every part of me. I want to be with you and tonight, despite what has happened today, I'm going to make love to you. We can and should be together forever," she told me as she guided my hands up and under the loose fitting top. Her breasts felt so warm, firm and rounded, I stroked her nipples with my thumbs and instantly she coloured up.

"Come, get onto the bed," she told me as she stood up and I did as I was instructed. I undid the laces of the trainers and Louise pulled them off, then she turned her attention to my top, gently pulling the sweatshirt and tee shirt off in one movement. Her lips were then planted upon my naked chest, kissing me from my tummy to my own nipples, and all the time I was calling her name and telling her that I loved her. She positioned herself so that I could remove her own top so as to reveal her exquisite body to me, and crouched over me just far enough away that I had to lift my head slightly to kiss and then suck each of her delightful breasts. Carefully she removed my remaining clothing and her own, when she felt the need to. I was aroused and she took full advantage of my state, bringing about more enjoyment for me, and her own state of readiness was revealed to me as I caressed the more intimate areas of her body.

She continued to make tender love to me, long into the night. Many times we shared orgasm after orgasm, and fell asleep with the new day's sun coming up over Truro, our naked bodies locked together, and our future was to be set from that day forever.

Chapter Thirteen

Thursday

We awoke to a gentle knocking on the bedroom door. I managed to find my glasses and after we'd covered ourselves with the duvet and repositioned ourselves in the bed I called out "Come in." Slowly the door opened and Marie stepped in carrying a tray holding a teapot and two cups and saucers, milk jug and sugar bowl, along with a plate of biscuits. Very softly Marie spoke to both of us.

"Good morning," she said, looking at us cuddled together in the king sized bed, for Louise had wrapped herself around me and I could feel her naked warmth close to my own naked body.

"And good morning to you," we replied together in our sleepy relaxed state.

"I hope you slept well," Marie asked as she placed the tray on the small bedside table. The cups chinked together as she put it down.

"We did," Louise said. "And thank you once again for all you have done."

Marie put her hand up. "You've both said thank you enough times now, there really is no need for either of you to say it again."

"Ok," Louise replied.

"Have you any idea what the time is?" I asked, as I didn't have my watch on and in my half-awake state couldn't remember where I'd put it.

"Its nine-thirty Andy," Marie told me. "And I'm just going to fix some breakfast. Would you like me to bring something up for you? Or will you be down?"

"Oh, I think we'll be down in about half an hour after we've had a shower," Louise replied to her. After Marie made her way out of the bedroom, we sat together in bed and drank the tea, managing to get two cups each out of the small pot, then Louise made her way to the bathroom, telling me she wouldn't be long.

I lay in bed with my mind going over what had gone on yesterday and the events had a somewhat haunting effect upon me. I was reassured by the words Stavros had spoken - It couldn't have been any other way. He was of course right. I was brought back from my thoughts by Louise calling to inform me that she had finished in the shower. As I entered the bathroom Louise was standing drying herself. I looked at her naked body and saw that now the bruises she had gained yesterday were beginning to reveal themselves. I touched them as I approached her but she didn't jump.

"Do they hurt?" I enquired.

"No," was her reply. "It's not as bad as last time and it helps because I know he won't be able to do anything like that to me again."

I had a shave and then a quick shower, and in less than twenty minutes we were ready to go down for our breakfast. Together we descended the staircase, Louise carrying the tray that Marie had brought the tea on. We made our way into the dining room via the lounge. Stavros was already sitting at the table and stood up as we entered.

"Good morning to both of you," he said, as he put a large mug back down on the table. "I trust you both slept well."

"We did indeed." Louise answered for the both of us.

"The boys have already eaten and gone off to work," Stavros told us as Nana brought in a fresh pot of tea. Marie stood at the open door that leads into the kitchen.

"Would you like a full English breakfast or something lighter?" she asked.

I looked at Louise. "Something light would be fine," was her reply. "Have you any cornflakes?"

"Yes indeed and I'll do some toast. Will that be ok for you Andy?" Nana enquired.

"Yes, that will be perfect, thank you very much," I said.

The five of us sat at the table and ate our breakfast and discussed what we would do with the day. All of us agreed that it might be best if we stayed in the house, at least until the police had been to take our statements. That was unless they wanted us to go to the police station. Nana and Marie had just cleared the table when I heard the doorbell ring. I looked at Louise. She took my hand and I could feel her shaking slightly. I too felt nervous. Nana made her way to the front of the house, and as she did so Stavros reminded us of the tack we were to take, adding that if there were any problems then we could demand to have a solicitor present.

We could hear voices and they got louder as Nana led them in the direction of the dining room. One voice I recognised as Inspector Jones, the other voice I couldn't place but it had a local accent. In an instant Stavros was up and as he passed me he winked. He made his way to the lounge door, opened it and went through into the other room. I could hear him talking but neither Louise nor I could make out what was being said. Then it went very quite and the door opened, Stavros came back into the room with us and closed the door as he did so.

"I have told them you are both still in a state of shock," he said very quietly to us both. "Things are looking good. The black guy has said he won't keep you long, just needs to confirm one or two things. And it's alright for Nana and I to stay with you both," he finished, as he gestured for us to follow him into the lounge.

Louise held on very tightly to my hand as we slipped into the big room and positioned ourselves on the settee. Both the Inspector and the other man stood as we entered the room.

"Mrs Shaw and Mr Jackson," the Inspector started, "I fully understand this must still be a very distressing time for both of you, in particular you, Mrs Shaw." He paused and both of them resumed their seated positions. "Seeing your husband die in such an awful manner couldn't have been easy, most unpleasant."

"Yes, it was terrible," Louise replied, and gave my hand a squeeze as her left hand came up to wipe away a tear. "Nana, do you have any more tissues please?" she asked.

"Indeed I have," Nana said. She made her way to the unit by the window, turned and passed a box of tissues to Louise.

"Thank you," Louise said in return, taking the box from her. "I'm sorry Inspector, this has been very trying you know."

"Yes it must have been, but if it is any consolation," the Inspector stopped again and looked at the other man. "I'm very sorry, it's very rude of me, I haven't introduced this gentleman. This is Sergeant Mitchell, the local man we assigned to look after you both, and he has some rather distressing news to impart to both of you." Jones paused and looked very closely at the two of us cuddled together on the big settee.

"Unfortunately, my initial theory about your husband's death was incorrect." He stopped again and I had a job to maintain a steady look at him. Louise sobbed just slightly and I suppose Nana and Stavros were thinking the same as I was: that our story may not hold up and we may have to use Jan after all. He may well be innocent but he did have a past, and good reason to have Gary out of the way.

"I have come to see you both today to inform you that," the Inspector stopped again, obviously trying to pick his words with some care, but before he could say any more Louise interrupted him.

"Stavros, could I have a drink of water?" she asked.

"Yes," he said, but before he could get up the Inspector stopped him.

"You may require something stronger, Mrs Shaw," he said. "Well, what I have come to tell you is that Sergeant Mitchell saw everything. I think it's best he brings us up to date with what he saw."

"Yes," the sergeant said, "It's better if I explain what I saw." His strong Cornish accent emphasised his words and what he was about to impart to us. "You see, I had taken up position in a very secluded spot, as instructed by the Inspector, to keep a safe eye on the both of you." He paused and looked across at Stavros. "When the call came from the Inspector I was in place very quickly and I could tell after that other fellow was shot by your husband, Mrs Shaw, you were in grave danger. I even had my gun ready. Yes, I'd been issued with one since being assigned to the case, but" he stopped and was now scratching his head and looking at Louise, "it wasn't me who shot your husband."

His words left me feeling a little lifeless. What was the man who had been sleeping on the job about to come out with next? Had he seen more than we had given him credit for, or was he just making things up as he went along? After all, Nana had said he was asleep when she'd seen him. Just how much had he seen? Louise pulled in tighter to my side and took hold of my hand, for she too was having her own concerns about what was to be revealed. I noticed the Inspector look at us; we must have looked very cosy, albeit still in a state of shock.

"I was about to take my aim when," he paused, looked at Jones and asked, "If you don't mind sir I think I could do with a drink, and something stronger than water."

And he was about to reveal the weakness that had been pointed out by Nana.

"Indeed, on this occasion I don't think it will do any harm. Perhaps Mrs Shaw and Mr Jackson would like that strong drink now as well," the Inspector said, adding, "I'll just have an orange juice."

With his words Stavros was up and over to the drinks cabinet and I watched him pour three very large brandies: one for Louise, one for the sergeant and one for himself. As he was out of the Inspector's and sergeant's eyesight he shrugged his shoulders, indicating he didn't know what was to come next, then he poured two large measures of malt whisky. Lastly he took a glass and filled it with orange juice. He passed the glasses to each of us: Louise first, and then much to my surprise a glass of whisky for Nana. She may well have been in need of it as her colour seemed to have drained from her. Then there was a malt whisky for me, and a brandy for the sergeant, and finally the orange juice for the Inspector. He then resumed his seated position with his own brandy glass in his hand.

I watched as Mitchell emptied the brandy glass into his mouth and then swallowed hard. Louise squeezed my hand and took a sip from her own glass. The sergeant then looked more composed. Like someone just having had a fix he was now ready to continue.

"Yes as I was saying, I was in position and could see what was going on."

"What, Gary holding onto Louise's hair?" I interrupted, almost trying to giving him a hand. "And the gun against her head?"

"Yes that's right. That's when I realised you were in real danger," he continued, looking at his empty glass. "I was just getting my aim correct," he carried on, as Stavros took his glass and refilled it. "I had him in my sights when from behind me I heard the shot that put paid to him. It was an awful experience, you both came so close to death." He took the fresh brandy glass and emptied it again in one swift movement.

"Thank you sergeant, that's put us in the picture," the Inspector said. "Is that an accurate account of what happened?"

"Yes," Louise and I said together.

"Well in that case, if you wouldn't mind signing these prepared statements it will be one part of this awful business out of the way," the Inspector replied, passing us the typed statements.

I looked at both of them and they were indeed a very good report of what had happened yesterday afternoon, in fact I couldn't have given a clearer account of the proceedings. We each signed our copy and returned them to Inspector Jones.

"So we know that Gary shot Rimes, but as it wasn't suicide and it wasn't the sergeant who shot your husband, then who was it?" the Inspector asked, as he glanced round the room eyeing each of us. Louise put her head into my shoulder and quietly sobbed.

"What we do know is the man who was with Gary when you got a beating was supposed to be finding out how things worked in this Country, with regard to the movement of the drugs. Well, let's say that is what we were meant to believe." Jones stopped and looked at me. I began to feel very uncomfortable and almost felt as if he was going to accuse me of orchestrating the whole affair, including Gary's death.

The Inspector crossed his legs before continuing. "But after the events of yesterday I made some very forceful enquires of my own." He paused, maybe trying to catch us out. "And I discovered I'd been kept in the dark about a lot of things. Only after a great deal of shouting at other people, including some very senior officers, did I find out this chap's name - Jan Van-Elderman, that is right isn't it Mr Jackson?" He was looking me straight in the eyes.

"Yes that's right," I replied. Well, it was more of a mumble.

"Then I also found out," Jones went on, "that this Jan has, or rather had, a bit of a grudge to settle with your husband on account of the fact it was his brother who was killed in Holland last year. You know, the one Mr Shaw was suspected of having something to do with." He stopped and took a drink from the glass he had been holding before he continued, "So we now consider Jan to be the prime suspect. It makes sense that he had every motive to kill your husband Mrs Shaw." He stopped looked long and hard into his glass and twirled the contents. "Now," the Inspector started again, "it seems to me that you, Mr Jackson, appear to be one step ahead of us in all of this and I'm wondering just where you've been getting your information from. I know you're not connected with anything to do with drug running, but you were able to inform me about Rimes before I'd found out any information, and that made me seem like a bit of a chump. I feel as if I've been wandering around in the dark," he finished, and put his half-empty glass on the coffee table in front of him.

"Well, let's just say I have one or two friends in unusual places and in times of need I've always been able to call upon them for help and advice, this being just one of those occasions," I told the Inspector.

"And where exactly does this gentleman and, I take it, his family, fit into this occasion," Jones asked looking at Stavros.

"It's like I've said," I started but before I could continue Stavros interrupted me.

"Inspector," Stavros paused. "Andrew came to me as a friend for some advice concerning," he stopped again and rested his chin in his hand, just for a few moments. "Really Inspector, you wouldn't want me to embarrass Mrs Shaw with the delicate details of why Andrew came to see me, would you?"

"No of course not," the Inspector replied, somewhat embarrassed himself.

"Listen Inspector," Stavros began, "we have a saying in the Greek village I come from. If you let a friend down then you let yourself down. That was why I was so willing to put Andrew and Louise up when he called and said they needed somewhere to stay, but until now I've been unaware of the circumstances that led to that request." Stavros stopped and cleared his own glass.

"Ok!" Jones said as he stood up. Then he turned and looked at the sergeant. "Would you mind going on out to the car, I'll be with you in a few moments. Just one other thing I need to discuss with Mr Jackson."

"That's fine sir," the sergeant said as he made his way towards the door that leads into the hall and putting his empty glass on the coffee table as he passed it. As he was approaching the door Nana quickly got up and followed him and was by his side as he got to the door. Faintly we could hear them talking as they made their way out onto the drive.

"I didn't tell you, Mr Jackson, we've brought your car back. I told you we found it in an old barn. We think it had been stored ready to be taken away, stolen to order as you might say. A lot of that goes on in London but I wasn't aware it happened out in the sticks. We've left Mrs Shaw's car parked at the apartments. It's locked up and will be quite safe, and here are the keys." He was still standing upright looking down at Louise and myself. Then he passed her the keys. "There is one other thing, and I understand this has been a very distressing time for you Mrs Shaw, but we are able to release your husband's body. No doubt you will require him to have a proper burial."

I looked at Louise as she looked up at the Inspector, her eyes red, almost sore. The sobbing had been genuine and not, as I thought, put on for the Inspector and sergeant.

"My dear," Stavros intervened, before she could speak. "I will take care of all of the necessary arrangements. You have no need to worry yourself about anything. Oh by the way, Inspector, if you don't mind me saying, the sergeant looked a little distraught. It couldn't have been easy for him you know, watching all that going on and not being able to intervene in any way to help." He got up from his chair ready to shake the Inspector's hand.

"No, you're quite right," the Inspector replied, taking Stavros's hand. "He looked most unwell when he came to see me after the shooting. You two had already left when he appeared from his hideaway. I'm not sure he was prepared for this sort of thing you know. Still, its over for him now, he'll be able to resume his normal duties after he's given a full account. I think we all need to be aware that Jan is about, and make no mistake he's still very dangerous and as far as we know still armed. If he turns up please don't try any heroics, I really don't need any more murders. I'm sorry Mrs Shaw, I didn't mean to be so flippant," he said, looking at my Louise.

I put my arm round her to offer her comfort, and just momentarily she eased away then came in close to me. I felt a little isolated. The events of yesterday coupled with what the police officers had said today were overbearing for me and I couldn't begin to think let alone understand what Louise was going through. The three of us accompanied the Inspector out to the drive, and there behind my Porsche was the Inspector's old Ford. He got into the driving seat and the sergeant made his way to the passenger side. As he opened the door he looked back. He didn't say a word. He didn't have to; his face spoke a thousand words. He climbed in and Jones started the car; a rattle of the diesel engine and a plume of thick smoke and they were on their way. The four of us stood and watched as the car made it's way along the drive until it had rounded the bend by the entrance and they were out of sight.

I felt empty and drained. We hadn't lied, but there again we hadn't been asked to tell the truth. We'd let them think an innocent man was guilty of this most necessary of crimes. Louise's hand felt limp and almost lifeless in mine. I looked at her and she was now sobbing uncontrollably. Stavros came to her side and led us indoors and Nana followed us.

"I knew it would be worse the day after." His words had a fatherly ring to them, as when comforting an injured child. "Come my child," he said, putting his arm round Louise's shoulder to comfort her. And as they made their way back into the lounge, I followed with Nana.

"The sergeant says he's going to leave the Police Force, this has been too much for him," she softly whispered in my ear.

By now Stavros and Louise were seated together on the settee and Stavros was holding her hands as she sobbed, the tears falling like rain drops, trickling down her soft cheeks and onto her red skirt, dark patches highlighted where her tears had fallen.

"Now you remember my dear, what I told you yesterday there was no other way, only to let you or Andrew die, or both of you for that matter, and I told you I wasn't prepared to let that happen. Now this is the shock coming out of you, believe me it is better this way than for you to become ill in months or even in years to come." He released his hold and Louise wiped her eyes and blew her nose. Nana passed her the box of tissues and Louise took a few more.

"But Stavros, we might just as well have lied to the policemen about what went on, we didn't contradict anything they said," she told him through her tears.

"Louise," Stavros started, looking into her eyes, and a firmness in his voice. "Would you prefer for those babies of yours to grow up alone in this world or grow up safe in the knowledge they will have two good adults to show them what's right and wrong and be there for them in times of need?"

"You know the answer to that question," was Louise's reply, shaking her head.

"Well, we still have to consider what Jan may decide to do if we let him go free. He's known for taking revenge and may still want to harm you and even your family. We could hand him over to the British police but," he paused and looked up at me. He could see I felt useless and was trying to reassure me as well as Louise.

"I think we need some more time to think about this and the options we have open to us." He stopped and stood up. The words had no sooner left his mouth than Louise was on her feet as well.

"I need to use the phone please." Louise said.

"My dear, as I told you yesterday, this is your home for as long as you are here, help yourself." Stavros told her.

As she passed me I went to take her hand but she pushed it away, turned and looked me in the eyes, and as if we were complete strangers told me, "I need to be with my babies, and Mummy and Daddy!"

"Yes of course. I'll take you home and we can be together," I said again, trying to take her hand.

"No, you didn't hear me Andy. I want to be with them and not with you!" she said, then turned and looked at a surprised Stavros. "I'm sorry, I don't mean to be ungrateful Stavros, but I do need to get away."

I felt as if I'd been stabbed through the heart. I didn't understand her reason, only a few hours ago we'd been in bed together as lovers looking forward to a new future together, now the woman I loved with every breath I took had rejected me and shunned me. A rush of anger came over me.

"No, you can't leave me now, we're in this together. I love you so much, I have to be with you. Please Louise, don't go without me," I began to beg her, grabbing at her hands, my anger replaced now with tears.

"Don't!" she retaliated. "It can't be, I have to go, please don't try to stop me, please Andy, don't!" she said, shaking off my grip on her hands, her cheeks flushed with colour. As she headed for the door Stavros signalled to Nana to follow but Louise turned and told her she wanted to be alone. I was beside myself; the pain of nearly losing her to a man with a gun, only now to be rejected, was too much for me to suffer. I broke down and cried and Stavros handed me another whisky before making his way into the hall, following Louise. I didn't want another drink. I needed her, and now alone I began to wonder what I was to do.

Stavros reappeared after a few minutes and came to me.

"I have tried," he began to slowly tell me, his fatherly eyes looking into my soul the way he had on that Easter Saturday when we had come to see him. "My dear friend, she has to be alone and wants to go back to her own surroundings for comfort and safety. I'm so sorry. I think I've got it wrong. I'm just as confused as you." He stopped and scratched his chin. "She has agreed for Marie to drive her to pick up her car and to go part way home with her." He put his arms out and I fell into them, as a son suffering great pain would. I looked up and Nana was also crying.

"Nobody must blame themselves for what has happened. I stand by my words of yesterday. There was no other way." He stood, releasing his hold on me, and hugged his beautiful daughter. Then he made his way out into the kitchen and Marie came back in with him.

"Andy, I will stay with her for as long as she needs me," Marie told me as she kissed me on both cheeks and gave me a squeeze. She then made her way into the hall and beckoned all of us to come to see them leave.

I stood on the driveway next to Stavros, and Marie opened the door of the car for Louise to get in. She didn't come to kiss me goodbye, neither did she look back. I was devastated, reduced to a wreck. I tried not to cry in case she should look back, but I was unable to contain my sorrow and my tears fell like rain. I was alone, apart from my good friends around me. The three of us stood and watched as Marie drove off down the driveway in her green Rover, and the car turned the bend that led out onto the road. I fell to the ground, with a pain in my chest so uncontrollable I felt my heart had been torn out. I hit the ground with my fists.

"Why? Why?" I screamed, anger and pain in my voice, my tears falling. I sobbed like a baby.

"Come, my friend," Stavros said, as he lent down to lift me from the floor.

"No, leave me. I want to stay here," I cried in reply, but he was having none of it and pulled me to my feet and led me indoors. Nana followed us, trying her best to comfort me but I was beyond any consoling. I had another two very large drinks and then I was beyond doing anything for myself. The drink had the effect of making me sleepy and at mid-afternoon I took to my bed and that's where I stayed until the following day. The drink and all of the events of Wednesday had drained me and I must have been in need of the sleep.

Chapter Fourteen

Friday

I awoke and felt across the bed trying to find my Louise, then came the realisation she'd gone and I was alone, and I cried again as I made my way to the bathroom and gave myself a wash. I couldn't even be bothered to have a shave or a shower and made my way down the stairs. Marie came out of the lounge to greet me as I reached the bottom.

"I followed her all the way to her home, Andy, and I stayed with her until her mother and father returned with the babies. They are such nice people," she told me as she hugged me. Then she continued, "I'm sure she loves you, but she is very upset. It's very difficult for you to understand, but as Stavros will tell you, time will make it better. It will heal and your grief will pass." She took my hand as if to lead me into the lounge but I turned and headed for the front door, and taking the keys for my Porsche off the telephone table I made my way outside and onto the drive.

"Take care Andy," I heard Marie say as I pressed the key fob and the doors unlocked. As I opened the driver's door that beautiful smell of Louise's perfume rushed out to greet me, and tears filled up in my eyes as I slid into the driver's seat. I turned the key and the engine roared into life. A feeling of pointlessness came over me and as I drove down the narrow driveway I didn't even glance back. Once on the main road I headed towards the dual carriageway I'd last driven on on Wednesday, and my driving now was completely reckless.

I glanced down at the speedometer - 160 miles an hour. I didn't care. I felt alone and unwanted and foolishly had no regard for anyone else's life, let alone my own. I raced along the outside lane passing everything; no adrenaline-rush, just anger and frustration, tears still in my eyes. What had gone so wrong that I couldn't be with her? I thought we had a future together, but it seemed as if I was destined to be alone, with all of this 'bloody money!' I shouted. I was running out of dual carriageway and slowed the car down. The realisation came over me there was no need to kill myself, for if I did then others would be let down and people would have reason to think I had played a part in Gary's death.

I pulled into a lay-by, wiped my weeping eyes, then turned the car round and headed back at a more controlled pace towards Truro and the safety of my friend's home, wondering all the way back whether I would be able to carry on alone without her. I did before I met her, I told myself, I would just have to pick up the pieces and try to move on.

As I got out of the car on the drive at Stavros's house Marie pulled up at my side on her motorbike.

"Andy, I couldn't keep up with you," she told me as she pulled off her crash helmet.

Yes, once again someone had been only a short distance behind me looking out for my safety.

"Come on, Stavros needs to talk to you," she told me as she turned off the engine of her bike. She put her arms around me and hugged me tightly.

Together we went into the house and made our way to the dining room and there sat Stavros at the table, today somewhat subdued. He looked up from the paper he was reading, and with a forcefulness I'd never seen before, he told me I'd been extremely foolish and not only risked my own life but also that of many others. Of course he was right, but I didn't feel like apologising, I was so full of my own grief it was almost consuming me.

"Now, Andrew, you need to listen to me and take note of what I'm going to tell you." With that direct manner and tone still in his voice and he went on, "I have spoken to Louise's Father and he tells me she is very confused and still upset. You must understand when someone has lived with constant fear and danger in their lives, when that menace is taken away it leaves a void, an emptiness that will take time to be filled, and that process may well mean leading a completely different life."

He was of course trying to tell me in the nicest way he could that her life may well continue without me being part of it.

"Nothing is fair in this life my friend." He stopped and looked long and hard at me. "I do know how you feel. I too have lost a love that had been part of my life. Oh yes, this old man may not show it on the surface but I too have suffered a broken heart. Another day I will tell you about it. Now, Louise's father Trevor and I have made the arrangements for the funeral. Sadly Louise would prefer if you didn't go." He stopped, but didn't remove his gaze. I felt like I'd been kicked in the stomach. That feeling of total rejection again, just how many more times would I have to be put down before it became acceptable.

"Is there any reason?" I asked.

"You didn't let me finish," Stavros said. "But Trevor thinks it will be ok if you are there but very much in the background, and I come with you." He paused and took my hand "Just to make sure you can get through the day and don't get into any trouble. Yes! You understand?" he had finished, I thought.

"I understand," I replied, in a very downhearted manner.

"The trouble is," Stavros said, opening the paper and turning it towards me, "you've made it to the papers again and this time for the wrong reasons."

And sure enough the headlines on this cheap tabloid read, 'Millionaire involved in shoot-out,' and the story then went into graphic but mostly fictional details of what had happened, nothing like what had taken place. I was furious, my sorrow replaced with an uncontrollable anger towards the gutter-press that had over-emphasised the relationship Louise and I had, adding lots of their own free detail.

"Bastards," I said banging on the table with my fists.

"I know my friend. Now you can see why Trevor thinks it's best if you keep a low profile at the funeral. The press is sure to be there and all of us can do without too much publicity," Stavros told me.

"When is the funeral?" I asked.

"It's next Tuesday," he replied. "I may well put a few of the boys in place just as in the past to keep an eye open for us. We can go to your house on Monday and I'll stay with you at least until Wednesday, but you must promise your old friend that you won't go and upset Louise. I know you won't intentionally upset her but," he paused, "don't let your heart rule your head. Please be strong, think of the love you had from her and try to console yourself with that. Time will heal."

"But she needs me with her now. I can protect her from all these people before they make anymore accusations," I pleaded with Stavros.

"Andrew my good friend. I don't want to fall out with you, but you must be strong now and in the future. It's not going to be easy, but we can do it together," he told me.

Then something occurred to me. Just how did the press find out? It wouldn't have been Inspector Jones who told them, he would have only reported there had been an incident and that would have been a brief statement. Now the article in the rag went into details that could only have come from one other person, and it wasn't any of Stavros's family.

"Is this the work of Mitchell?" I asked, anger still in my voice.

"Now, my friend, you are thinking like the old Andrew I remember," Stavros replied, a smile on his face. "That is the conclusion we have come to, but this time his loose tongue has put him in a very tight spot and given us just a bit of an advantage. You see, if it was he who spilt the beans then he can't go back on his words without the risk of perjuring himself in a court of law, and that of course puts the blame on Jan Van-Elderman."

"But he will deny he had anything to do with the killing. I hate that word." I stopped, and the memory of seeing Gary die came flooding back to me. "No, we saved other people from his tormenting and bullying ways."

"Well, we may be able to give him the option of not having to deny it," Stavros replied, and went on, "You see, my cousin has just arrived in Falmouth. He is the captain of a large container ship and he will happily take an extra passenger on board for a little trip around the globe if requested to do so. All we need to do is convince Jan that it's his best option."

"And what if he doesn't agree to go willingly?" I asked Stavros.

"Well, then we may have to persuade him that this is his best choice, or we hand him over to the Dutch authorities. It won't be difficult to smuggle him back into Holland and leave him in some convenient spot for the police to pick him up," Stavros said.

Marie came back into the room with some fresh coffee and toast. I didn't feel like eating and as soon I'd taken a mouth full had an overwhelming urge to be sick, mainly due to the fact I hadn't eaten anything other than breakfast the day before.

Marie suggested she might be able to find out if Mitchell was responsible for the story in the paper by going to some of the sergeant's haunts. Stavros agreed, but only if Andreas or Demetri went with her. She agreed to the proposal and a timetable of when she would leave was drawn up. Nana was able to give good information as to which pubs the officer drank in and agreed it was best if Marie was to go on account he hadn't seen her yesterday on his visit. It was also felt best if the sergeant was left to let his mouth run away again, for all the time he was talking he was digging a bigger hole for himself.

Early in the evening after we'd had a light supper the boys unceremoniously brought Jan to the house. He was blindfolded and his big hands were tied behind his back. He stood in the kitchen doorway almost obscuring the light that had been shinning through it. Both of Stavros's sons stood on either side of him and Nana sat by my side at the table.

"Now," Stavros began "before I have my boys remove your blindfold will you promise me you aren't going to try anything foolish. I really have had enough excitement for one day without someone else being very silly," that comment referring to myself. Nana gave my hand a squeeze and whispered, "He doesn't mean it really."

The Dutchman's reaction was far less polite than Staveros's request.

"I'm going to kill the fucker that has done this to me as soon as my hands are untied," he bellowed.

"That wasn't what I asked you, and I don't think you're in any position at the moment to do any killing," Stavros told him very calmly and calculatedly. "I should like to point out there is at least one lady present and another one may well be joining us soon, so I'll ask you again and this time I expect a more respectful reply."

"I don't know who you are or what you want," Jan replied, still angry and confused, continuing, "but you've made a big mistake, I can assure you of that."

Stavros signalled to the boys to pull up a chair for Jan to sit on. They had to push him into the seat. Once Jan was seated Stavros stood up and removed the black blindfold that was covering his eyes. He squinted as the light penetrated his eyes, and slowly he regained his focus and looked round the room. To his right and left were Stavros's sons, then he refocused his attention on me. I felt in no mood to be anything but unpleasant to his prickly comment.

"I know you," he said, his light blue eyes now peering into mine. "I stopped Gary from killing you in the lane a few weeks ago."

"Oh yes," I replied, "I never got round to thanking you did I, but you could have stopped the entire beating, but you chose not to." There were many other things I wanted to add but for the moment they would keep.

"Yes I could, but," Jan stopped and looked at Nana sitting by my right hand. For comfort she had taken my hand.

"Oh, you won't be so lucky next time," Jan said, and continued, "I take it he doesn't know you're with his wife; that is Mrs Shaw?"

Instantly Stavros spoke to the boys in Greek and whatever he said Nana could understand because I just about to tell Jan it wasn't Louise when I felt Nana's foot kick me under the table.

Stavros looked hard into my eyes but it was Nana he spoke to. His stare was to draw my attention to the fact that Jan may not be too well informed and it would be wise if I let my head do the thinking, at least for a little while.

"Louise," he said, maintaining that piercing stare, "will you go and see if Marie is ready to go out?"

"Yes I will," she said as she rose from the table, not adding her customary 'father' to her reply. That exchange reinforced what I thought - Jan might not know Gary was dead.

"Yes," Jan started, "I may well tell him about this very cosy rendezvous and see what his reaction is. That is, before I kill him!"

That confirmed it, he didn't know Gary was dead. But just what did he know, and what were his reasons for being in Cornwall, in particular so close to my apartments? The other thing it confirmed was we still had all of our options open to us, but it was left to Stavros to do the interrogating of this big man.

"Tell me," Stavros began, "why should anyone want to harm Mr Shaw. From what I've heard he's not such a bad guy; well, no worse than yourself."

"Why should I tell you anything? You're not the police, and there's nothing you can do to hurt me," Jan replied.

"Well, you'd be quite surprised as to what we can do to hurt you, but on one point you are right: we're nothing to do with the police. Let's just say we're inquisitive as to what has been going on and what brings you to this part of the Country," Stavros told him. "Now, we do know you are interested in the drug market, and I don't mean the things to make you better when you've been ill. On the other hand we could just hand you over to the police, they'd be more than happy to send you back to Holland. We know one or two people there who would like to have a chat with you. Or shall we lock you up again in that safe place we have reserved just for people like yourself?"

"Well, the drug thing is what I'm here for," Jan started. "Looking into the operations side of things, just to see how it's moved around."

Stavros stood up and picked up the blindfold. "Take him away, he's not going to tell us anything we don't already know," he said.

"Just a minute," I said. "What were you doing by my apartments? That's where you were found, you hadn't been near Gary for weeks." I looked long and hard into his eyes and they still had that menacing look I'd first seen on the Thursday in the lane. Then I thought one more question might loosen his tongue. "What do you know about a man called Rimes?"

Jan's expression changed instantly. I'd touched a nerve. His eyes now had an angry look to them.

"He's an acquaintance of my brother, well let me say was; you see, my brother is dead," was Jan's reply. The word 'dead' had a poignant ring to it, little did he know that Rimes was also dead.

"Had an accident did he?" was Stavros's quick question.

"Yes, an accident at the hands of that bastard Gary, that's why I'm going to kill him when I catch up with him, he killed my brother!" He tried to stand up, his whole body flexing with the strength he was exerting but the boys stood their ground and pushed him back into the seat. Jan continued, "Gary was meant to be bringing some material back into this Country last year from Belgium but he got all responsible and took offence over the type of things he saw. My brother tried to have a careful word with him and Gary went berserk, saying he was offended by what he had seen. My brother came off badly on the receiving end of Gary's fists and died two days later. Just over some books with pictures of some kids in! I managed to catch up with Rimes the other day and we had a chat about Gary, he'd only just come back from Belgium. Then I saw Rimes in the village where Gary lives and I followed him, thinking he might lead me to the bastard, but then my hire car broke down. I was walking along the main road, when someone bundled me in the back of a van."

"And these books were to be handed over to Rimes?" I asked.

"It was later when I found out that Rimes was involved. Gary was just supposed to leave them at one of his pick-up points, the ones he uses for movement of the drugs. It was a new line my brother had got into."

"But my friend, your brother was a customs official, he wasn't meant to be above the law. Enforcing it was his job, not breaking it!" Stavros said to him.

"So why are you telling me this! He's dead now and I'm going to give Gary some of my own law, that's right, Van-Elderman's law!" was Jan's angry reply.

"But then you'll face prison in this Country as well, are you really prepared for that?" I asked.

"I told you I want to kill the bastard and I'll willingly go to jail," was Jan's instant response.

"Well, I've some news for you," Stavros started. "It would seem someone has beaten you to it."

"What do you mean?" Jan asked, a puzzled look on his face.

"I mean Gary is already dead," Stavros told him. Jan's face changed again, this time a look of disbelief etched right across it. Would he be so willing to go to prison now, when he knew the police suspected him of the killing, that was the burning question I longed to ask, but he had questions of his own.

"I don't believe you, how do you know he's dead?" was the first thing he asked.

"Because, my friend, we've had the police here today asking questions. Andy should know, he saw Gary get shot," Stavros told him. Jan's face still had that puzzled look upon it. "Oh, just one other thing, Rimes is dead as well," Stavros finished.

Jan looked at me as if asking for corroboration of what he had just been told. I made him wait just a few moments before I put him out of his misery.

"He's right," I said, looking into Jan's now half-closed eyes. "You got beaten to the job. I was with Louise, you see." Suddenly my mind went back to the awful events and I realised I'd made a slip that Jan might be able to pick up and before I could say any more he did.

"Well, she didn't look too upset to me if her husband has just been killed," was his quick-fired reply.

"It's only to be expected," Stavros intervened. "The man was a thug and a bully, you of all people should know that having seen Andy beaten up in the lane."

"So," Jan said as he sat back into his seat, "he had more than one enemy. Well, I'd like to shake the hand of the person who killed him."

Stavros looked at me, then up at his two sons. Little did Jan know just how close he had got to that person.

"Why do the police suspect me of his murder?" Jan asked.

"It seems as if someone has been giving them information as to what you were really doing in this Country," Stavros told him. "Perhaps you let it slip before you came over, but they knew an awful lot about you and what you've been up to back home."

"You could be making this up," Jan said. The words had just left his mouth when the door opened and Nana stood in the doorway.

"Well my friend, why don't you ask the lady yourself," Stavros said to Jan.

What a gamble, I thought, we really are tempting fate. Nana hadn't been in the room and was completely unaware of the conversation we had just had. Now Stavros was going to risk our entire future on what could easily be considered a foolhardy question. But just as Jan was about to ask that question Stavros looked up at Demetri. Quick as a flash Greek words rolled off his tongue and Demetri replied in the same tongue. I knew we had been saved: not only did they have this fast exchange of words but Demetri made his way into the kitchen, slamming the door as he went.

"What question does he want to ask me darling," Nana said to me as she resumed her seat, taking my hand as she did so.

"Jan wants!" I was stopped by Jan shouting at Nana.

"Is that bastard of a husband of yours dead?" he almost screamed at her.

"Well, the answer to your very direct question is yes, Gary is dead," Nana said, tightening her grip on my hand.

"You don't seem to be upset in any way and where has your wedding ring gone, you don't appear to be wearing it," Jan said looking hard at Nana's left hand.

"You only knew him for a short while, I was with him for too long to remember. He made my life hell. I'm glad he's at rest," Nana replied to Jan's questioning. "I've left the ring off so as to help me forget," and with those words Nana started to cry, removed a tissue from her sleeve and wiped her eyes.

"Now look what you've done," Stavros said to Jan, anger in his voice. "She has held up so well until now and you being rude has brought all this pain back."

Jan just shrugged his shoulders and grunted, he just couldn't care. He must have had a great deal of hatred inside for Gary.

"So what do you plan to do with me?" Jan asked.

"Well," Stavros began, " It depends on just how you behave, if and when we untie your hands."

With those words he snapped his fingers and Andreas turned and went out into the kitchen leaving just the three of us. Stavros looked long and hard into my eyes. I couldn't care what happened to the Dutchman, but this had put Nana in possible danger. It was a difficult act to maintain, we were all in danger of letting something slip. It would only take the smallest of comments to put doubt into the mind of Jan and it was anybody's guess what he may do in the form of retaliation. Stavros turned his attention to Jan.

"I think it might be best if we don't take that risk," he started to tell the big man. When the boys returned in Demetri's hands were a cloth and a small file of glass. In an instant he snapped it and just as Jan looked to see what the breaking sound was, Demetri covered Jan's nose and mouth. It only took a few seconds for him to fall under the influence of the chloroform; without time to fight back he was out for the count, and slumping forward his head fell to the table with a thud.

"It's best this way," Stavros told all of us, continuing, "My cousin will take him for a little ride, maybe drop him off in Greece. It depends where the next port of call is. They will keep him under lock and key until they are far enough away and isn't a danger anymore. It's best you two boys take him back to the safe place until we can get him on board the ship, tomorrow will be soon enough to take care of that," he finished and between them Andreas and Demetri lifted the big man up one at each shoulder. Then they made their way out of the house via the back entrance.

"That was very close," I said to Stavros. "I'm not happy about Nana playing at being Louise."

"Sometimes we have to take a risk," Stavros replied looking directly at me. "And you should know all about risks, after this mornings little escapade."

Those words brought the memories flooding back, and again I began to feel very lonely. I'd had no word from my Louise, all I had as reassurance were the words of Marie: saying she had got home safely and Marie was sure Louise loved me.

Demetri and Marie went out for the evening to investigate the stories in the paper. That was the only paper we had read, but it was sure to have made it into the others and I was to read a full and more accurate account the following day.

Stavros, Nana, Andreas and myself were left together. We had a few bottles of wine, not that I felt in any mood for company, even that of the reliable friends who had saved my life and the woman I loved. I made for my bed before Demetri and Marie returned. I heard them come home, but fell asleep soon after.

Saturday

Stavros woke me on the Saturday morning. He came into the bedroom with a large mug of tea and placed it on the bedside cabinet. It must have been nine o'clock, and the sun was pouring though the half-drawn curtains. A new day had arrived and I was still alive, but the pain was deep in my heart and wouldn't go away, as Stavros could tell as he stood at the side of the bed looking down at me. However, his words gave me some encouragement to get up.

"Andrew my friend, you need to get up, we have some news for you from last night," he said, and a slight smile formed before he continued, "We also have a copy of The Times for you to read. I know it's your favourite newspaper, too big for me of course, but they have a much more accurate account of what happened on Wednesday. I think it will clear up a lot of doubt in people's minds."

I sat up in bed drinking my tea after he had left, after informing me Marie was cooking an English breakfast and so as not to spoil it I should be down in twenty minutes. This morning I had a shave and shower, but all the time my mind was on Louise and what she might be doing. I was unable to put her out of my thoughts.

The boys had already gone off to do their Saturday morning business by the time I'd got down and it was just the four of us for breakfast: Nana, Marie, Stavros and myself. The conversation during the meal was dominated by Marie's visit to the drinking establishments frequented by the sergeant. Sure enough they had located him, and his mouth was running free, helped by copious amounts of beer purchased by reporters looking for the best story.

"It was like he couldn't help himself," Marie told us. "His tongue just ran away with itself. It will be like that for a few more days yet, just like vultures coming to pick over the bones of this man's foolish talk."

"The one thing it has helped do is force the Post Office to make a statement," Nana said, passing me a copy of the Saturday Times.

Well, the account of the incident in The Times was far more accurate and it took up the story from the latest account it had published with regard to the fraud investigation. It went as follows.

The Police and Post Office can confirm that the two men shot on Wednesday were both employees of the Post Office. The younger man, a Mr Gary Shaw, had been under investigation for a considerable time by the Post Office in connection with irregular transactions using official Post Office transport together with a long-term redirection of mail to a PO box. The Police, the Fraud Squad to be precise, had been called in to assist as a matter of course, due to the nature of the investigation and a concern that drugs may also have been involved.

The Post Office has now launched a separate enquiry into how one of their own investigating officers could have been the subject of an investigation by the Serious Crime Squad. This individual's own boss was unaware of that investigation or for that matter the implications of the outcome.

A very embarrassed senior Royal Mail representative read a brief statement saying all of the allegations would be fully examined. New procedures would be drawn up to ensure that no Post Office employee would be able to set up a long-term redirection of mail without it first being approved by his manager, and it would only then be allowed to continue for a maximum of three months. The use of official Post Office transport for private use has always been a disciplinary offence and that ruling would be tightened up and new checks on the routes and methods of monitoring that transport will be brought into place as soon as possible. And in the fullness of time a report will be issued.

Police were satisfied Mr Shaw took the life of Mr Marcus Rimes after a heated discussion with regard to the importation into the Country of pornographic and paedophiliac material. A spokesman for the Police indicated another individual had been responsible for the shooting of Mr Shaw, but they were not at this stage prepared to release the individual's name as investigations were still continuing.

At no time was Mr Andrew Jackson or Mr Shaw's wife Louise linked to the killing of the two men, in fact the Police spokesman was quick to reassure the Saturday Times reporter both of these individuals had been ruled out of the enquiry.

As long ago as Easter the two were interviewed by Police, investigating the much published fraud enquiry within the Post Office.

Mrs Louise Shaw, the Police spokesman said, was taken against her will to the apartments, where she had spent some time with Mr Jackson during the Easter holiday. Mr Jackson had made his own way after Mrs Shaw had called Mr Jackson. Neither of them where harmed at the incident and the Police say they have been ruled out of the investigations.

The land and property at which the murders took place is owned by multi-millionaire Andrew Jackson. A spokesperson for Mr Jackson said Andrew and Mrs Shaw had spent Easter at the apartments, which are rumoured to have cost over four million pounds. Other than that there is little to link the two people, but they have been seen in local restaurants and on one occasion were spotted shopping in the capital of the county.

Mr Jackson has been dogged with bad luck since acquiring his fortune. His wife of nearly twenty years left him, setting up home in America after the divorce and it has been suggested the settlement for that alone was over ten million pounds. He was forced to leave a considerable sum of his new wealth in the United States, where it originated, and underwent a long and expensive investigation into his wealth, due in no small part to the way he inherited it.

We reported at the time that banks up and down the Country had queues of people wanting to see records and looking for long-lost rich relatives. The Government was forced to intervene and tighten up on the inheritance laws.

That's not to say that it can't happen in this Country. It's a known fact there are millions of pounds held in locked bank accounts all over the Country, money where people have died and had no surviving relatives. Not that it could match the sum Andrew Jackson awoke to find he'd acquired, conservative estimates put it at two hundred and fifty million, but some financial experts say its nearer three hundred million when all of the property he has since bought is taken into account.

It is only speculation, but a source close to the family said he had set his sons up in business at a cost of over two million pounds.

Mr Jackson and Mrs Shaw have been staying with friends in Truro since the incident. He is, as we have already mentioned, a frequent visitor to the Duchy. In fact his land borders that of the Prince's, but it is understood the two men have never met.

He also owns a substantial piece of land in Scotland, along with a number of farms and forestry land, together with his own private loch specially stocked with salmon.

"Well, they got most of it right," I said, still with the overwhelming feeling of loneliness. "Apart from Louise being here. Oh, by the way, who's the spokesperson?"

I looked across at the hand which had gone up on the other side of the table; Marie's.

"It wasn't difficult to find the man from The Times," she said, "he was the one smartly dressed and drinking orange juice. The information I gave him should keep him off us for a few days anyway."

"Thank you," I replied, "you're always around me, protecting me, I don't know what I'll do next week when I'm on my own."

"My friend, you'll have me near you, and some of the boys," Stavros told me, adding, "Just to make sure no harm comes to any of us."

I spent the rest of Saturday trying to relax, but it wasn't easy. Every time the phone rang I thought and hoped it might be Louise, but it never was. The phone is used as a business line as well for the domestic calls to the house, and quite often the calls were someone wanting to buy an item they'd seen in the shop.

I didn't venture out into the hall other than going to the bathroom, and then the evening came and it was time for bed. That time couldn't come soon enough, for some reason it was the one place I could find comfort and a small amount of safety. I found no difficulty in sleeping.

Stavros put it down to the shock still coming out of me, but in reality it was where I could rest with my thoughts of Louise, telling myself it would have been easier to accept her death than for her to walk away from me. I dreamt of her as I slept in that lonely bed, the bed we had made love in after Gary's death, her words "I want to be with you now and forever." I gave myself comfort in believing she had meant those words; who knows, one day we may be together again.

Sunday

Sunday was to be much the same as Saturday. We spent a lot of time talking about the past. The papers were once again full of the story that had by now gripped the county: how could one man with so much money enter the area and no one know who he was? The cheap papers paid particular attention to the drugs issue, using words like 'rampant problem' and making all sorts of accusations about the size of the drug market in the Country's favourite holiday region. One paper described it as being out of control and as bad as in the centre of London. I couldn't argue for or against any of the comments, drugs weren't my 'thing'. I'd never had anything to do with them, and my knowledge was limited to a few pints of beer on a Sunday and a glass or two of wine or whisky in the evening. The speculation would continue for some considerable time before the press would find another poor victim.

I was also in a very fortunate position, at the end of the day. I was financially able to retaliate. If I wanted, I could sue if any of the allegations really did offend me. Others were not so fortunate. I had read of what the press was capable of doing to a man's reputation. As Stavros told me, I had done nothing wrong and had nothing to fear.

The broadsheet newspapers, on the other hand, gave the drugs issue a miss, concentrating more on my wealth and where it had come from. In fact for the most part they all gave a very good lesson in history with regard to my family background and the way in which the money had come into my hands. One of the papers even paid me the compliment of saying I'd spent my new found fortune wisely so far. It quoted other individuals by name, who had won the lottery and managed to squander the entire fortune within weeks, as was the case with one poor soul who was now back to square one; financially penniless.

I, on the other hand, was back to square one emotionally, without the woman I loved and no amount of money would buy her and I felt as if I'd gone round in a complete circle. And all of this talk about money reminded me that you can't buy happiness, dreams are free and even the biggest fortune won't fulfil those dreams and bring them to reality if they involve the love of another person.

Marie and Nana cooked the most delicious of meals and it was accompanied by a few bottles of Stavros's favourite wine, but it didn't take away the empty feeling I had deep inside. My thoughts went ahead to the next day, of returning to my big empty house, and to try to take my mind off the future I suggested we go for a walk. To my surprise all agreed. We left the house and intentionally I was leading away from the town. We made our way the long route to Boscadwen Park, but sadly I was spotted by a reporter and we had to beat a hasty retreat and return home via the back streets of Truro. It was fortunate for me that we had all gone out, for I'm sure if I had been on my own I would have been hounded by the reporter, and the one would soon have turned into a pack.

Once again I made for the security of my bed before darkness had arrived, and lay still for a long time wondering if Louise would see me on Tuesday. What would her reaction be if she were to see me? Maybe it would make her understand that I really did care for her. I would have given anything to have her back with me, but I fell asleep thinking that Tuesday could only bring the worst and she may not even see me.

Monday

I returned to my home late on the Monday afternoon, followed by Stavros in Marie's car, after a very tearful departure. It wasn't just me who shed tears, both of the girls were upset, and understandably so. I had been with them for four days, and during that time they had given me a great deal of support. I was going to miss them and in turn they said they would miss my company. As for Andreas and Demetri, each of them had been a tower of strength and I informed the ladies they had nothing to worry about as long as the boys were about.

The house was much as I'd left it on that fateful Wednesday morning. The road works had all gone as I had expected, and apart from some dirt on the pathway outside my house you wouldn't have known there had been any 'ongoing work'.

Christine had been in and moved the post and put it in the study. She had also had the newspaper cancelled. Apart from that the house remained as it was; my packed bags still in the bedroom where I had left them and the airline tickets still on the writing bureau along with some loose change.

It was almost the end of April and the empty house had a coldness about it which chilled me to the core. What had in so recent times been my place of happiness and delight now had an overbearing effect upon my very soul, an emptiness that gripped me with every room I entered. The feelings I'd had of security were soon to be replaced with an overpowering sense of solitude.

William came to see Stavros and myself in the evening, he made a big fuss of me and I'm sure I saw a tear in his eye. It must have been a tear of sympathy, and it helped to know that my eldest son was trying to share some of my pain. He was pleased to see our old friend Stavros and they sat in the conservatory talking while I half-heartedly prepared a meal. William said Natasha wouldn't come as she was too upset. She was, as I have already said, a very sensitive young woman. William told me she sent her love. He didn't stay for a meal as he an appointment to keep later in the evening, but wished Stavros a fond farewell and told me he would see me soon, adding if there was anything I wanted then I only had to call. I couldn't ask him to get my Louise.

Stavros and I ate in the dinning room and we managed a bottle of wine. It was suggested by my guest that an early night might be in order, for tomorrow was going to be a long and difficult day. Before we retired for the night Stavros made a phone call to his home in Truro. I heard him confirm with Marie that the boys were in place, just to keep an eye out for us.

The day after the funeral I was to be alone, locked away in a tomb full of memories, with just a small hope that the woman I loved so much would call me, or even better come to me. First I had the difficult and somewhat painful task of attending the funeral of her husband and I had to remain at a distance. A promise I had given to people who in only a short space of time I'd taken to; I mean Diane, Louise's mother and her father, Trevor. And those were the thoughts that took me off to sleep, now back in my own bed, but a bed I had also shared with Louise.

Tuesday

And Tuesday was with us soon enough. The funeral was at eleven, plenty of time to get to the church in the village where Louise lived. Stavros had a call on his mobile from the look-out boys informing him they had found a convenient position for us and we would be able to observe what was going on and not be seen ourselves, just inside the churchyard. We had a light breakfast and even had time to look at the papers. Stavros had taken the walk to the newsagents to collect them, he had also arranged to restart the delivery of my daily copy of The Times, not that I would feel like reading it, but today I did make the effort. It helped to pass some time before we set off to the tiny village.

I was sitting in the conservatory reading. The Post Office issue was there again, but this time with some very powerful news. The article went on to explain at least a dozen senior managers had been suspended following the investigation into the misuse of official transport and suspected trafficking of drugs around the Country using official Royal Mail vehicles. More suspensions and possible dismissals were expected within the next few days, and it could not be ruled out that more arrests wouldn't take place as a result of the continuing investigation. A spokesman for the Royal Mail confirmed the issue was on a much larger scale than anything they had expected to find.

The report also went on to say that the inquest into the death of the two Post Office employees in Cornwall on Wednesday concluded that Mr Gary Shaw took the life of Mr Marcus Rimes. Mr Shaw, a Post Office transport driver for nearly ten years, was killed by person or persons unknown, but the coroner took into account the evidence given by Sergeant Mitchell that at the time of his death Mr Shaw was endangering the life of his wife Mrs Louise Shaw. The coroner ruled 'in this case the verdict was unlawful killing by person or persons unknown'.

The police were still looking for a man seen acting suspiciously in the area on the day in question. Then, as with all news reports, came the punch line. The funeral of Mr Gary Shaw is to take place today at St Mary's church in the village of Chillingston, where he lived with his wife Louise and two children, Sarah aged six and James two.

Then came what seemed like a real sting in the tail, almost a twist of the knife. Mrs Shaw was recently seen in the company of the multi-millionaire Mr Andrew Jackson. Mr Jackson is not expected to attend the funeral. His whereabouts is not known at this time but it is thought he is still staying with friends in Truro.

"Have you seen this Stavros?" I asked my old friend who had now joined me in the conservatory.

"Its much the same in all of the papers my friend," was his reply, as he thumbed his way though his smaller paper. "I'm afraid I can't get on with those big papers, you know."

"Well, they won't be expecting to see us anyway," I said, still feeling despondent.

"That, my friend, doesn't mean we can afford to be complacent," Stavros said, looking up from his paper. "You can be sure that the press will be about in force, we can't take any chances, you in particular will need to be on your guard. If just one reporter gets sight of you then the entire pack could easily descend upon you, or if for that matter you try to make contact with Louise then think of what they will do to that poor woman. She may not be able to stand the pressure, please think of her as a," he paused, "think of her as a delicate flower, the most beautiful of orchids you would handle with utmost of care. Even if she never comes back to you, my friend, she will respect you for giving her space, space to carry on living."

"But Stavros, if I'm seen then it would deflect the attention from her, give her more space," I replied.

"Andrew," Stavros started, "remember I told you to let your head rule your heart, now it's the other way round. You must be strong, you will have to dig deep. I'm going to be by your side all the time. Unlike at the apartments this time you will be able to see me, I won't come out from behind a wall. If you need to, draw on me for strength, I've told you that you are like a son to me. I shouldn't have to remind you of that."

With those words I took this strong and powerful man's hand.

"I'll never forget the kindness and," I paused, not sure if I should say the word to another man, but it needed to be said, "the love you have given to me. I will never forget what you have done for me and for Louise."

"Somethings in life are a pleasure to do," Stavros began, and gripping my hand he went on, "You too are a gentle and sensitive person with strong emotions; not a fault, I must add, for the world is made up of all sorts of individuals. It would not be good if we were all the same." He stopped again. "I've seen you cry, no shame in that, but you don't see my heart cry for you because you are now one of my own. If I could take away the pain believe me I would."

He released my hand and looked at his watch. "It's nine forty-five Andrew, time, I think, we were making a move, yes?"

"Yes it is," I replied, and getting up from the settee I made my way upstairs and got the jacket to my suit. I'd put on the navy one, the same one I'd worn when I'd taken Louise out for dinner back in March. That now seemed so long ago, like a dream. When I came back downstairs Stavros was waiting for me in the hall.

"We will take Marie's car," he told me, "but you will have to give me good directions."

We made our way out onto the drive after I'd set the alarm, and just for a moment I stood by the car. It was a dull day with no sun and was very overcast, but it was quite warm and it forced me to ask the question, "Do you think it will rain?"

"No," was Stavros's reply and he went on, "the forecast is for cloud all day, clearing tonight. Come along, we don't want to be late." There was just a touch of forcefulness in his tone. I truly was one of his own.

So at ten o'clock we set off to the village church. I gave directions. As we approached Stavros caught sight of one of the boys, the same ones that had been outside of my house for that week before all of this had taken place. He directed us to the far end of the church, we parked the car well out of anyone's view and walked back towards the churchyard. There we were met by one of the other men. He was a little older and as he shook my hand his words of comfort brought a lump to my throat, "It will soon be over and done with."

We stood next to some trees which gave us added cover, and I had a clear view of the driveway leading to the church. By my left side was Stavros, to our rear two of Stavros's men kept a lookout behind, just in case the press should start to wander round the churchyard. From where I stood I could see two or maybe three reporters and also a few photographers.

"Now," Stavros whispered in my ear, "if that lot get wind of us we will have to make a very quick exit, do you understand?"

"Yes," I replied, still looking at the gates leading into the churchyard.

"The boys will make sure we get away safely," Stavros said.

He had no sooner said the words than I saw the hearse pulling in through the gates, closely followed by two other cars. Louise was sitting in the first car together with her father and another woman, but I didn't know who she was, and there was no sign of her mother. I could see as they got out of the car that the two ladies were dressed in black. Louise was wearing the long coat she had on when she came to my house after we'd both got a beating, the other woman was wearing a three-quarter-length coat. Trevor took Louise's right side and the other woman her left.

In the second car were four men, but I had no idea who they were. I assumed they were football mates, not much of a turn out for someone who had spent a lot of time in the clubhouse after matches. All of the entourage were just waiting to proceed into the church when there was a flash of light quickly followed by more and more flashes, the photographers had started in earnest. I felt myself take a step forward, then the hand of Stavros on my shoulder, and heard his words, "Remember your head!"

I pulled back. "Have they no respect?" I asked.

His reply was quite simple. "No."

I looked again at my Louise. She looked tired and drawn. This had taken its toll on her and she was looking very frail. Her father was giving her all the support he could, a small but strong man. As they made their way into the church behind the vicar I got a better view of the other woman. Judging by the looks I would say it was her sister Jackie, but I was to have to wait to have that confirmed.

We stood in silence while the service took place. I don't think they were in the church for more than twenty minutes before I saw the doors open and the vicar appear, followed by the pallbearers, Louise and her father, and the other woman. The four men slowly came out behind and appeared to be somewhat uncomfortable, followed by some other people, but not many. From where we were positioned I could just make out the grave. Louise seemed to be staring into it long and hard, not looking to her left or right, shedding no tears. She had shed enough over the years. Slowly the coffin was lowered into the ground, Trevor cast the soil into the hole, and as the vicar said his closing words a small gap appeared in the clouds, no shaft of light, just a glimpse of blue sky between the dark overshadowing grey clouds. It would be a long wait before I was to notice any blue light in my life.

Gradually the people who had attended the funeral started to drift away, and we watched as the vultures from the media threw question after question at my poor Louise. I even heard my own name being mentioned and more photographs were taken. Slowly the cars left. I felt Stavros's arm round me, gripping me, passing his strength to me. Louise had said her goodbyes to all who had bothered to come to pay their respects - to all except me and our friend Stavros.

What both he and I noticed, was Trevor didn't get into the car to return with the others but walked off into the other side of the churchyard. Only the vicar was left, along with the sexton. The vicar made his way inside the church and the sexton to the new grave and the job of filling it in.

Then as if from nowhere Trevor appeared by our side, his sudden arrival even catching Stavros's men by surprise.

"Andrew," he said as he approached us with his right hand outstretched. "It's good to see you," he told me, gripping my right hand with his vice-like grip and putting his left hand on my shoulder. We came together for a necessary embrace. "And this must be Mr Stavros," he said, as he turned his attention to my companion.

"No one calls me Mr!" Stavros replied, taking his hand with both of his. "That is, only the taxman or my accountant," he finished, with his usual raucous laugh. He cut himself short as suddenly he remembered where he was, but it didn't bother Trevor for he had a smile on his face indicating he had seen the funny side to his greeting.

"My friend, everyone calls me Stavros, and so should you," he looked behind him and nodded to the men who had come a little closer, and with his signal they withdrew to their original positions. "Trevor, it is my pleasure and privilege to meet you. You're Louise is one of the most beautiful women I have ever seen. You are a very lucky man to have such a charming daughter."

"Thank you," Trevor replied, then went on, "And how are you bearing up Andrew?"

"Well," was all I could say before Stavros interrupted me. I'd wanted to pour my heart out to this man, the man who could get a message back to my Louise, the message being I loved her and longed to see her.

"Trevor, it is very hard for Andrew, but he is coping well. We will get him through this difficult time and you will be looking after your Louise, Yes?" he finished, and looked at me with determination in his eyes.

"We will indeed," Trevor said and went on. "This is such a mess. Louise has told us what happened on Wednesday." He paused. "I must thank you for saving her life. The man was a brute and a thug; sooner or later it would have caught up with him. But Andrew, you mustn't blame yourself. You didn't get her into this mess, you made her happier in that short space of time than I, or for that matter anyone, had seen her for such a long time. I'm sure she loves you. But at this moment she is very confused, also very tired. We need to ensure she gets plenty of rest and you need to look after yourself." With those words he put his hand back on my shoulder and I drew in close to this man I'd taken to so warmly.

"I didn't see Diane," I remarked.

"She stayed at home to look after the children," Trevor replied, and continued, "That was our other daughter, Jackie. She has been a great support to all of us, especially Louise. They always were very close, but when she married that pig of a man she almost cut herself off from the rest of the family." And her words came back to me from a week ago. "I gave up my friends and most of my family for you, Gary."

"It's not much of a turn out for someone who thought he was very popular, I must say," Trevor said. "The four men in the other car were from the football club, of course, but no-one from the Post Office as he'd managed to disgrace himself, you know, doing the things he had."

"But my friend how, did you manage to get across to us without the press following you?" Stavros asked, looking somewhat puzzled.

"Stavros, I was a bank manager, you get used to dodging awkward customers. It almost becomes second nature to find a different route to the other side of the banking hall if there is somebody unpleasant in and you don't want to see them." He paused before continuing, "I told Louise and Jackie I was going to visit the grave of my grandmother and I would make my own way back to the house, it's not far, only a ten minute walk."

Then suddenly all of our attention was drawn to the church entrance as an old dark-blue transit van came screaming in through the gates, almost knocking into them. The van pulled up outside of the church doors. The press had by now made their way to Louise's home, or that of her parents, so it was fortunate there was no one standing outside. Both doors opened and two scruffily dressed men jumped out of the van, just for a moment they stood and looked around the graveyard. Stavros signalled to his men, a warning to be on their guard.

"Oh that's all we need," Trevor said, scratching his head.

"Do you know these men?" Stavros asked, moving slightly in front of me as so to give me some protection.

"Yes, unfortunately I do," was Trevor's somewhat nervous reply.

I looked across at these two individuals. The man who had got out of the driver's side was the older of the two. I would say he was in his fifties, about five foot six and very broad, his hair cut very short. As he turned to talk to the other man I could see he had an earring in his right ear. The other man was much younger, in his late twenties. He was taller, about five ten, and much thinner. His long dark hair was tied back in a ponytail, and both were dressed in jeans and sweatshirts. The older man slammed the van door and called across to his companion.

"Looks like we're too late."

"That's Gary's father," Trevor softly told us.

"And the other man, my friend, is?" Stavros asked, snapping his fingers behind his back to draw the attention of his men to these unsavoury characters. His two men came closer to take the view.

"The other man is his nephew, both of them are very nasty, I wouldn't trust them. I remember them from Louise and Gary's wedding. Obviously the younger man was only a teenager but they all got blind drunk, most embarrassing, not sound people at all. Gary's father," Trevor paused and held his chin in his hand before continuing, "Len, that's his name; well he's been in and out of prison, mainly for petty crime and fighting. Perhaps that's where Gary got it from."

As we stood looking at these two men the doors of the church opened and the vicar reappeared. He was standing in the porch and Gary's father shouted at him loud enough for us to hear.

"Has my boy's funeral taken place yet?" He started to make his way in the direction of the vicar. We couldn't hear the vicar's reply, for he was a small, softly spoken man.

"Well, what time was it?" Len shouted at the vicar.

The reply prompted Len to look at his watch. He walked back and kicked the door of the van. Yes, now I could see the likeness. The vicar made his way towards Len, and put his hand out to offer some comfort, but he was pushed away in one angry movement. He almost fell to the ground, but after regaining his composure he pointed in the direction of the new grave, and both men made their way to the grave which by now had been filled in by the sexton. He'd been the last to leave, after the press.

We stood very still as these two big men glared down at the ground where Gary had been buried.

"The younger man's name is Mark," Trevor began. "The rest of his family are dead and he's been living with Len for a few years now. I remember Gary telling me Mark's mother, father and two sisters were killed in a car crash. His parents were very drunk. Mark was the only one to survive. Of course Len says it was the other person's fault, but the driver of the other vehicle was also killed. But that's him, even when faced with the truth he can't see it. He brought Mark up after the accident."

Then on the gentle breeze we could hear Len's harsh words of anger.

"I'm going to get the bastard that done this."

"Yes, and I'm going to help you!" was Marks reply, nodding in agreement.

"What about Gary's mother?" I quietly asked Trevor.

"Left them years ago, hasn't been seen for a long time. Just disowned them, well Len and Gary. Then of course there was the other son." Trevor paused. "Kevin, was his name. Strange that, a really nice man, so different from the other members of the family. Very sound sort of chap, kind and considerate, I think he even went to university, but I can't be sure. Again, he hasn't been seen for a significant amount of time."

The two men made their way back to the van. Mark took out a packet of cigarettes.

"Do you want one?" he called across to Len, now by the driver's door.

"Yes," he replied and Mark threw him a cigarette.

For a few minutes they stood by the front of the van, the smoke rising into the air and drifting across in our direction. It's smell reminded me of the days when my father used to stand in the garden smoking after he'd had a fall-out with my mother. We watched them stub their cigarettes out with their feet. Len then spat on the ground.

"Bastards," he shouted, anger and frustration in his voice as he stamped on the cigarette butt again.

"Where we going now Len?" Mark asked.

"Lets go to the pub and bid our Gary a decent farewell, then we can decide where we have to start looking, you know, to find out who killed him," was Len's reply.

"Yes, that's a good idea," Mark said.

They both climbed into the van, Len started the noisy smoky diesel engine and they reversed out of the churchyard and turned in the small bay in front of the entrance gates, and were on their way.

Their manner and actions worried me. So much so I asked the question of Trevor I'm sure was on Stavros's mind.

"Where is Louise staying?"

"She's staying with Diane and myself along with Jackie and the children." He paused and looked into my eyes before continuing, "You've no need to worry, he won't come to our place and cause any trouble. If he does, then I'll call the police. It's a bit strong, all this melodrama, anyway, he hadn't had anything to do with Gary for such a long time. Never about when he was a child either. As I've said, either in prison or the pub."

"If you like a few of my boys will stay for a couple of days," Stavros said to Trevor.

"No, we'll be fine. Anyway, after he's had a few pints Len won't remember what he went into the pub for, and as for Mark, he can't remember his name half the time. Had a bump to the head in the car accident and did some damage, really he's quite harmless," Trevor told Stavros.

"Look," Trevor said, taking my hand, "I'd best be getting back, you know, before I'm missed." He gripped my hand harder, but I felt a need to put my arms around him. He did the same to me.

"Tell her," I started to say, with a lump in my throat and tears welling up in my eyes.

"I will, and I know you do," Trevor said before I could finish the sentence, then he went on, "Maybe one day she will feel well enough to see you Andrew."

Then he released his hold on me and turned to look at Stavros. They came together as lifelong friends.

"Trevor, I look forward to the next meeting," Stavros said.

"I do as well, and once again thank you for all you've done," Trevor said, and with one last look at me he turned and walked back in the direction he had appeared from, then he was gone out of sight between the headstones of this old village churchyard.

Now I stood with just my trusted friend by my side, the trees swaying to the gentle breeze blowing through them, a knowing deep inside of me, I was to be alone very soon and would have to manage as best I could. We went back to my house, taking the precaution of parking Marie's car in the side street. Stavros said we could soon be expecting some unwelcome visitors to the house in the form of the press and would need to be on our guard. If they'd taken the time to go to the church, then my house wouldn't be very far down the list of places to visit afterwards. My own car was safely installed in the garage well out of the view of any marauding photographer. We spent the rest of the day talking over what had happened and just how unpleasant those two individuals were and what lengths might they go to in order to fulfil their curiosity. I ordered some food from the local takeaway, and Stavros and I ate in the dining room and drank two bottles of wine.

Wednesday

The day was with me in lightening speed and I awoke with the most awful of self-inflicted headaches. The morning was slow to pass. We had breakfast and copious amounts of coffee. I was in need of the coffee more than Stavros was. Twelve o'clock came and he sat me down and gave me a lecture. Whether I wanted it or not there were some things he needed to tell me, things I had to promise I would do and others that I wouldn't.

"Now you need to listen to what I am about to tell you," he said, sitting opposite me in the conservatory, with a firmness in his voice, like a father telling a child he has had enough sweets. "You remember I told you, your head must rule your heart, well when I have gone it will be very important for you to do just that. It will be very tempting and also easy for you to pick up the phone, or maybe write a letter on that fancy computer of yours, but you mustn't, you would only be harming yourself in the long run. If and when she is ready," he paused, the phrase had an unpleasant ring to it, "as I say, if and when she is ready she will contact you, but you must prepare yourself for the eventuality that she may never." He stopped, the words had an end-ness to them which hurt, and he could see the pain it caused deep inside of me.

"On the other hand in a few days or weeks she may feel the need to contact you, then we will be able to delight in that coming together. But you of all people must not force it. As I told you only the other day she will respect you for giving her space. You may never see her again and I know the thought is hard to carry in your heart. It is like a massive weight, but time will make it lighter." He stopped again and took my shaking hands. "Andrew, do you promise your old friend Stavros that you won't do anything foolish?" he asked.

"I promise you I won't." I told him, as my tears started to flow. It had been a few days since I'd shed any tears, mainly due to the fact I'd had his company. He'd helped me occupy my mind on other tasks and duties around the house, but now I knew I was soon to be alone and a feeling of being cut off would take over my life, along with the hurt and even anger, anger which comes from not knowing. Some people may be able to blot those feeling and emotions out, but I wouldn't be so fortunate.

"And I want you to look after yourself. Keep eating, use the confounded computer thing to order your groceries with, if you don't feel like going out. You need to eat, what will Louise think if she turns up and you have the shape of a rake about you. You understand?" he asked me.

"Yes I will," I told him.

"There is just one other thing I need to tell you." He paused, his right hand came across and took mine, and then he stood up and in the process pulled me to my feet, in the same way he had on that Easter Saturday. His embrace was immense, his presence, power and strength all coming together, then his words, "You know each and everyone of the family love you, for you and that young woman are part of my family, we have told you. Any time you want to come to our home with us you can. Andrew I love like I love my other two sons and Nana," and with those words he kissed me on both my cheeks, then quickly continued, "Come! You will be thinking Stavros is going soft in his old age."

Having made my promises to him I made my way into the study and wrote him a cheque for five thousand pounds.

"Stavros, could you please take care of putting the apartments in order, and the remainder is for the funeral expenses," I said as I passed him the cheque.

"My friend, this is more than enough. I shall give you the remainder when we meet! Yes?" he replied.

Stavros had already brought his bags down, they were in the hall and he was just getting ready to leave, when there was a knock on the door followed by the bell being repeatedly rung.

"Let me," Stavros said in a manner indicating he knew who would be at the door. As he made his way to open the inner door he gestured for me to go back into the study. I did as instructed. I stood by the doorway watching the flashes from the photographers flashguns bounce round the walls of the hallway. I could also clearly hear the conversation that took place. A barrage of questions flew at Stavros as soon as he opened the outer porch door.

The questions were coming from members of the media. Did he know my whereabouts? How long had I known Mrs Shaw? Had she been in contact with me? What were our plans for the future? The last one really did hurt. "What future?" I asked myself.

Stavros's reply to these questions was as I should have expected.

"My friends, I know nothing!" he said emphasising his Greek accent. "He's not here, I only bring his car back and now I leave to return to my home."

I heard him close the porch sliding door and call me from the hall.

"Andrew, it is safe for you to come out now," Stavros said softly, then picking up his bags he went on, "I must go now. I won't come back in, it will look too suspicious, but before I go I'll draw the curtains in the front of the house." He put his bags down and did as he said he would, and in no time he was back in the hall.

"My friend, I will speak to you soon! Yes!" were his final words to me as he set off on his journey home. He pulled the door closed and as he slid the porch door I heard another stream of questions fly at him. I just caught his muffled reply and he was gone.

I made my way into the kitchen, made another cup of coffee and took it into the study. There, underneath the tickets for our trip to Scotland on the bureau was my diary.

Sitting at the table I opened it, looking to see the last entry I'd made. It was the night I'd taken Louise out for dinner, a private note I'd written to myself and underlined.

'She looked so beautiful, if I hadn't loved her before, then tonight I would have surely fallen in love with Louise Shaw.'

Printed in the United Kingdom
by Lightning Source UK Ltd.
105250UKS00002B/111